PENGUIN BOOKS

# SHORT GIRLS

Bich Minh Nguyen is the author of the memoir *Stealing Buddha's Dinner*. She teaches at Purdue University and lives in Chicago and West Lafayette.

# *Short Girls*

BICH MINH NGUYEN

PENGUIN BOOKS

PENGUIN BOOKS

Published by the Penguin Group
Penguin Books Ltd, 80 Strand, London WC2R 0RL, England
Penguin Group (USA) Inc., 375 Hudson Street, New York, New York 10014, USA
Penguin Group (Canada), 90 Eglinton Avenue East, Suite 700, Toronto, Ontario, Canada M4P 2Y3
(a division of Pearson Penguin Canada Inc.)
Penguin Ireland, 25 St Stephen's Green, Dublin 2, Ireland (a division of Penguin Books Ltd)
Penguin Group (Australia), 250 Camberwell Road, Camberwell, Victoria 3124, Australia
(a division of Pearson Australia Group Pty Ltd)
Penguin Books India Pvt Ltd, 11 Community Centre, Panchsheel Park, New Delhi – 110 017, India
Penguin Group (NZ), 67 Apollo Drive, Rosedale, North Shore 0632, New Zealand
(a division of Pearson New Zealand Ltd)
Penguin Books (South Africa) (Pty) Ltd, 24 Sturdee Avenue, Rosebank, Johannesburg 2196, South Africa

Penguin Books Ltd, Registered Offices: 80 Strand, London WC2R 0RL, England

www.penguin.com

First published in the USA by Viking Penguin,
a member of Penguin Group (USA) Inc. 2009
First published in Great Britain by Fig Tree 2009
Published in Penguin Books 2010

1

Printed in England by Clays Ltd, St Ives plc

ISBN: 978–0–141–03917–6

www.greenpenguin.co.uk

Mixed Sources
Product group from well-managed
forests and other controlled sources
www.fsc.org Cert no. SA-COC-1592
© 1996 Forest Stewardship Council

Penguin Books is committed to a sustainable future
for our business, our readers and our planet.
The book in your hands is made from paper
certified by the Forest Stewardship Council.

In memory of my grandmother Noi

*(1920–2007)*

short
girls

# Van

After Miles left, Van began checking the security alarm every time she entered the house. She had nightmares of the alarm failing, losing the password of her and Miles's wedding date. Pressing those numbers made her remember his hand on her back, guiding her through dance steps. They had practiced in a ballroom class, then in his apartment, Eric Clapton singing "Wonderful Tonight" over and over. She didn't tell Miles that the lyrics bothered her: Why must the woman only look wonderful *tonight*?

The rooms hushed around her, the open floor plan stretching forth on the hardwood. Though they'd moved in almost three years earlier, she still felt vaguely like a house sitter. She was careful to keep the hand towels neat, her shoes lined up in the mudroom. She circled the first floor, making sure the blinds were drawn, and turned on all the outdoor lights. She lingered in front of the television, for going upstairs seemed almost unsafe, a yielding of territory. Someone could trap her there. She thought of places to hide, to buy herself time between the breach of the alarm and the arrival of police: behind the armoire in the bedroom corner; in the cedar chest in her closet.

She could just fit into it, her small body folding into the tight darkness, the lid clamping down like a set of perfect teeth.

Van spent most of her time in the TV room, where she lay on the sofa between the windows so that someone standing in the backyard would not be able to see her. Only in bright daylight did she want to peek outside. It was always the same Ann Arbor subdivision, the houses as new and graceful as hers, with brushed-brick facades and wrought-iron sconces. Cars nested in garages. Streets rounded into cul-de-sacs. "Para-noi-a," Miles sometimes sang softly when he caught Van squinting through a slit in the blinds.

Those first two weeks of Miles's absence, Van had waited for someone to confront her. She was certain her coworkers would read in her face what had happened. She prepared answers. A business trip. A big case, confidential. But the days went by and no one at her law office asked her if she was okay. Her friends e-mailed their usual brief messages about work, pictures of their kids. Her sister Linny did not appear on her doorstep to crow about how much she'd always disliked Miles. Van nearly convinced herself that he *had* been away on a business trip. It was almost easy to go along, letting her world split from that one day in February into separate versions of reality.

How little anyone knew of Van's real life.

Even so, she kept checking the caller ID. She didn't stop expecting to see Miles's cell number, and hated how her heart jumped whenever the phone rang. But it hardly ever did. A week before he left, Miles had added their number to the national Do Not Call list. Van wondered if it was a planned courtesy, that she might exist untroubled by telemarketers while sitting down to her solo dinner.

She had not been the kind of teenager who could talk for hours on the phone with a friend; that realm had belonged to her sister. When she and Linny called each other they ended up using their father as an excuse: Who was going to visit him next? Had he said anything about Thanksgiving? How was he doing all alone in that house? He was the spool around which the thread of their conversations wound.

Van's father didn't like phones, not even to acknowledge birthdays. In college, she could go almost an entire quarter without hearing from him. His calls, when they came, seemed random. He would want to know where a friend of his could find good sushi in Ann Arbor. Or he'd ask, *Do you remember where I put the pliers? Were there any D batteries in the house?* As if she were still there, or should be.

But now he was reminding her to come home.

After twenty-eight years of stubbornness her father was finally taking his oath of citizenship, letting go at last of his refugee status and the green Permanent Resident Alien Card. He had taken the test, handed over his fingerprints, had his background checked—the last of all his friends to do so. To celebrate, he was throwing a party in the old style, the way all of the Vietnamese families in their town used to gather in the late seventies and eighties, finding relief in their free-flowing beer and language. It would be a reunion, a remembrance of their collective flight from Vietnam and settlement in America— 1975 all over again. Van, who was born in a refugee camp three months after her parents arrived in the States, knew only her mother's description of the dusty barracks and tents at Pendleton, and the startling cold of their first winter in Michigan. She didn't understand why her father would want to return to 1975.

"It's the last hurray," he insisted when he first told her his idea for the party. "We come a long way, baby."

After Van had left for college her parents decided to live on separate floors of the house they'd had for twenty years, a sixties ranch in Wrightville, a suburb of Grand Rapids, Michigan. They'd fallen into the arrangement after yet another petty argument—which potted dendrobium at the home and garden center looked the healthiest—blew up into a two-day fight. The Luongs had always done this, scratching at each other's words as much out of habit as anything. But this time when Thuy Luong told her husband to go sleep in the basement "like a dog," he stayed there instead of slinking back upstairs. When Van went home for winter break she found that he had actually moved to the basement. He had shoved aside the old fold-out sofa they'd had since their first apartment in the States and set up a futon right in front of the big-screen TV, a clunky first-generation model that would soon be replaced by newer and newer models, to which he'd add an elaborate sound system, with speakers hidden inside wooden figurines of Vietnamese fishermen.

The basement had always been his domain. Van was going on nine when they moved into that house, and she had helped him partition off a section of the floor to create a studio for his company, Luong Inventions by Dinh Luong, for which he often ditched his "everyday money" jobs in tiling and construction. He kept his sketches tacked up on the faux-wood paneling, along with photographs of himself trying out his prototypes. His most successful invention—or least unsuccessful—was the Luong Arm, a tong-like gadget devised to help short people reach items on a high shelf. He had sold more than a hundred Luong

Arms to various friends in the Vietnamese community. But the product had never been quite right—the mechanical grip could grab a light basket, but lost control with plates and glasses. When Van graduated from college, her father gave her a prototype as a gift, saying, *Short girls have to take care of themselves.*

In law school, when Miles first came over to her apartment he had spied the Arm immediately. It lay on top of her kitchen cabinets, where Van had stored and forgotten it because she couldn't see that high up.

Amused, Miles examined the Y-shaped instrument and held it like a divining rod. "Will this lead me to gold and riches?" He steered it toward her.

"It didn't for my dad," Van replied.

She showed Miles how it worked: put the wrist through the velcroed brace, hang on to the wand, and use the thumb to work the lever that opened and closed the tongs. Miles wanted to try it, aiming for a thin-necked vase in Van's kitchen cupboard. "Don't," she said. "It's the only one I have."

"I've got it." He secured the grip and drew back slowly to set the vase on the counter. But it slipped from the Arm and crashed onto Van's linoleum floor.

When Dinh Luong settled into the downstairs part of the house, he bought a set of safari-print sheets from JCPenney. The basement, with its low ceilings and movie-worthy darkness, was perfect for running *Die Hard* and Indiana Jones DVDs until he fell asleep. He got a mini-refrigerator to store his beer and bought a George Foreman grill from a garage sale. When he cooked he made turkey burgers with pickle, dipping each bite into *nuoc mam* sauce. When he got cold he used a space heater that made the basement smell like Linny's old curling iron set on high. Van worried that her father would burn the whole house down but he had laughed at that. "I'm an inventor," he said. "I'm not destroying—I'm *making*."

Upstairs, Van's mother and sister made changes too. They gathered up Dinh Luong's infomercial orders—the food dehydrator, the vacuum sealer, the automatic shoe polisher—and left them on the basement steps. Mrs. Luong painted their bedroom lavender, and threw out the pile of *Popular Mechanics* magazines her husband had saved in the bathroom. They didn't ignore each other, didn't quite divide the house in two, but it was clear to Van that they had come to some sort of resolution about their space: they just didn't want to have to see each other very often. Linny, a senior in high school then, used the opportunity to spread out her clothes and music, stay out late while their parents were so distracted.

Van was secretly glad that they hadn't just given up and divorced. In her mind they couldn't—they were too conjoined, had known too many years together. Ornery as old house cats, they needed each other's presence without ever admitting it. They could have gone on like that for decades, Van knew, living together but not together, meeting only occasionally when Van's father needed to get some towels or utensils from upstairs or when Van's mother needed to use the washer and dryer. And maybe they would have if Thuy Luong hadn't collapsed in her best friend's nail salon that May, 1994, nine years ago; Van was finishing her first year at the University of Chicago and Linny was about to graduate from high school. At the hospital, the attending physician had been fairly sure that it was a stroke, rare for a forty-two-year-old, though they never knew for sure because Dinh Luong had refused an autopsy. *She wouldn't want it*, he said, and the pronouncement gave a strange comfort to Van, made her think that in spite of all the arguments, her parents had known, after all, a river of intimacy. The fall after Mrs. Luong died, Linny started community college and moved into her own apartment, and their father returned to the upstairs part of the house for good.

When nighttime started its descent over Ann Arbor—less swiftly every day, Van noted, grateful for hints of spring—she wondered what it would be like to coexist with Miles, each living on a separate floor. Would she rather have him in the house, secure in his nearness, or would it make her insane, force her to eavesdrop on his phone conversations with people she didn't know? Watching television in her usual way, lying on the sofa so that everything on the screen appeared sideways, Van was glad that Miles could not see her like this. If he were home she would be sitting up with a glass of wine, playing an indie movie since Miles called network television a scourge on the brain.

Van knew that she would have to go to Wrightville for her father's party, and that questions would follow her: *Where's Miles? How's Miles? When are you and Miles having a baby?* She had begun to plan her answers, simple as tabbed files: *He had a case. He's doing fine. We're in no hurry just yet.* The last one a lie she had been telling for more than two years.

Van pictured her father shuffling up from the basement, stepping into the kitchen. If in a good mood he would wave hello and pat her on the back, saying, "Where's that Chinese boy?" It's what he'd been saying since the first time Van brought Miles home. They were engaged by then, and Van's father had inspected the prongs that held the diamond in place and said, "Good thing we love Chinese food."

If Van had dated a fourth-generation Chinese American in high school—if there had been any to date, if she had dated at all—her mother would have wept and her father would have forbidden it. Those were the days when they were strict about Vietnamese boys who would grow into suitable husbands for Van and Linny. Once, during Van's junior year, her mother had tried to make her go on a blind date with a son of a cousin of a friend who had just settled in the area. Van had outright refused. But a few days later Pham Ly was sitting at the kitchen table when she came home from a Sunday trip to the downtown library. He was gawky and full of smiles, his cheekbones sharp and shiny. In those days, phrases like "fresh off the boat" embarrassed Van. By now it had become hip or funny, one of those bits of language people were trying to reclaim. They're so *fobby*, her friend Jen Ye had said affectionately about her own parents. Van often thought the word applied to her father too.

Pham had been in the States for less than a year and his accent showed it: warbled, clotting the sounds he couldn't yet pronounce. Mostly he spoke in Vietnamese with Van's parents, and the three of them shouted with laughter over jokes Van could not understand. Sullenly she ate her mother's fish soup, wondering where Linny was. Even in tenth grade, Linny had things to do. She was always going out; she dated Van's classmates. By then they hadn't been close, hadn't really talked to each other without squabbling, in years.

Their parents were erratic in their rules, probably because they could never unite in enforcing them. Mrs. Luong could scream at Linny for coming home at two in the morning, but

Mr. Luong would have forgotten it by the next day. He might announce, "You're grounded until further notice!" (a phrase he had learned from TV) but it would be his wife who would have to make it stick. Linny, taking advantage of the disarray, slipped around the questions so that their parents often ended up interrogating *Van*—what she had been doing after school, and who had been there, though she was more likely to play Trivial Pursuit than a drinking game.

At the end of dinner Van's parents suddenly retreated, leaving her alone with Pham, who had become flushed and cheerful from the Budweisers Mr. Luong had offered him. "What you doing tonight?" Pham asked her. The dinner, the company, the beer had turned his shy smile slick, and Van looked away. "I have to study," she said, making sure to emphasize her English, using a cold voice she didn't know she had. It was something that would come in handy later, in law school. Then Van got up from the table and fled to her room.

By the time Van left for college her parents had pretty much given up: any Asian was a good Asian. They had seen enough of their friends' children dating white people to realize that. Van wondered how much she'd had her mother's wishes in mind when Miles came into the picture during law school. Her mother had once said they probably had relatives who were part Chinese, their heritage handed down through centuries of rule. Chinese, Japanese, Korean—here in America, it was all the same.

Van changed the channel—*The Golden Girls* starting on Lifetime—and fought the desire to call Miles and tell him that she was going to visit her father. The idea of leaving town and coming back and never saying a word about it to him made her shiver. How would he know where to think of her?

She worried she wouldn't be able to keep up the lie, at least not with Linny, who might stare her down, narrow her eyes, and in that way force the real story. Van knew, too, something harder: it had been six weeks, and each day meant a greater separation, a further burrowing of the truth. One day, she would have to open her mouth and speak it.

# 2

# Linny

Linny would not dress up her apartment for Gary: let him see the stains in the bathroom grout, the laminate countertops, the Magic Chef range so narrow two of her pans barely fit on it at the same time. Let him lie in her bed strewn with her discount designer clothes, then glance out the windows at the alley and the row of brick buildings whose windows were almost always blinded shut. Here in Wicker Park, hipster girls punked up their hair and slouched in coffee shops while skinny mothers with their Bugaboos ordered chais to go. Linny used to take their orders, standing behind the counter in her assigned apron, five years ago when she quit school and moved to Chicago.

Gary's house in Lincoln Park took up three stories. The cherry floors gleamed seamlessly, inviting his kids to slide down the halls and crash into each other. The furniture was covered in fabrics with names like *faille* and *habotai* that Gary's wife, Pren, had studied in her textile classes before she switched to art history. In the kitchen, Tuscan tiles bordered quartz countertops, showing off the six-burner two-oven range the nanny used to cook the dinners Linny pre-made at her job. Linny would not compete with that house. She sat in her IKEA lounger and waited a full minute before answering the buzz that announced Gary's arrival.

For three years now Linny had been working at You Did It Dinners in Oak Park, just west of the city. Each day, moms filled the company kitchen to assemble two weeks' worth of meals in two hours: chicken enchiladas, spinach lasagna, citrus-glazed salmon, all piled into plastic bags and tin pans ready to be pulled from the freezer and popped into an oven. The owner of the company, Barbara, billed the experience as a social event. *You'll get to know other mothers in the area!* her flyers promised. The women sipped wine as they layered chicken breasts with provolone cheese, comparing their kids' schools and sports and their summer vacations. Linny's main role was to put together the meals for customers who couldn't be bothered to make the trek to Oak Park. ("Can we call these You Didn't Do It Dinners?" she'd asked Barbara.) That was how she met Gary, bringing a new supply of burritos and chicken bakes to his family. As she stacked the pans in his freezer he asked her questions about the company, how she liked it, what her favorite dishes were. They flirted for months until the day she found him at home by himself, the nanny out at the zoo with the kids. Gary kissed her that day, leaning her against the stone counter. Linny, who had just broken up with a boyfriend of a year, found something irresistible in the idea of a married man. The ease, the allure. No chance of commitment. She had only intended to see him a few times anyway. But now, four months into it, the thrill was turning into something like caution. Even when alone she was looking at the clock.

Linny had told Gary that her favorite You Did It dish was the chicken Marbella, with orange rind, olives, and figs, though in truth she didn't really care for any of the meals. The company aspired more to Applebee's than *Gourmet*. It was what the customers wanted, Barbara said decisively. The most popular items were stuffed shells, chili, three-cheese macaroni, and a concoction called taco rice. Even the more high-reaching dinners—chicken tikka masala, apple-rosemary glazed pork tenderloin—tended toward a salty ooze and chew, a flattening out of the palate. Not that Linny felt entitled to highbrow menus; neither she nor Barbara had been through formal culinary training. Alone in the company kitchen sometimes, they traded stories about their mothers' cooking or restaurants where they'd waitressed. Barbara was divorced, her two sons in college, and she'd started the business after watching a talk show about mom entrepreneurs. She had recently dyed her blond pageboy auburn and changed her last name back to Hull. She was the first boss Linny had ever cared about.

On the days when women weren't prepping meals in the kitchen, Linny and Barbara formulated new dinner ideas. The ingredients couldn't be too complicated or time-consuming; everything had to appeal to a family of four; and the foods had to transition well from freezer to oven or stovetop. Fish was the main obstacle, and they had tried out countless versions of salmon, halibut, and the bland favorite tilapia. As Linny had quickly discovered, You Did It's customers were urban moms with suburban roots. They carried designer bags but coveted old-fashioned stews and macaroni and cheese. Fancy logos they could handle; fancy ingredients, as Barbara said, often intimidated them. So Linny combed through cookbook aisles in used bookstores and flipped through Crock-Pot recipes from the 1970s, jotting down ingredients and ideas in a notebook.

In the past few months Linny's recipe notes had expanded, reaching toward questions beyond her job. Who bought all of the star fruit in the produce section? What about kumquats? Which herbs had Mrs. Luong preferred in her *banh mi* sandwiches? Did her mother ever cook with persimmons or only eat them raw? Linny realized she was writing notes toward another anniversary of her mother's death and it became a comfort, as though she were calling forth her mother, bringing back the hours they had spent in the kitchen together when Linny was a girl.

Though a year younger than her sister, Linny had been the one to take over the cooking duties when they were growing up. When their mother stayed late at Roger's Department Store to get overtime pay and their father retreated to his sketches and basement studio, Linny made spaghetti, stir-fries, and sloppy joes. She followed her mother in the kitchen on weekends, paying attention to the shape of *goi cuon* summer rolls and *banh xeo* crepes. She learned how to cook *pho* soup, chicken and vermicelli, caramelized beef and shrimp. The directions made logical sense to her in the way sewing also did; every stitch, every ingredient, depended on the others. Linny was hemming her pants and piecing together her own skirts by the time she was ten. After the requisite home ec class in seventh grade in which Linny learned to make cupcakes and potatoes au gratin, she began getting cookbooks from the local library while Van checked out the classics she needed to learn the "canon" (a term that Linny associated for years with the weapon, literature as a threat or death blow). The home ec teacher, pleased by Linny's interest and by the sewing skills she'd learned from Mrs. Luong, had given her a Home Economics Certificate of Achievement at the end of the school year. It was the only award she ever won in school. Unlike Van, Linny grew picky about what she ate. She had always refused mealy tomatoes in winter and insisted on dark chocolate over milk. She became as fastidious about her meals as she did about her feathered hair and highlighted cheekbones.

One day while Linny got dressed in a room at the Westin, Gary pulled the notebook from her handbag and flipped it open. " 'What about kumquats?' " he read out loud, falling back in laughter as Linny grabbed the book back. From that moment on the word *kumquats* became his code word. "Did you bring me any kumquats?" "When can I have some kumquats?" He e-mailed the word *kumquats* to say, *meet me*.

They met around Michigan Avenue and in the Loop, in business hotels filled with out-of-towners. Linny especially liked the modern anonymity of the Swissôtel, and the Inter-Continental for its spectacular Moroccan swimming pool and the bleachers from the days when the Olympian Johnny Weissmuller, the future Tarzan, swam for crowds. Linny had gone up there once to watch golden arrows of sunset slanting into the turquoise water.

She always declined rides back to her apartment, preferring to take a cab or train. She hated saying good-byes in a car, that lingering moment of awkwardness when pulling up to the curb: one could leap out of the car too quickly, or not quickly enough. And she never invited Gary to her place, though he had asked more than once to see it. "Why?" she asked.

"What do you mean, why?" He laughed easily, something Linny had liked about him from the start. "I want to see where you live."

She brushed off his request. "I like hotels."

It became almost a game between them, Gary asking to come over and Linny saying no. She cited her messes, the small size of the place, the lack of a king-sized bed. The more he pushed, the more she resisted. She found herself unwilling to give him this, needing to keep something of her own between them.

People who met Linny would not have guessed that she lived in an apartment filled with mismatched housewares from discount stores. She had never managed money well. She could drop hundreds on a pair of shoes but kept a card table in her dining area. The dulled floors in her studio needed refinishing and the exposed ductwork seemed to invite the cold of Chicago winters to linger—but at least the place was hers. She thought of it as protective gear, outside of which her identity could be swayed, up for grabs. There were times, out on a date, sitting in a low-lit restaurant, when Linny had the sensation of just waking up into a parallel dimension, as if she were viewing herself from another place, another body altogether.

Now Gary was walking up the three flights of stairs to see her apartment for the first time because he had something to tell her. "Let me see where you live. Then we can talk," were the words he used.

Linny's friend Sasha, the one person who knew about Gary, said it had to be one of two things: he was going to dump her or he was going to dump his wife. Either way, better to be on your own turf, she advised.

Gary kissed Linny as soon as she opened the door, letting

the early April chill of his jacket seep into her thin sweater. She stood on her tiptoes, having forgotten to put on her heels. Linny had always preferred tall men. Her senior prom date had been a six-foot-four basketball star. She hadn't cared that they looked comical dancing together, Linny's head tilting back so she could see him.

With one quick gaze Gary seemed to take in her apartment's meager square footage, the wood veneer furnishings, the bare walls save for the one faux-vintage wine poster Van had given her for Christmas a few years back. It showed a woman bursting out of a spray of grapes, a thin vine coiled around the fruit and up her body. Gary sat down on the slipcovered sofa, noticing the stack of *Saveur* magazines, the old sewing machine that had belonged to Linny's mother, and the television that took up one corner of the room.

Once in a while, in hotels, he agreed to watch TV with her. He was amused by her penchant for sitcom reruns and History Channel shows about lost civilizations. Television was one of her oldest habits, originating in her first memory of childhood: she and Van planted in front of it, spouting cartoon dialogue to each other, and pretending to be Laverne and Shirley. The television had been a mainstay for the whole family, all of them gathering on the nights Mr. Luong wanted to see *Superman* or championship figure skating. It had brought more voices into the house.

Gary's dark brown hair, silvering so slightly that he sometimes appeared to be walking in mist, was getting too long, starting to curl against the cashmere scarf he slowly unwound from his neck. While an El train raced by he spread his arms in a grand gesture and said, "Finally, it is all revealed."

"Disappointed?"

"Never." Gary looked around again. "But where's the bedroom?"

Usually they had sex as soon as possible, as if to get it out of the way. This time, as Linny led him to her room, she decided against it.

He landed himself on the bed, the metal frame creaking. Linny remembered that the bulb in the ceiling fixture had gone out. "I love being surrounded by all of your things," Gary declared, finding a lace-trimmed camisole lying on the duvet. He held it up to himself. "What do you think? Is this me?"

He grabbed at her and the mattress dipped, the whole bed lurching. Breaking free of his grasp, Linny nearly fell to the floor.

"I had a feeling you'd want to talk first," he said. It seemed to foretell good news, a spark of hope thrown into Linny's chest.

"I'm such a good hostess, I even bought a bottle of cabernet," she said.

In the kitchen Linny opened a cupboard to take out two wine glasses, the only ones she owned. She kept everything on the lowest shelves because, like most kitchens, it was built for someone taller. As a girl, Linny had perfected a method of reaching things—an easy one-armed balance on the counter, the other grabbing a sack of sugar or box of cookies. That was when her father invented the Luong Arm. Though he had never said so, she was certain she had inspired the idea.

Gary stopped at the refrigerator to look at the photos held in place with food magnets—cheeseburgers and sundaes, a wedge of iceberg lettuce—that Barbara had given her. He peered closer at one photograph. "Is this your sister?" It was from two Thanksgivings ago, Linny and Van with their plates of turkey and stuffing Linny had made, while their father stood in the background, staring at something off in the distance. Linny couldn't remember why she had that picture on her fridge. "I can see the resemblance, but her face seems broader. Rounder. Your cheekbones and lips are fuller. Your eyebrows have shape. I don't think I've ever even noticed eyebrows before." He finished his assessment. "How much older is she?"

"One year."

"It's that turtleneck."

It was true that Van favored cotton turtlenecks neatly folded over. She had a collection of big square sweaters, sturdy chinos, and cardigans from J. Jill and Talbots.

Sometimes in high school, Linny would see her from the end of a hallway: Van leaning into her locker, reaching up for her books, probably thinking about exams. She was all alone with her binders of equations and symbols, history dates and metaphors. Linny would see her like that and feel sorry for her. And Van, lost in her own world, would close her locker and set off down the hall to her next class. It wasn't that she didn't have friends; they were like her—the ones who did Model UN after school and didn't care about clothes. But why weren't they ever around when Linny caught a glimpse of her? Why did Van always seem to be so alone, her long straight hair pushed back into a limp ponytail?

Gary said matter-of-factly, "You're prettier."

"Am I supposed to say thank you?"

He smiled. "I like this place," he said instead. "I like how spare and modern it is." When Linny rolled her eyes he insisted, "No, really. You've got everything you need and it's all yours. Independent. I'm a little jealous." He put a hand on Linny's shoulder so that his thumb grazed her collarbone.

Linny pushed the wine bottle toward him. "We're supposed to be having a talk, remember?" She paused to let the noise of a passing train subside.

"That must get old, hearing the El all the time."

"I don't even notice it anymore," Linny said, a lie. She heard it every time, wakened to it each morning. The familiar rumble, rolling in and out of the station just a few blocks down, reassured her that she wasn't in Michigan anymore, not in small towns or at state schools dreary with late sixties architecture.

"Let's go out for dinner," Gary suggested suddenly, and Linny was surprised. They almost never did that. "Let's go to that sushi place down the street."

It was not yet seven. A few miles west of here, the nanny and the kids would have already finished eating—perhaps the vegetable lasagna, or the enchiladas Gary's five-year-old son loved. Linny knew how many dinners remained, the frozen blocks neatly labeled. Soon she would have to get started on the next round.

Or perhaps Pren was home tonight, taking care of the kids because Gary had already called to say, breezily, audaciously, that he was working late. Linny imagined Pren clearing the table, her honey-colored hair falling into her eyes as she put the plates into the sink. She was almost as tall as Gary, slim, able to retrieve whatever she needed from any cupboard. Linny imagined her thinking of her husband, whose downtown office faced the lake with its boats in warm weather. His windows darkened with the evening. So many late hours, followed by an inching drive home on Lake Shore. The word *traffic*, Gary had said, always bought him an extra half hour.

When Linny and Gary walked out into the cold evening, he tucked her arm in his. On Milwaukee some of the storefronts were framed with dotted lights, stringing together vintage shops and cafés, boutiques devoted to stationery, shoes, and angular-looking clothes. As Linny glanced up at the awnings she felt a wayward burst of contentment. It came out of nowhere, overriding the dark mood she had nursed for the last week. She could feel herself being drawn into a self-conscious fantasy—the two of them, out in the open, Gary seemingly unworried about running into someone he or Pren knew.

But the moment evaporated with the ring of a cell phone. Linny's. When she saw it was her father she dropped the phone back into her bag.

Through some tacit agreement Linny and Gary never asked about each other's calls, but this time she volunteered, "My dad." She didn't explain that he was no doubt going to remind her that she had to return to Michigan for his citizenship party, and that she ordinarily didn't hear from him unless he had a specific question—when was she next coming home; where could his friend find good *pho* in Chicago; how would he get spilled Sriracha out of a white shirt. That was how he communicated, and when he did he needed to be answered right away. He hated voice mail and would call four times in a row until she picked up.

A gust of wind blew right through her coat and she paused, breathless. Gary tugged her closer. "Is he calling because of me?"

She laughed. "He doesn't know you exist."

"What about your sister?"

"I would never tell her anything."

"I know you said you weren't close."

"I wouldn't tell her because this isn't real," Linny said. "Also, she would freak. She's married, remember. Not that *you* care about marriage."

"Well, you and I are both good at keeping secrets," Gary said. "Maybe that's why we get along so well."

Linny considered this as they crossed the street to the sushi place. Perhaps he thought they got along because they never fought. Linny was careful to avoid becoming the soap opera girlfriend. She and Gary joked about their relationship, used words like *tryst* and *dalliance*. He was remarkably easygoing about cheating on his wife, Linny had said to Sasha. They did not talk about the future, and only once did Linny slip up. It happened accidentally, a month into their scheduled meetings. Lying in bed, Linny had said, "I like the silver in your hair."

"My dad had gone completely gray by the time he was my age. To think, thirty-eight used to sound ancient to me."

"It's not gray, it's silver," Linny said. "I wonder what it'll look like next year."

Gary patted her arm, saying nothing, and instantly Linny understood the mistake she had made.

Heading back home that day, Linny had blushed to herself. She had, as her mother had told her once, too much pride. It kept her playing a casual role, as if she could walk away from Gary at any time and never drop a word of bitterness. Linny had expected him to be a restless, nearing-middle-age man looking for some diversion. But he spoke fondly of his wife. While he liked that Pren's consulting work took her out of town every week, he also admired her accomplishments. Pren had scored with a Rauschenberg piece for her job; Pren had bought smartly for someone at a Sotheby's auction. At home, Pren designed their new sunroom. She had a closet devoted entirely to shoes, handbags, and scarves.

Linny tried not to react to such comments, though once she'd snapped, "How does Pren like my chicken piccata? I went straight from the hotel room to the kitchen."

To Linny the very idea of the future had become dangerous, like leaning over a balcony on the twentieth floor.

At the sushi restaurant Linny and Gary kept celadon mugs of green tea between their hands. Gary studied the menu while Linny adjusted her coat on the back of her chair, wound her hair into a rope over one shoulder. Her cell phone rang again and this time Linny turned it off.

"Your dad again?"

"He doesn't like to leave messages."

"Why?"

"It's just how he is. He and my mom fought a lot." She thought about telling him how they had practically split the house into his-and-her spaces, but let the moment pass.

"Maybe they were just figuring things out. My parents were high school sweethearts. I don't remember ever hearing them argue. But you know what I found on his computer the last time I went home? The biggest stash of Internet porn you can imagine." He looked over the menu again before closing it. "I might try that sardine appetizer special."

"How long have they been married?"

"Forty-five years. They're very into celebrating it, so I'm dreading their fiftieth."

"Do you feel a little weird," Linny said, "celebrating that? Don't you feel like a fraud or a hypocrite?"

"A fine question, miss." He was always entertained by these kinds of remarks—*spouting off at the mouth*, he called it. "But to answer: no. We all have our own arrangements. My dad's got his porn. I've got you."

Linny didn't laugh with him. Two Asian guys were sitting at a table nearby and she hoped they hadn't overheard. She hoped they weren't looking at her as the age-old stereotype, Asian mistress to a white guy. *Typical*, she imagined one whispering to the other. *Fucking Twinkie.*

She set down her mug of tea too hard, splashing her hand. Gary glanced at her, finally registering her tenseness, but then the waiter came by. Gary ordered edamame, miso soup, and three rolls. No sardines.

When Linny's mother died, her parents had been married nineteen years. They had never done much to acknowledge their anniversary, instead speaking of their years together as if the numbers were battle scars. Linny knew she could never talk about these kinds of things with Gary. Their meetings were too temporary. She didn't want to describe how her parents had scrambled onto a ship leaving Saigon in 1975; how her mother had given birth to Van in the refugee camp in California; how sponsors brought them to an apartment with stone-colored walls painted in a series of fan shapes that would become Linny's first memory. That, and her parents arguing in Vietnamese, their voices raging in the hall between the bedrooms while she and Van sat on the sofa bed watching TV; outside, a new correctional facility rose up near the freeway. Then the move to the house in Wrightville and Linny and Van

separating into their own bedrooms. And, years later, her father settling in the basement, and she and her mother realizing he planned to stay there. *What happened?* she'd wanted to
ask him, her mother, and never did. Later she supplied her
own answer: *Work. Other people. America.* It was the immigrant's
answer.

Linny watched Gary neaten the cuffs of his shirt as if preparing for a negotiating session.

"Think you'll stay in Chicago forever?" she asked.

"Pren loves it."

Linny had only met her a couple of times while dropping off
dinners from You Did It, and found her just as Gary had described: tall, with ice-princess looks but a Southern charmer
personality. She didn't baby-talk to the kids, seven-year-old
Alexis and five-year-old Charlie, who were generally cheerful
and well behaved, absorbed in their own friendships, school
projects, art classes. It was only when Linny saw them that she
felt any guilt.

Pren, short for Prentice, her grandmother's last name, was a
traveling art consultant, a job she loved. She was often flying to
some corporate city—Hartford, Atlanta, Denver—to help businesses and law firms choose art for their offices and lobbies.
"Like Whitley on *A Different World*," Linny had blurted out
when Gary first explained the job, but he had just looked at her
quizzically.

Gary, who'd grown up solidly middle-class in Cincinnati, met
Pren during their senior year at Northwestern. They married as
soon as they graduated, partly, Gary said, so they could share
an apartment, which Pren wouldn't do without the ring on her
finger. For a while they lived downtown, where Gary worked in

finance, and Pren drifted from one administrative assistantship to the next before finally landing the art consultant job. After Gary's second promotion they bought the house in Lincoln Park, on a leaf-thick street walkable to the zoo and the Green City Market, and when Alexis was born Pren hired a nanny. She found that she didn't, after all, want to be the stay-at-home mom she had always assumed she would be. It was the nanny who had driven Pren to seek out You Did It Dinners. "Anna's great with the kids, but her cooking is a little too trashy," Gary said. "Pren came home once and found us all eating Frito pie. She sort of lost it."

"We have tamale pie at You Did It," Linny said.

Pren was almost too nice, in the way some white women tended to be when they complimented Linny's smooth skin or slim figure. Van probably would have called it patronizing. Linny had imagined what her sister would say if she knew about Gary. Maybe, *You should be ashamed*. Or even simpler: *you're immoral; a homewrecker*. In high school, Van had told Linny she was on the verge of becoming a slut, the dreaded word that could ruin any girl's reputation. Stung, Linny had lamely shot back that at least she wasn't becoming a geek.

Van didn't understand the power of holding a boy's interest. She had never stolen someone's boyfriend or flirted with guys at a party just to make another girl jealous, just to feel what she was capable of breaking. The first time Linny took her clothes off for Gary she realized: there was satisfaction in knowing he was married to a woman like Pren.

"Have you done this before?" Gary had asked her.

"No," she said, though she had ended more than one relationship by starting a new one. "Have you?"

"No." His hands on her thighs. Did she even believe him?

Once in a while, as she prepared a family's supply of mush-room chicken and smothered chicken and lemon chicken, Linny thought of Pren picking up the phone to call You Did It Din-ners. How that one day led to the possible precipice of her own marriage, teetering further each time Linny opened a hotel room door to find Gary waiting for her.

After bowls of ginger ice cream, after Gary set his American Express card on the plastic tray that held the slip of the bill, he reached across the table and touched Linny's hand.

"So," he said. He paused, just long enough to make Linny worry. She watched as the Asian guys left the restaurant, letting in a burst of air.

"Go ahead."

"So, Pren got fired. A stupid reason, a stupid mistake she made—it doesn't matter. But she decided it was a sign. She's coming home to stay."

"Oh," Linny said, though she was wondering if that meant they would no longer need meals from her. No more deliveries—the thin band of excuse holding her and Gary together unrav-eling.

"She wants another child."

"And you?"

"It's what she wants."

Linny focused on the restaurant's textured green wallpaper and the brass sconces that shifted their light upward. The smell of warm rice and masago, the steam curling out of teacups—all seemed sharpened by her growing anger. She thought of Pren's big hazel eyes and beauty-pageant hair—never stringy, never frizzy. In that tall limestone house she surely hummed to herself, holding her wedding rings up to the glow of her Simon Pearce lamps.

"We'll still see each other at lunch or after work, as often as I can get away during the week," Gary said quickly. "Weekends are harder, but we'll work something out."

Then Linny did something she had never done before. She got up and left, heading past the green walls, the tables laden with plates of tuna rolls. She walked right out of the restaurant. Gary turned around to stop her but she moved fast, knowing he was stuck there until the waiter ran his credit card. She felt vaguely like she was on television. But she could not bear the sight of Gary's face one more minute. She couldn't bear to hear his plans, to feel herself pushed into a role she had never aimed to have.

Back in her apartment Linny sat in the dark, catching her breath. She counted how long it might take for Gary to pay the bill and walk back to her building. She measured the minutes, but he did not arrive. Outside, someone rummaged through one of the dumpsters in the alley. Linny had often watched people there, astonished at their findings: bags of bagels and hot dog buns; sweaters and baseball caps; once a toaster and a bonsai tree. She had seen a man carry away the blue floral tablecloth that had been her mother's, stained with the half bottle of balsamic vinegar Linny had spilled on it.

Usually Linny liked this furtive view, but tonight she wished her apartment faced the street, gathering up all the noise of the cars, the El, the drunks who always had something to say. She wanted to see how Gary looked as he left the restaurant and walked toward his car. She wondered if he had a parking spot on the street, and if maybe he was standing in front of her building at that very moment, deciding whether or not to come up. If she were hiding in the back of his car, would she hear him singing out loud to himself? Would she feel a change in the atmosphere as he drove eastward, closer to his real life?

3

# Van

The day after Miles left, Van opened the yellow pages to *H*. She went to her laptop and typed *Ann Arbor hotels* into a search engine, doubling and rechecking her research in the way she'd always done with work. She had ruled out the possibility of his staying with a friend; he wouldn't relinquish the privacy of his story in order to gain a few days in a spare bedroom. He would have gone to a hotel. But they lived in a college town; there were no W Hotels or hipster boutiques here, the kinds of places Miles preferred whenever they traveled. The Bell Tower Inn was stuffy and brocaded, too conspicuous. She couldn't picture him at the stodgy Campus Hotel either. Still, she called. No, each front desk clerk told her, no Miles Oh was registered. She dialed the Holiday Inn, the Embassy Suites, places he probably would never choose. She tried to think of what fake name he would use. Was he so afraid of her? What did he think she would do?

A certain fear kept Van from calling his cell phone. He had once told her a story he had heard, about a guy who had saved the dozen or so messages a desperate ex-girlfriend had left on his machine. The guy had played them over and over for all of his friends, laughing at her humiliation, at the quaver in her voice as she begged him to call her, to see her, to love her again.

It wasn't the same, Van told herself, to get in the car and drive around Ann Arbor, circling the building where Miles worked. She was looking for his dark red Land Cruiser and the first three letters of his license plate: LSM. To her the letters seemed to spell *lissome*. Which described Miles exactly. He was lissome, lithe, a self-sustained vine.

Out on Saline Road, Van stopped at McDonald's to get a coffee. It was late morning, just a few minutes before the switch from Egg McMuffins to Big Macs. At the pay window the smell of the grease made her both queasy and hungry, and she asked for an order of hotcakes. She parked facing the road and began to eat with her hands. The cakes were rubbery and soft, and when Van closed her eyes she thought of the slight pillow of flesh that had cupped her mother's arms. Miles hated fast food. Once, coming back from work, she had stopped for a furtive order of fries, wolfing them down before she got home. But Miles had eyed her sharply, sniffed her hair. "Ugh," he said. "What have you been doing?"

She stopped eating the hotcakes, and when she looked up she saw a dark red SUV waiting to exit a gas station across the street.

She threw the McDonald's bag into the passenger seat and jerked the car into gear. The Land Cruiser was merging into traffic and she went after it, cutting off a Civic hatchback, not slowing down until she and the SUV were nearly side by side. Van thought she could stay in Miles's blind spot, follow him right along to his destination. She was giddy, flushed with the kind of excitement she remembered from her first major court victory—a deportation case—three years ago, right after the New Year. She'd considered it an auspicious way to begin the millennium. Her client had wept with relief and later, in the darkness of her own bathroom, so had Van.

Up ahead a light turned red and the Land Cruiser braked. She slowed down, then suddenly decided she *wanted* him to look. She would show herself to him and see how he reacted.

Van pulled up next to the big car and faced Miles. The guy sitting in the driver's seat was listening to a rap song, nodding along to the beat. The SUV was dirty, an older model. It wasn't a Land Cruiser after all, but a Nissan Pathfinder. And here was a kid with dirty hair under a baseball cap, probably an undergrad at the university, driving a car his parents paid for. He didn't even notice Van.

Van made a right, heading back home. Of course it wasn't Miles. Not even close. He could have been anywhere in southeast Michigan. She pictured him sitting at a hotel restaurant, lingering over newspapers and coffee. Or maybe he was truly gone, on a plane, or already landed at his parents' house in San Francisco. He was still sleeping in that carved wooden bed they always shared when they visited. Wherever he was, he was unreachable. She could hear his voice in the back of her mind. *Did you really think you'd find me like that? Where's the logic in that, Van?*

There wasn't any logic. Just the long stretch of road, and Van going solo from one end to the next. The winter sky had locked itself down on Ann Arbor; every year it refused to relent until May. Van skirted the university she had loved for its law school, for bringing her to Miles, to get to the house that had been built just for them. She had no context, no way to think of Ann Arbor without thinking of Miles.

All her life with him she had been eager to get home. Every party, every social gathering, every going out was just a working toward the close of the evening. Van loved nothing more than the departure from a party, and Miles's old-fashioned insistence on helping her with her jacket. It was satisfying to know how each night would end: just the two of them, Van ushered out in the crook of his arm.

At home, his steps were gentle on the hardwood floors. His suits were a slim gabardine. He walked to the kitchen and called out to her—did she want a glass of wine? In the living room Van would clasp her hands together, wanting the whole day or night to pour into their house, where no one else had ever lived. She liked reminding herself that it was hers. That the history of the house began with them. Van touched the eggshell walls and thought, what more could be wanted?

In law school all kinds of girls went after Miles. Fellow students, undergrads, glam girls, co-op vegetarian girls, girls of all races. Van watched them. They held their drinks just so at parties, tilting their heads when they laughed. They asked him for dates outright. Miles was sweet and boyish yet utterly self-possessed, the kind of person who was never seen at four in the morning cramming for exams.

Van thought of herself as the kind of girl guys either overlooked or talked to because they needed her study notes, or because she represented a break from the exertion of trying to get with the hot girls. The few guys she had dated in college had hailed from small towns like hers; they majored in classics, and were so earnest and quiet that the relationships faded away without argument. She would never have thought to throw her hat into the ring that surrounded Miles. But she hung on to the times they interacted—small talk after orientation, even just exchanging hellos in the hallway. He could make Van—probably everyone, she supposed—feel not just noticed but *seen*. When they walked by each other he would break into a smile as though he couldn't help it. In their second year of school, he had taken to teasing her about her disciplined study habits, her perfect answers whenever she was called on in class. While most of their cohort, like Van, could spend hours going over tort reform, Miles took a blithe approach to classes, as if the entire enterprise of law school were something of an after-thought. He was also taller than most Asian guys she knew, a point that Van's father, later, would often mention—with admiration or envy, she wasn't sure.

Van, who had dutifully joined student Asian American Asso-ciations in college, had theorized that most midwestern Asians in her generation fell into one of two groups: politically aware and vaguely uncomfortable yet always claiming pride in their skin, or blissfully ignorant and unworried about the whole race thing. But Miles, who had grown up on the West Coast, whose great-grandfather had landed at Angel Island, had the confidence that came with growing up fourth-generation, surrounded by other Asians. He was politically aware *and* cheer-ful. He didn't get riled up about racism or affirmative action, and if Van did she felt strident next to him, out of date. She had almost felt sheepish admitting that her interest in law had be-gun in college, when she first learned about Vincent Chin, the Chinese American who had been beaten to death in 1982, in

Detroit, by an autoworker and his son who ended up serving no jail time. But Miles had been impressed by her motivation, called her studies noble.

It was a day in September, their third year of law school, when he sat down next to her on a limestone bench outside the library. Van, who had been waiting for her friend Jen Ye, felt suddenly jittery. She hadn't talked to Miles since the semester started, had heard that he'd summered at a firm in San Francisco.

"Aren't you going to miss this?" he said.

Van took just a moment too long to formulate a response, so that Miles laughed and said, "Yes, I'm talking to you."

Van turned red, tried to laugh too.

"I mean this suspended time," Miles elaborated. He looked out at the quad that lay before them. The sections of cropped grass looked crisp in the fall sunshine, and the stone pathways cutting through them matched the graceful gothic arches of the buildings they decorated and held. It was all very East Coast–looking to Van, sort of *Dead Poets Society*, though she wouldn't say that to Miles.

"Yes," Van said finally. "I already miss it."

Before she could say anything else, Miles stood up and began walking away from her. Van started; she wanted to call him back.

He went five steps, maybe ten. Then he turned around, his shoulders casual, hands in his pockets. He was smiling. "Well?"

Van missed lunch with Jen that day, forgetting all about it until that night when she had to call to apologize and explain. She was not an absentminded type, but she found it difficult, when in such close proximity to Miles, to think about other people. It was a feeling that would lessen only a little over the years, and she never lost the riveted, almost dizzying sensation he could inspire in her just by stepping into her line of vision.

And just like that their relationship happened. He showed up at her place at unexpected hours, so that Van learned always to be dressed, her studio apartment clean, just in case. He called her to say, *Let's get dinner in twenty minutes*. On Saturday mornings they would join the breakfast crowd at Zingerman's, where Miles, wearing the thin glasses he donned at such times, would read *The New York Times* and buy cheeses and stuffed olives for later in the day. For the first time in her life Van prepared for each date. She took to daily moisturizing her hands and feet. She kept her clothes ironed and hangered. She fussed with her hair, wishing she had paid attention to Linny's lengthy experiments with hair spray and hot rollers, her constant search for something called volume.

Within weeks Van's friends began declaring them a couple, although one did remark, "I had no idea you even knew each other." Van understood that to strangers they seemed a fine pairing: two Asian people, simple as that. But the people who knew them probably paused to figure out how easygoing Miles and shy, serious Van had ended up together.

Gracefully tall Jen Ye, who seemed a closer match for Miles save for her first-generation Ohio upbringing, said, "Looks like he's over that big heartbreak." When Van said she didn't know what that meant, Jen apologized. She knew all the gossip about their classmates and told Van, "Some long-distance girlfriend left him. Apparently she was very moody and dramatic. I thought you knew. But it doesn't matter. The important thing is how much he adores *you*."

And he did adore her, had said so from nearly their first day together, even if Van sometimes wondered at that. She felt—couldn't help it, in spite of what her women's studies professors would have said—chosen.

A couple of months after they started dating, Van discovered the pictures. Three of them, framed, perched on a windowsill in Miles's bedroom, revealed when Van lifted the blinds to let in the light.

He lived in a small apartment off Packard Street. All of the furniture belonged to a property management company, which favored cast-offs from the university building and maintenance department. Miles liked to play being a bachelor, wearing boxer shorts while eating Bell's pizza, splayed on the mustard-colored sofa. But his bedroom hinted at his real self: pale blue sheets freshly laundered; desk cleared of all but his computer; dusted bookshelves; walls decorated with framed black and white photographs of a lone silo, a car with a flat tire on the side of some derelict road, a tree split in half by lightning. Van had assumed that Miles had taken the photos, since he often talked about his interest in photography, architecture, and design. He had taken a number of art classes in college and kept an ornate-looking camera in his closet.

On the windowsill, the pictures of three women looked out at Van. A brunette of uncertain ethnicity—Armenian, Van guessed. An Asian girl with ungodly cheekbones and a smile-less, burning stare. And a freckled girl with clear hazel eyes and a pile of blond wavy hair.

Miles was taking a shower, so Van pulled out the biggest

photo album from his bookshelf. The pictures, organized chronologically, interspersed Miles and his family with images of the three women. Here was Miles at a beach, his arm around the blonde. Here Miles and the Asian girl were dressed up, holding glasses of champagne. The women looked happy, taller than Van, well dressed. These were pictures they could look at without shame for the rest of their lives. Van flipped through the pages quickly and put the album back. She sat on the bed, overcome with a searing sense of bitterness she had never before experienced. It felt like a puncture, an invasion.

When Miles emerged, Van was making the bed. She had left the window blind up so he would know that she had seen the photographs of the women. When he didn't acknowledge them, Van nodded toward the black and whites on the wall and said, "Did you take those?"

"A friend who's a photographer," he replied, opening his laptop to check his e-mail.

"What about the ones in the window?"

Miles looked up, amused. "Are you jealous?"

"I just wondered who they were."

He went to the window and introduced them. "This is Maya, Diana, and Julie. Ladies, meet Van."

She knew she was supposed to play along. "And where do they live?"

"All over. San Francisco, New York." He still had a curious smile on his face, as though he had just uncovered a secret dirty habit of Van's. "They're just friends now, Van. I've known them for a long time. You can't be jealous of my having friends. I never understood people who aren't mature enough to be friends after a relationship ends."

"Did one of them take those photos on the wall?" Van tried to keep her voice light.

"That's Julie."

Miles came over to Van and put his arms around her. He smelled of citrus soap and shaving cream. "So jealous," he said teasingly into her hair.

The rest of that year, whenever Julie's name popped up—Julie had done volunteer work in Cambodia; Julie had e-mailed him to say she was spending six months in Italy—Van felt that same puncture, a tightness that stayed with her for hours. Julie was the heartbreak girl, and Van imagined her arriving in Ann Arbor to reclaim Miles with her effortless good looks and artistic photography. Whenever Van was alone in Miles's room she would stare at the photo of Julie on the windowsill, half hating her, half in awe of her. These women were a part of his past, Miles said. He believed in respecting that. *Don't you?* he would add, and Van would agree. All that school year, she worked hard to contain the jealousy, which Miles had called the least attractive emotion. There was no way to express her discomfort with the photographs without acquiescing to the label of insecure girlfriend. So Van continued to wake up beneath the gaze of Julie's art, convincing herself that Miles was right: What was so wrong, after all, with staying friends with one's exes? She knew, by then, that in order to keep him she would have to sweep away what bothered her. And she did want to keep him. She wanted, with a fierceness that daily rebloomed, to have what the other women could only eye, or remember, from afar.

Several times, Van almost told Jen about the photographs, but she could imagine her friend's response. Jen was the one person who seemed unwilling to be fully charmed by Miles. "If he tries any harder not to be interested in law school he's going to have to drop out," she had remarked once in her deadpan way.

"Half the people here don't want to be lawyers," Van had defended him. "I think Miles is looking at law as an option rather than the rest of his life. He didn't even go out for any of the journals."

That's when Jen dropped the news that actually Miles's bid to join the *Law Review* had been rejected; Jen knew because she had dated the editor. Van, who had aimed for the journal on race and law, only shrugged and said, "Happens to a lot of people."

She chose to admire Miles for not throwing himself into the intensity of school, for not competing the way everyone else did. It was spring then, they were the class of 1999, and their classmates talked endlessly about where they were headed next, where they might be ensconced in time for a new century. Van could see the curtain of their three years slipping down, and a new one lifting behind it, and she was glad when, in the impatient shuffle toward graduation, Miles responded by drawing them away. They spent a weekend in Saugatuck, near Lake Michigan; skipped class to spend four days in Chicago, where Van did not bother to call her sister. For spring break Miles took her to San Francisco so Van could meet his parents in the Italianate foyer of their house in Pacific Heights.

When Miles proposed, sitting on the bench outside the law library, one month before graduation, Van cried out of surprise and relief. He said he loved everything about her, from the confidence of her arguments in mock trial to the static in her hair. He loved her devotion to immigration law and her funny, frog-like laugh. She was smart and clear-headed and she knew just where she wanted to go in life, he said, so why waste any time?

*But where will we live?* was the first thing Van asked after saying yes. She had accepted a position at the International Center in Detroit, where she had worked the previous two summers. For months she had expected Miles to move back to California. She had wondered if he would ask her to go with him; she had wondered when and how their relationship would have to end.

Looking at the ring Miles pushed onto her finger, Van imagined herself in the early morning chill and fog of the Bay Area, applying for jobs at immigration firms. In an instant she resolved to do it. But Miles surprised her again. "You've got a great opportunity at the IC," he said. "We're not going anywhere." He went on to say he had taken a position at the in-town office of Volker, Voss, and Williams, which Van knew well as the corporate-law giant of the Midwest. The *Midwest*, she thought, the word itself sounding so humble. She couldn't picture Miles staying here, not joining their classmates who had been hired at multinationals.

He wouldn't hear her objections. "You've focused so much of your work on immigrant law in this state, Van. You should stay a while. Maybe not forever, but for now."

It was the right thing to do, he insisted, and everyone who heard about it told Van she was lucky, and did she realize that men never put their wives' careers first? Even Jen was impressed. Van's father, over the phone, told her she was lucky to be marrying a lawyer, seeming to forget that Van was one too.

Only Linny expressed disapproval. "Hold on," she said when Van called with the news. "You're getting married to a guy you haven't even dated a *year*? Are you sure about this?"

"Of course I'm sure," Van snapped, irritated at how typical her sister was, always looking for flaws.

"Okay," Linny said, full of reluctance. "But I've seen women get married just because they want to be married."

Van flushed, remembering how her sister had bragged about her dates in high school. *I don't think a guy has* ever *called you*, Linny had once said with a laugh. She probably resented Van's having found anyone at all. "You're hardly one to be doling out advice. When was the last time you had a serious relationship? You don't even know Miles."

"Yeah, but I know you."

"What is that supposed to mean?"

"Nothing." Silence. "Forget it."

"I've already forgotten it," Van said, hanging up.

By fall she and Miles had moved into an apartment together, taken the Michigan bar exam, planned the wedding, and started looking at houses in Ann Arbor. With a down payment drawn from his trust fund ("Trust fund!" Jen had exclaimed. "That's so nonimmigrant."), he had started looking at older neighborhoods, with homes that had "character" and original leaded windows, near the arboretum. But these tended to be smaller than the houses going up in the new subdivisions north of Ann Arbor, and it didn't take long before Miles warmed up to the prospect of everything new, everything theirs. Like the wedding, plotting out the house became one of his projects, and he could spend weeks discussing maple versus cherry wood, one lighting fixture versus another. It had all seemed daunting to

Van. To her, words like *escrow* sounded like a threat, in spite of the course she had taken in real estate law. As Miles had once dryly pointed out, Van was as certain in the classroom as she was uncertain in real life. He scheduled meetings with architects who weren't, as he told her, cookie-cutter types at all but the kind who happened to create beautiful new construction.

Van had never lived in such a place, surrounded by hygienic gleam and newness. The prospect was as alluring as it was guilt-making, especially in contrast to the cases she dealt with at the International Center. But it was too late to think about guilt. By December she and Miles had married in San Francisco and gone to St. Barts for their honeymoon; by the following summer they had moved into the new two-story colonial home, so much larger than Van had initially expected, with its rosy bricks and black shutters, the double garage carefully hidden from the street front, in a subdivision named Birch Crest Hills.

Of course, Miles had invited the three framed women to the wedding. To Van's relief only Diana had come, and Van had been so busy talking to other guests that she didn't have time to scrutinize her smiles. Maya and Julie had sent regrets—Julie probably wandering around India or Tibet, no doubt taking pictures. When Van and Miles moved into their house, the framed women disappeared along with Julie's black and whites. Grateful for his silent tact, Van took it as a sign of how well Miles understood her. How much he truly did love her. She was glad she had suppressed the urge to throw away the photos or say something about them. Now that she and Miles were married it was all worth it. Like a strange hazing she had survived.

Van couldn't help feeling that in the space of two years, from the day Miles sat down next her on that stone bench, her entire life, her future, had been formed. There were moments when it didn't seem real—this house, this husband. Then she would look at Miles's left hand and feel a profound sense of victory, her boat glided into its correct, sheltered slip.

Even her job seemed to cooperate. At the International Center, a hub of immigrant law in downtown Detroit that brought Latino, Asian, and Middle Eastern communities into its fold, Van worked with asylum seekers, refugees, and immigrants looking to sponsor relatives. Each weekday, and most Saturdays, Van listened to Spanish-language CDs while driving the hour commute to the Center. She had started taking Arabic language classes too, because the Detroit area had become the Arab immigrant capital of America. Jen Ye worked in the district attorney's office nearby, so the two of them often went out for lunch together. Driving back home in the evenings, Van would plan all the conversation pieces she could set forth over dinner: what one coworker had said to another; someone's extraordinary story of escape and refuge; the morass that was U.S. immigration policy.

Yet Ann Arbor, and their house of soft lighting and speakers that emitted carefully chosen jazz music, often seemed an unbridgeable world away from the IC. Miles, who had gotten interested in gourmet cooking, would spearhead most of their dinner plans and Van would play the role of sous-chef. Secretly, she found their kitchen a little intimidating: the stainless steel hood that hovered over the range; the island that housed a built-in wine refrigerator. The drawers had a special track that slowed their progress, like antilock brakes. It was a beyond-bourgeois kitchen, Van sometimes thought, calling back the dulled laminate counters in her parents' house, the cupboards that rained sawdust in the cooking pans.

Like everything else in the kitchen, the cabinets had been a product of Miles's many magazines and home decorating websites, all of them jammed with pictures of gleaming stone counters and streamlined appliances. He had spent hours weighing one cabinet pull against another, lining them up to ask Van's opinion. She never got over feeling that she was being tested whenever he asked her to make a choice. She was a suburban girl who had married a city guy, and that truth never left her for long. When at last Van touched the slim cabinet pulls done in satin stainless steel, Miles beamed. "Exactly what I was thinking," he approved.

Birch Crest Hills, with its curving roads and wide lawns, brought to mind Van's father's best friend, Truc Bao, who had predicted his own fate by changing his first name to Rich and then amassing a fortune from dry-cleaning franchises in the west Michigan area. Rich Bao had a huge house—a McMansion before anyone knew the term—but Vietnamese American taste. That meant puffy white leather sofas, too much brass and gold, heavy mahogany tables, and floors of green marble tile. As kids Van and Linny had been in awe of such clear wealth, admiring it like a house out of a soap opera. It wasn't until she got to college that Van understood the guttural depth of the word *tacky*. Van and Miles's house might be all new, but it would be nothing like Rich Bao's.

Miles had grown up with parents and grandparents who had done well enough to afford private schools, resort vacations, and Qing porcelain without a second glance at the bank accounts. Miles had learned to drive with his mother's Lexus; he had backpacked in Europe twice; had even, in high school, been named homecoming king. In so many ways he embodied an immigrant dream of immersion and status, and Van felt the burden of having married up and into it.

Where their house was concerned, Miles knew how to speak of art and architecture. He might point out a curve of wall that looked very Bertrand Goldberg, or a lamp in a store window that was an obvious Nelson rip-off. Van tried to pay attention, though it was many months before she realized that the designers Charles and Ray Eames were not brothers but a husband-and-wife team. Van noticed, though, that Miles's tastes kept shifting. Even as their brick colonial had risen from its cement foundation pushed into the frozen Michigan earth, every other sentence Miles spoke seemed to carry the phrase *mid-century modern*. He hesitated just once, when Van asked if it was all right to pair modern furniture with the traditional-looking colonial. He answered, finally, that the contrast itself was modern.

Before the kitchen plans got under way Van had asked for customized counter and cabinet heights. It had been her father's idea, the first thing he suggested when Van mentioned the new construction. He calculated that counters two inches lower than standard would be optimal, but even one would make a difference. "Think of the comforts," he urged, and Van had to admit that it sounded pretty good. She'd never been in a kitchen that didn't seem designed for a tall person.

Miles had laughed. "I love your dad. He's hilarious."

"But it does make sense," Van said. "Actually, it would be kind of a dream come true."

"Well, what about me? I'm not short."

Except for their ongoing debate about pets—Van wanted a cat but Miles thought only a dog would be suitable when they had a kid old enough to want one—they rarely argued. When they did, though, it could become epic, Miles's mood darkening for days even after Van, the first to give in, apologized. She knew she was going to lose this argument too, when Miles insisted that custom counters would affect the resale value of the house. "People will say, that's the house for short people. You can't expect someone as short as you is going to want to buy this place."

"We might not sell," Van found herself saying. A four-bedroom house in a top school district—that was enough for her.

"Van, come on." The case was closed.

She never told her father that she gave up on the idea of a kitchen customized for short people. He had only visited them once, anyway, while driving back from a friend's in Detroit. He had barely glanced at the kitchen; the mere fact of the house sealed his affection for Miles. "You see how he'll always take care?" he said to Van, disapproval built into his voice as if she were already neglecting her husband. So the only consequence was that whenever Van dragged out the Luong Arm or used the step stool that she kept stored in a corner cabinet she felt a slight flare of irritation toward Miles. Sometimes she planted it on the floor louder than necessary. But Miles, if he noticed, didn't say. He was on to another project—his office upstairs, or built-in bookshelves for the family room, which he refused to call the TV room.

Van came to realize that Miles needed these projects, that without them he could grow alarmingly restless. That was when he would take jabs at Ann Arbor or the state of Michigan, calling it provincial or down and out, depressed, flyover country. Then Van would redouble her acknowledgment of the sacrifice he had made in settling there. She would steer the conversation toward decorating the guest bedrooms, or landscaping the backyard. She told him, finally, that she would be willing to move anywhere he wanted, whenever he wanted. It felt suspenseful, waiting for him to make up his mind about leaving this place for good, heading out to one of the coasts where, surely, people felt more tied to the national conversation. But no new jobs materialized, and as long as Miles didn't bring up the subject, neither did Van. After a while, she started hoping that in spite of his complaints, maybe he preferred their life in Ann Arbor after all. At any rate, it was easier to let the lid on the topic fall shut.

Mostly, life seemed more or less tranquil, orderly, the way Van had always pictured marriage should be. While she brought home sweets and baked goods from her clients, Miles brought ideas for the ongoing decoration of their house. He didn't talk much about his work at Volker, Voss, but he didn't seem unhappy there either. In her mind Van plotted out the years ahead: a child, maybe two; a couple weeks of every summer in San Francisco and at his parents' beach house.

But all of that was before Vijay Sastri.

He had been a client like many others, in the States as a student, hoping to secure an H-1B temporary worker visa through an engineering firm that wanted to hire him. Van had filed his paperwork, chatted with him about his wife, about which restaurants they liked best in the area. Vijay was going to settle in, work his way up the salary rung, eventually buy a house in one of the suburbs; his children would grow up completely American, shun Vijay's customs for those of their white friends at school. It was going to be the typical immigrant story.

But then Vijay got arrested, called Van from a holding cell. It was November 2001 and blustery, the roads thick with blackened slush. And Van had known even then, long before she presented his case, that she couldn't save him, couldn't keep him from the fate of deportation. Still, the loss—her first and only—hit her hard. It hit Miles too, seemed to shake him into a state of mind, of intensity, she'd never seen before. Then Van's whole life seemed to become a tumble, a spillage, Miles arguing again with her about what they were doing here in this blank Michigan landscape. It was in the haze of those days Van learned she was pregnant, and the news became the one thing she wanted to pin down, a thumbtack on a map of her world. She wanted to keep Miles there with her. Until that too, like the well of certainty she had started to think her life could be, became the thing that never was. Uncontainable. And, in retrospect, the beginning of that moment when Miles walked into the house and told her he didn't want to live with her anymore.

At home after her phantom car chase around Ann Arbor, Van checked the phone for voice mails. None. In the kitchen she buried the McDonald's bag in the trash. The garbage bin, built into the cabinetry, smelled of the shrimp shells she and Miles had peeled two nights before. He had sautéed them with garlic and scallions and chili oil, making jasmine rice in the fuzzy-logic rice cooker.

As if to test how alone she was, Van opened one of the cutlery drawers and tried to slam it shut, but the drawer returned primly to its place. She moved on to the cabinet doors, which had little felt-like stubs that prevented the doors from banging shut. She pulled back the door to the baking pans and kicked it as violently as she could. She did it again and again to hear the muted slams.

Van had always hated how mournful and slow Sundays felt, full of regrets, full of errands that didn't get done. The work week loomed the way the school week had when she was a kid. She had nothing to do this Sunday, especially, but wait for her husband to call or come back. It was her only motivation to shower and dress. If Miles came back, he would find her checking case files at the kitchen counter, not drowsing in front of the TV. He would find her a natural part of the house and the message would be clear: they belonged in the same space, where each room blended into the next, leading toward the soaring ceilings and windows. Walls and walls of a taupe-colored paint, a shade called Evening Fawn that Miles had chosen.

When the phone rang Van's heart dropped. She was so certain of Miles that she didn't check the caller ID before answering.

"I'm having a party," her father's voice announced.

Van tried to hide her sigh of disappointment. "What for?"

"Citizenship. I'm a hundred percent American. The letter come in the mail yesterday."

"Congratulations, Dad." She was actually relieved to hear the news. She had been the one to fill out the forms, inspecting every detail. Immigration was known for rejecting applications that had even one error, making the wait of two years or more even longer. Van had also paid the hundreds of dollars in fees, knowing they were a main part of her father's refusal to apply in the first place. She had brought each round of her father's documents, fingerprints, and photos to the Detroit immigration office in person. All of this her father had taken for granted, as he did whenever he asked her to help one of his friends with some paperwork. "Just in time too," she added. "It's really a good thing we sent your application when we did."

"What you mean?"

"INS is being taken over by the Department of Homeland Security. It's going to be a huge mess."

"It's no difference to me."

"Well, it will be to a lot of people," Van said irritably.

"The ceremony is in April," her father went on. "Two months from now, on the last Friday. I'm having a big party on the Saturday. Everyone's coming. Vien's family is coming from California, everyone in town—everyone. So you and Linh and Miles have to be there. Friday and Saturday."

"The ceremony's at the Gerald Ford Museum, right?"

"Yes." He always said the word with an inflection that indicated *obviously*. "You be there, Van. You and Linh and Miles."

Only her parents and other Vietnamese people called Van and her sister by their real names: *Van* pronounced *Vun*, *Linh* instead of *Linny*. Van had become so used to the Americanized versions of their names that *Vun* sounded strange to her. It belonged to another person.

"I'll tell you what else. Someone told me about a chance for a television show, so I'm working on something new." For years he had been fantasizing about QVC or the Home Shopping Network, envisioning himself a Vietnamese version of the gadget-master Ron Popeil. That description, in fact, was one Van had used, laughing about him with Miles. *My dad thinks he's the next Ron Popeil.* Miles had gone along, always calling Van's father an "eccentric character."

"I thought you were still perfecting the Luong Arm."

"I've been doing that already," her father said. "And you

remember the invention that comes up out of the water, from the submarines?"

"The periscope thing. I know." He'd been working on that for years now, a viewfinder device to allow short people to see over people's heads in a crowd.

"The Luong Eye. It's a good one, but I've got a better one now. I realized on the TV, it's smart to have a series. The Luong Arm and the Luong Eye. Then people remember. Wait to see my other idea too."

"It sounds great." Out of habit she was careful not to break his chatty mood. He got like this once in a while, usually spurred by drinking, and at such times could keep Van on the phone for twenty minutes. Their more typical conversations went no longer than a commercial break.

Van wandered into the TV room and lay down on the sofa. Her father was still talking but she only half listened. Looking up at the vaulted ceiling, she remembered how anxious he had been on the day of his citizenship exam. She had jumped up from her chair in the waiting room as soon as he was done. "They ask me, 'Who is Betsy Ross?' I don't remember that in the book you gave me," he said, referring to the exam guidebook she had sent him. "So I say she was married to a big president. The lady laughed. But I passed the test." He didn't seem that happy about it, so Van took him to lunch at a Chinese buffet. They ate mostly in silence, her father repeatedly getting up for more king crab and fried shrimp. Several times he seemed to forget where they were sitting, and Van had to wave at him to call him back.

Now she interrupted whatever he was saying about the party. "Dad, I have to go."

"Don't forget the party."

"I know."

"Tell Miles I say hello." He always said this.

"I will."

Van kept the phone nearby as she slumped on the sofa. She told herself to get up, maybe clean the tortilla chip crumbs from the kitchen counter. She told herself to do some work. Instead she covered herself with a throw blanket, curling into the warmth. She lay there for a long time, unable to fall asleep, realizing slowly that she did not expect to hear the sound of the garage door lifting.

During their first winter in this house they had spent so much money on heating bills that she started to turn the thermostat down a couple of degrees and wear a zip-up sweatshirt in the house. Miles laughed at that, asked where her Jimmy Carter cardigan was, and said it reminded him of something her father would do. In fact, it was something he did do. So Van took the layers of sweatshirt off, let the heat run high. They simply paid the bills. And the novelty and freshness of such open space faded into footfalls and whispers and the eeriness of late night when it seemed anything at all could come crashing through one of the high windows. Van sometimes thought that if she were a bat, or a crow, or a pigeon, she would have tried it. She would have set the glass to shattering, sailed through someone else's house, used up all the space that humans never reached.

# 4

# Linny

Linny had lived in Chicago for five years, enough time to inure her to the touristy crowds on Michigan Avenue where suburbanites traveled great distances to shop at Nike and Banana Republic. Still, whenever she approached the city from her Wicker Park neighborhood she couldn't suppress a little catch of joy at seeing all those skyscrapers coming into view. They created a chart on a graph that she could follow. Even on a day like this one, the second week of April, cold and gray, the buildings seemed to collect the gathered gleam from Lake Michigan and throw the light back into the air.

Sometimes Linny imagined running into Pren here, on the northern side of Michigan Avenue, between Barney's and the Drake Hotel, where Linny's friend Sasha ran the Paolo Francesca Salon. It was easy enough to get there from Lincoln Park. Linny had walked the reverse route, heading north past all of the doormen buildings in the Gold Coast to get to Lincoln Park itself, then down a side street lined with oaks, toward Gary's limestone house with its wide front stoop and bay windows. Most of the families Linny cooked for lived in homes that carried a similar sense of tidy well-being, a scent of children with freshly shampooed hair. How many of them ate her dinners night after night, the parents checking the large-font instructions to know which temperature their ovens should bear?

Before answering the ad for You Did It Dinners, Linny had lasted eight months as Paolo Francesca's receptionist. She sometimes returned to get a free haircut or manicure, but mostly just to get after-work drinks with Sasha. They used to wait tables together, back when Linny first arrived in Chicago, and over the years had shared countless stories about dates and jobs gone wrong. Sasha had grown up in a working-class neighborhood just outside the city and made no secret of her desire to get ahead. She always knew what to do on weekend nights, bringing Linny to parties and lounge openings, places that tried to lend out a sense of being somewhere significant.

When Linny arrived at the salon, Sasha was neatening a stack of fashion magazines in the waiting area. "I can't wait to get out of here," she said. "Are you wearing a new jacket?" It was a habit they had, appraising the ebb and flow of each other's wardrobes.

"Sale," Linny began to reply, but was interrupted by a client swathed in a plastic Paolo Francesca cape. Blond highlighting foils twisted the woman's hair into an alien look.

"Excuse me," she said, drawing her arms out from under the plastic. She touched the edges of her forehead gingerly, as if afraid to know what was there. A bride-to-be, Linny decided— diamond ring flashing, getting ready for the big day. "I thought someone was going to give me a pedicure while I'm waiting for this color to take?"

"We'll be right there," Sasha said, putting on a customer-service smile that Linny knew well, and used herself, when the mothers gathered in the assembly-line kitchen.

"Well, I've been waiting." The woman turned to go back, but paused to point at Linny. "Are you doing the pedicure?"

"What?" Linny's word came out like a bark.

The woman, realizing her error, began to laugh. "Oh, sorry, I just thought—"

"Someone will be right with you," Sasha rushed in. She escorted the woman back to the inner rooms of the salon, glancing back at Linny to mouth the words, *Fucking bitch.*

Linny waved a hand to indicate, *Don't worry.* It was not the first time she'd been mistaken for the manicure girl.

During her time at Paolo Francesca, Linny had quickly tired of the brides that clouded up every weekend. They arrived doughy-faced in button-down shirts and left shimmering, haloed in veils, their updos anchored with bobby pins and a shellac of styling cream. Eventually they all looked the same, or wanted to, with heavy "natural" makeup and an inevitable strapless dress. Salons like Paolo Francesca promised, and often delivered, the magic of metamorphosis. But Linny had seen the process too up-close.

She had spent much of her adolescence perfecting her own hair, makeup, and nails, but realized that doing so for other women was worse than a chore. Besides, she had always vowed never to become just another Vietnamese girl running a nail shop. Even though Paolo Francesca, with its steel counters and relentless techno music, was far removed from the strip-mall joints where some of Mrs. Luong's friends worked, the very space of white on a woman's French-tip manicure never failed to remind Linny of those striving, Lancôme-wearing Vietnamese women in Wrightville. Linny would shudder just driving past all those nail salons with orange adhesive letters spelling out signs on the window. *Nails by Kim. Nails by Hoang.* Or the worst, *Oriental Manicure.* Where bargain-conscious white women who stopped in to get their nails done always believed they were being gossiped about in Vietnamese. Where the same whiny soap opera music would blare from a boom box, the same Vietnamese magazines would cover the tables, and the same odor of nail polish remover and incense would linger in the air. Linny had promised herself that she wouldn't end up filing other women's nails for a living.

She'd never told Gary, or any guy, about that. As far as Gary knew she would be working at You Did It Dinners forever. He once said he admired her work ethic, whatever that meant. He spoke of his middle-class background as if it forged a connection between them, when he had no idea how Linny had really grown up, first in that little apartment, then in the ranch house in Wrightville. The voices of her parents rising in argument while Linny and Van increased the volume of the television.

In the week since she had left Gary at that restaurant he had started leaving her enough voice mails to make her cringe. Where once she used to call back immediately, engaging in the banter that would lead to their next meeting, now she felt like she was part of some show. When he said, *Come on, Linny. Bring back your kumquats,* Linny wanted to tell him, *Do you know how you sound?* But instead she didn't answer at all. Just that day, working in the company kitchen at You Did It, Linny had realized that for months now she had fancied herself a stand-in wife, the kind who kept her man fed. Had Gary ever thought that, too?

At Paolo Francesca, waiting for Sasha to grab her coat and bag, Linny tried to picture Pren stepping into the salon, holding forth her hands so Linny could get to work on the nails. But the image didn't last. Pren was too polite, for one thing. And try as she might, Linny never could sustain a vision of her and Pren in the same room for long. Linny just didn't belong in that sphere.

Although Pren surely understood, as Linny did, how beauty equaled currency. Linny had figured that out even before middle school, when she memorized makeup tips from *Cosmo* and *Glamour* while standing in the magazine aisle at the grocery store. Linny put in long hours experimenting with shadows and liners, trying to make her eyes look bigger, deeper-set, less Asian. She painted plum colors up to her eyebrows and applied three coats of mascara. She ran peroxide-soaked cotton balls through her hair to create caramel highlights. Van, meanwhile, didn't use any makeup at all. She bit at her nails until they bled; she called Linny vain. Coming home from an afternoon at Woodland Mall, Linny would see Van sitting at the kitchen table, surrounded by school and library books. Linny would avoid her sister's gaze, walk right past her without saying a word. Even then, she thought, Van was too full of worries, always thinking ahead.

When their mother returned from work, her hands cramped from a full day of sewing, she would smile to see Van studying. "Good girl," she would say to her. To Linny Mrs. Luong would shake her head, make a low noise at the back of her throat to express her thoughts about Linny's bird's-nest hair and rainbow makeup. She wasn't home enough to control how Linny looked.

Mr. Luong would be holed up in the basement, working on the Luong Arm or Luong Eye, occasionally popping upstairs for tea or to make announcements to his wife and daughters. He liked having them a captive audience, especially when they were eating. A favorite topic was statistics about short people.

"The average height of American men is five feet nine and one-half inches. That is tall. We live in this country with some of the tallest people. That's America. But for guys like me, like Vietnamese, it's five feet three. American women average height is five feet four inches. But girls like you, five feet.

"Did you know you girls are called petite? Petite is women five feet four inches and shorter than that. I think they should say five feet two inches.

"Did you know that men who are short have hard times getting jobs?"

When he went on like this about the plight of short people in America, Linny, Van, and Mrs. Luong tended to tune him out. Van would continue reading; Linny would watch TV; Mrs. Luong would clean the dinner dishes. It was no use to challenge him in any way, though Van, in her teenage years, sometimes tried. *What about tall people?* she'd ask. *They have problems too. Maybe even worse than us. My friend Keri is really tall and she has just as hard of a time.* To which their father would always counter, *This is a country of tall people.*

Usually Dinh Luong liked to lecture at them, needing little response. He would start off with a confidential tone in his voice, almost charming, beginning sentences with "Did you know." When he got excited he would misuse idioms, like the time he told them all to "cut me some slacks" and Linny and Van had howled with laughter. He would go along with the joke until the moment it went too far—no telling when that would be—and then he'd command them to shut up and listen. He would flick his daughters' chins to make them face him. He would jab the off button of the television so violently the set would tremble. He would pick up keys, a newspaper—things that wouldn't break—and throw them into the living room.

Mrs. Luong reacted to these outbursts with deliberate calmness, so Linny would do the same. *What did knowing any of this information change?* her mother would ask while Linny folded her arms, silently agreeing with her.

But Van played Mr. Luong's game, always more willing to be the dutiful daughter. Perhaps as a way to diffuse his fits of anger, she even went to the library and gathered a list of famous short people, starting with James Madison, at five-four the shortest U.S. president, and including Beethoven, Joan of Arc, Mother Teresa, and of course old Napoleon, whom Mr. Luong didn't like because he resented the idea of the "complex" that Van had repeatedly explained to him. At first he thought it referred to a "non-pole" complex. "Just because the short people can't be tall like a pole," he fumed. "Now we can never get mad or be the boss without getting called a complex! Plus then people say we have the *short* temper. Not fair."

Such a focus—who was tall, who was short—became woven into their lives, so that a person's name couldn't even be mentioned without one of them wondering or stating out loud that person's height. In sixth grade when Linny had been assigned a report on David B. Steinman, architect of the resplendent Mackinac Bridge, Van piped up that Steinman had stood barely five feet tall. "And," she added prissily, "he was one of the most successful and famous bridge designers ever."

"Very good," their father had praised her. "You know to keep track." He had offered Van a big smile, rare enough to make Linny feel forgotten.

Linny knew lots of families lined their kids up to record their height, but to her father it wasn't just for fun—it was a living record of their identities. Whenever Linny complained about wanting to be taller he would reprimand her. "Not about being tall," he said. "It's about being being just as equal as tall people."

"Well, that problem would be solved if we just were taller."

"No, Linh. It means we want to be *smarter*. If you not seen as equal you do whatever you can to make equalness happen. Why you think I invent things?"

In the final tally Mr. Luong was five-foot-three, Van five and one-eighth, Mrs. Luong four-eleven-and-a-half, and Linny four-eleven. In Linny's seventeenth year, Mr. Luong had noted, "That's it for you."

"I could still have a growth spurt, you never know," Linny said.

He shook his head. "It's done. Now you got to do work by yourself."

Linny had heard her share of lame short jokes—*How's the weather down there?*—*Do you want a booster seat?*—*Oops, I almost stepped on you!*—but that was the first time she felt sorrow, real hurt, at the fact of her height. She had wanted, at least, to be as tall as Van.

Her father said, "It's not your fault. It's your family."

Linny had never heard him say such a thing before. They

stood there for a moment, looking at the pencil marks that crept upward on the hallway wall. The lowest mark belonged to her at age eight, when they had first moved into the house.

Her father admitted, "You maybe drink more milk to be same as Van. Too late now."

When Linny started acquiring boyfriends she bragged to Van that she liked being short: she could make even the scrawniest guy feel tall and powerful. "What scrawny guys?" Van had countered with a sneer. "No one's short in this town but us Vietnamese, and you only date white guys."

"You don't go out with *any*body."

By high school, their roles were set. No going back: Linny would join the popular girls at lunch and Van would get praised by her teachers. School felt like floating—or inertia, one of the few things she remembered from science class. The path of least resistance. Linny managed to date a lot of boys without quite being labeled, in spite of Van's ominous predictions, a slut. She was elected to Homecoming Court (though the title of queen went to leggy Melissa Heinke). She was, in fact, invited to every dance from the moment she stepped into ninth grade. Meanwhile, Van went to debate tournaments, took Advanced Placement classes, headed up the school's quiz bowl team, eventually earning a partial scholarship to the University of Chicago.

Linny went to the local community college, and when those two years were up began a series of moves from one state school to the next. Each place seemed the same, for in each place she found herself seeking out boyfriends because she didn't know any girls to hang out with, didn't know how to keep friendships with them. Her high school group had scattered, and some were even getting married, a leap Linny couldn't fathom. She took classes in fashion merchandising and marketing, always losing interest before declaring a major. At four o'clock on a winter day, darkness already falling, Linny would find herself in the middle of a campus, surrounded by new trees and buildings resembling those in an industrial park, and she would need a minute to remember where she was.

When Linny dropped out of school for good and moved to Chicago with a boyfriend, her father and sister told her she would waste her life without a degree. But Linny found satisfaction just writing down her city address. Growing up, most of the kids she knew said they couldn't wait to get out of west Michigan. *Chicago* was the word they revered, nearly as bright a beam as *New York*. And Linny was the one to achieve it. She lived with the boyfriend long enough to meet a new one at the restaurant where she worked, and move into an apartment with a few other people he knew. During the day she worked retail jobs, aiming to get her own place, finally borrowing the security deposit from Van. During her two years of bumping from one college to the next, her overriding goal had been to have a place by herself. She couldn't stand any more kitchens overflowing with other people's dirty dishes, dried spaghetti sauce everywhere, and girls, whether they lived there or dated someone who did, who kept stealing her clothes. She couldn't bear the same drinking games, the pizza boxes, the stained sofas and the people on them, soaking up each other's cigarette smoke.

In her own apartment in Chicago, Linny wasn't afraid to be alone. She was more afraid of the opposite: letting someone encroach, scatter the order of the small household she had created for herself.

\* \* \*

Sasha selected the new Henry Hotel for drinks, since it was two blocks from the salon and close to the stores around Oak Street. They often browsed together, using shopping as another way to talk. Holding up four-inch metallic heels, they talked about their friends, complained about their love lives, conjured new ways to assess the situation of Gary and Pren. Lately, such conversation had been making Linny feel stalled, impatient. A couple of weeks ago she had even walked to her neighborhood library to see if they had any course catalogs from DePaul or the University of Illinois at Chicago. But, thinking of her sister's dreaded question, the one everyone asked—*What do you want to do?*—she left before talking to the librarian. Van's voice followed her anyway. *Is* this *what you're doing with your life?* Linny didn't want to answer the question; she wanted to erase it.

When Linny and Sasha settled at the bar of the Henry, a collusion of copper tables, mahogany, and mosaic tiles, Linny said, "This place looks confused." She pointed at the blue pendants snaking down from the ceiling and the garish faux-coral webbing across the walls. "It's creeping me out."

"Forget about it," Sasha said. "Tell me the Gary update."

But Linny had no more information than what she'd already relayed over the phone. "He wants to keep seeing me, as he says, even while trying to have another child with her. Which is just—"

"Fucked up," Sasha supplied. She set down her martini and added, "Are you into that? Because you're looking at a huge mess."

"I know." Linny had seen Sasha through her own tangled

relationships; they had always been able to advise each other straightforwardly, without too much judgment—a rare thing in a friend, Linny had learned. "Everything is suddenly more real, when I've been preferring the make-believe. With him and with work."

"Work?"

"Oh, you know—how You Did It Dinners is this whole make-believe world of home cooking."

"Is Pren going to start coming in and putting together her own meals there? That'll be loads of fun."

Linny hadn't considered this scenario before, but now she saw Pren securing one of the white aprons that bore the whimsical company logo and stepping up to the trays of ingredients. She would probably go for the fancier menu items Linny and Barbara were about to roll out. *Exotic* was the word Barbara kept using whenever Linny suggested ingredients like harissa and lemongrass, fenugreek and coriander.

"Maybe she knows."

"She doesn't," Linny insisted, though she wasn't so sure anymore.

As Sasha beckoned the bartender for another drink, Linny glanced around the room. She expected to see the kinds of people she always saw in bars and restaurants around here, their faces eased by money and alcohol, their bodies still tense with all that the workday had troubled and not resolved. Men in ties, women with highlights in their hair.

But then Linny saw her sister's husband fitting right in, sitting at the far end of the room, at a table with a woman who almost looked like Van, except her hair was too long, too studiously flipped.

"My brother-in-law is here," Linny said, and Sasha immediately swiveled to take a look.

"Is that your sister?"

When Linny shook her head, Sasha raised an eyebrow. "What the hell kind of family do you have?" she joked.

In the mirrored wall behind the bar Linny saw herself and Sasha reflected against shelves of liquor—Sasha's pale skin glowing within the frame of her big wavy hair, Linny's own narrow shoulders flanked by bottles of Maker's Mark and Courvoisier, the favorite drink of her father and every other Vietnamese guy. Linny glanced over at Miles and the Asian woman again. They were drinking white wine, their elbows leaning in toward each other on the table. It was startling to see him out of context, and disturbing to see him with someone other than Van. Maybe they were both lawyers, working on a case in Chicago. Perhaps Asian American lawyers gravitated to each other the way Asian kids in college did.

Linny couldn't help thinking that Van could do her hair like that woman, with layers and lowlights. She remembered how she'd suggested just that at Christmas, the last time they saw each other, saying, "Do you ever think about doing something different with your hair?"

Van had touched her shoulder-length pageboy self-consciously. They were in the kitchen, Van helping Linny prepare dinner. "I like it like this. It's easy to take care of and it's a classic style."

"All I know is, you shouldn't have the same hairstyle for years and years."

"Is that what your magazines dictate?" Van was cutting up

potatoes slowly, though Linny had tried to teach her how to use the knife more efficiently. Van worked with too much caution, afraid of the blade.

"I'm just trying to help. You could look so much better if you only tried."

"I happen to think there are more important things in life. A college education, for instance."

That was how their conversations usually went, filled with barbs, veering toward each other's weak points.

In the Henry Hotel bar, Sasha wondered out loud if the woman with Miles was a girlfriend. Linny didn't want to respond to that. She kept an eye on them as they finished their drinks, rose from the table with their jackets and shopping bags.

"Let's find out," Sasha murmured. Miles and the Asian woman would have to walk past Linny at the bar, would have to say something.

He seemed not at all flustered when he stopped to say hello.

"How are you?" Linny replied. They always spoke to each other with near-formal politeness, never venturing beyond topics he brought up, like real estate in Ann Arbor and Chicago. He always remembered to ask dutiful questions about Linny's job, though they never failed to sound condescending. Linny once made the mistake of telling Van he was suspiciously nice. "One of those rich, been-here-for-generations Asian American guys," she'd said. "And calculating, like a lawyer." Van, furious, had said, "Trust me, Miles couldn't care less what you think of him, and neither could I."

Linny introduced Sasha, and though she was curious about the Asian woman, she had a feeling she might find out something she didn't want to know. It made her nervous enough to long for a cigarette, though she hadn't smoked since college.

"This is Grace," Miles said, and the woman smiled. She and Linny sized each other up for a moment and it only took that second for Linny to know: Chinese girl, second- or third-generation, from an upper-middle-class family. Dark jeans, cashmere sweater under a short jacket, a named handbag. Her lipstick was glossy and her eye shadow held a hint of shimmer. She was thin and angular, nearly as tall as Miles, the kind of girl who could wear a shapeless tunic and look good in it. Linny envied those rare tall Asian girls, though she never admitted it out loud. Sometimes, catching her reflection in a dressing room mirror, Linny remembered the pencil marks in her parents' house and felt indignation, even shock, at the unchangeable fact of her height: *she* should have been a tall girl.

Miles interrupted the stare-down. "She's a lawyer in our firm."

"You have a case here?"

"We don't have meetings on Saturdays, thankfully," Grace answered. Up close, Linny saw that they actually had similar hairstyles, layered with side-swept bangs.

Turning back to Miles, Linny said, "I haven't talked to Van in a while."

"She's fine." His tone was mechanical, almost dismissive.

"Is she here?" Sasha asked loudly. "I'd love to meet her."

Miles barely let his gaze rest on her. "She's in Michigan," he told Linny. Then he touched Grace's shoulder. "We should get going."

As they sailed across the shiny stone floor toward the lobby of the hotel, Miles's hand drifted to Grace's back, as if escorting or protecting her. It was the kind of gesture Linny had seen him use with Van.

All at once she snapped awake. She slipped down from the barstool. She hurried to the lobby and crossed it, heading toward the hidden bank of elevators. Rounding the corner, she spotted Miles and Grace stepping into the same gold-toned car. Her impulse was to jump in after them. But instead she stopped in front, in full view. Her face was what Miles saw as the doors closed.

Later, after Linny and Sasha had questioned and rehashed the whole scene—was Miles cheating on Van so brazenly? and what, if anything, should Linny say to her sister?—she found a seat on a bus heading west to her apartment. The days lined up in front of her—more meals, menus, her father's citizenship party—and Linny thought of her sister driving through her sub-division in Ann Arbor, deaccelerating, directing the car into the driveway. She pictured Van just sitting there, almost unwilling to move. How well Linny knew that feeling, every time she re-linquished an off-street parking spot to drive somewhere, and every time she returned, circling blocks to find a space. During winter storms some people dug out their cars in the morning and left lawn chairs in their place to stake a claim; trespassers would find their cars keyed. Whenever Linny did nab a space she felt a mixture of relief and dread. *Now I have to get out of the car*, she thought at those times. And she always did, even though she dreamed of driving on without a map, or even steering her way to a garage at the airport, abandoning the car there, and buying any ticket she could afford. For the first time, it oc-curred to Linny that maybe her sister had fantasized that very same thing.

# 5

# Van

When Vijay Sastri called, patched through by the International Center's answering service, Van had been setting the table for a late dinner while Miles stood at the stove, tasting the shrimp and red curry dish he'd prepared. *I'm at the police*, Vijay told her, his voice shaky. *In the town of Northville*. A car accident. He'd been an anxious driver since getting carjacked at a gas station the year before, and when he missed a stop sign and plowed into the passenger side of a Cadillac, he panicked and tried to drive away from the scene. But a police cruiser two blocks over had heard the crash and pulled Vijay over. The officer was the one who found the gun, stashed under the passenger seat of Vijay's car.

Taking this all in, Van walked away from the table, toward the other end of the house. *What were you doing with a gun?* She wanted to scream. But all she said was, *Do you know if they called Immigration yet?*

Vijay had no idea. *Will you come here to help me?*

*You're going to need an attorney who does criminal law.*

*Why? I am not a criminal!*

*You can't get a gun license unless you're a citizen or a permanent*

*resident. And if you had a gun under the seat you would need a license*
*for a concealed weapon. That's why they arrested you. Vijay—are you*
*listening to me?*

From the living room Van saw Miles leaning against the
counter, waiting. He had set out the bowls of shrimp curry and
rice, brought forth two bottles of imported beer. It was one of
Miles's thoughtful dinners, and Van was going to ruin it all.

If Vijay had been drunk-driving, or simply a bad driver, Van
knew she could have kept him in the country. But certain
offenses—drug possession, domestic violence, and firearm possession without a license—were pretty much nonnegotiable.
The case went to trial in January 2002, a time when judges were
less than generous with immigrants. Still, Van worked and re-
worked the language of her argument. She sometimes even believed the judge would understand how Vijay's carjacking had
propelled him to a gun store, afraid for his safety. He hadn't
known about needing a license. And he hadn't realized that he
was risking deportation. Why would he chance everything—
his home, his livelihood, his job, his ability to support his family back in Hyderabad? There were so many things, Van said,
that immigrants didn't yet know.

But the judge on the case was known for his strictness, and
Van shouldn't have been surprised when, after all of her preparation and worry, all those nights when she worked instead of
going to bed with Miles, the deportation decree came down
anyway. She would always remember the way Vijay's eyes closed
upon hearing the decision. She would remember the stifled cry
of his wife and her slow walk out of the courtroom, the sky-
blue fabric of her sari sighing around her ankles. Van dreamed
about them sometimes—a hot climate she did not know, filled

with the smell of motorcycle oil, the vague images of dust and yellowed sky that she had borrowed from her mother's descriptions of Vietnam.

The night of the decision, Van and Miles had driven in silence to downtown Ann Arbor to have dinner with a couple they'd known in law school. Van had wanted to cancel but Miles said it would be rude. He was angry about the Vijay news, and Van was stunned to realize that he blamed her.

Van pointed out a parking spot on Main that turned out to be in front of a fire hydrant. With an exasperated sigh, Miles pulled away from the curb too fast and almost hit another car going past. Van jumped in her seat, letting out a little scream, and that's when Miles had growled, "You're not helping! Why can't you ever pay attention?"

He made a U-turn in the middle of the street to catch a spot that another car was leaving. As he parallel-parked he said, "You need to think about what you're doing. I think you need to step up."

"I don't want to talk about this."

"It's not the classroom anymore. This is life. These are other people's lives. This is the stuff that matters."

"Shut up, Miles." She'd never said such a thing before, and he turned to her with a look that sharpened into contempt.

"Is that in your arsenal of great argumentative tactics?"

"What do you think you're accomplishing here?" Van burst out. She felt a kind of wild panic trembling in her chest and she put her hands there as if to contain it. She wanted to point out that he'd acted almost resentful of the time she'd spent on the case. Over the Christmas holidays they'd flown to San Francisco to be with his family and she had stayed in their room, working, while he went to parties with his parents and older sister.

"I'm trying to help you, Van. You need to acknowledge that you failed. What are you even doing at that International Center?"

"It was a nearly impossible case. Everyone at the IC said that."

"If those excuses make you feel better, fine. But they don't help anyone else."

"Go to hell." Even as Van said it she hated herself for falling back on such words.

"You do not speak to me that way." The more out of control Van felt, the more calm Miles seemed to be. He opened the door, and the car began making a ping-pinging noise. "I am going to dinner with Ed and Jamie. You are not." He removed the keys from the ignition, halting the pinging. Before Van could think of another thing to say, he slammed the door and started walking across the street toward the restaurant where their friends—his friends, in truth, stopping by Ann Arbor for a nostalgic visit—were probably already sitting at the table with drinks, waiting to receive his composed, surely convincing story of how Van had gotten stuck in Detroit on some case.

Van, stuck in Miles's car without a key, had a moment of fury rush through her. She considered storming after him into the restaurant, letting Ed and Jamie know just how he'd left her there. She considered sitting there until he returned, though it was so cold she could already see her own breath. Finally, she considered leaving altogether. It was the only moment of their marriage that she had truly contemplated what it would be like to leave him. To clear the house of her belongings before he could get back from the restaurant. In the end, she did what Miles probably expected. She took a cab back to their house and went to bed.

He woke her up in the darkness, sliding next to her, offering an apology, and Van took it even though she could still repeat exactly what he'd said to her in the car. The words had an enduring effect. At the Center, Van began shying away from deportation and asylum cases, focusing instead on simpler petitions for spouse and child visas. It didn't help that Miles had always criticized Van's hour commute to work and the Center's drafty, asbestos-laced building where, in the depth of winter, Van had to pile on sweaters.

And then Van discovered she was pregnant, something she thought she could trace back to the very night of Vijay's deportation, the argument in the car, then the sex in the middle of the night after Miles had whispered, *I'm sorry.* The news gave her a fresh hope that they would recover, dispel the tension from the house. Miles had been the one, after all, who had wanted to start trying sooner than the three-year mark they had vaguely agreed on before they got married. After September 11, he had gone through a range of reactions—a loud-spoken desire to move to a *real* city; a wish to live closer to his parents and sister—before settling on the need to have a child. *Why are we waiting?* he suddenly asked. He went to the bathroom and opened the drawer where Van kept her birth control pills. *What do you say?* He handed her the packet, and she tossed it right into the trash. And the effect of the pregnancy worked. Miles started talking expansively about the future, about the books, gadgets, and education their child might require. He looked at fancy strollers online and kept a list of baby names, favoring Andrew or Justin for boys, Sophie or Amelia for girls.

When Van resigned from her job at the Center it was easier to agree with Miles about the commute, the asbestos, the immigrants and social workers chain-smoking around the perimeter of the building. It was safer to come back to Ann Arbor. And so, a little over two years after her first day at the International Center, she left with another job already in hand at Gertz & Zarou, a small practice in town that only handled corporate H-1Bs and permanent resident applications. It happened fast, even easily—one day she felt like an immigration lawyer, the next she was more of a paper-pusher.

It was in her second week at Gertz & Zarou that Van had her first ultrasound appointment and heard, instead of a heartbeat, the static of nothingness. The video monitor showed a wobbly empty sac, flickering around the edges. Blighted ovum, the doctor called it. Meaning nothing had ever really grown in there. They scheduled a D&C and Van went home, utterly unprepared for what she would say to Miles. Coming on the heels of Vijay's deportation, it felt like another failure, or at the very least a punishment, a sign of her inability to hold any world together.

The whole thing hit her harder than it did Miles, which Van's pregnancy books, in the small space devoted to miscarriages, had said was normal. Fathers-to-be just didn't get attached, they said, the way mothers-to-be did. Miles said, "The bright side is you *can* get pregnant." But it only deepened Van's reticence. She tried never to cry in front of Miles—he thought crying a sign of weakness or manipulation—but for the few days that led up to the D&C procedure she allowed herself to tear up, if she was alone, while watching television. She couldn't help looking on the loss as a sign of her lack of responsibility. Van had been unable to provide shelter to anyone. And every subsequent month she got her period the blood was her confirmation.

In the drawer of her nightstand Van still kept the baby name lists, along with her ovulation charts, her basal body thermometer, and books with titles like *Seize Control of Your Fertility*. February, right before Miles left, had marked a full year of their trying to conceive again after the miscarriage.

They had agreed to try for a year before going the way of fertility tests. Miles was adamant about this. He wanted it to happen the *natural way*, he said, and he was certain it would if only Van would relax. He grew annoyed by her charts and temperatures; he thought she was obsessive. He'd read that a woman could disrupt her ovulation with so much stress and planning, and he refused to have sex just because some thermometer said so. Each month Miles read the news of no news in Van's face, and the more sex Van sought, the more he didn't feel like it. The previous fall, Van had finally said she was going to see her doctor about a fertility drug called Clomid. *Let's just see a little longer*, Miles had replied. Probably Van should have paid more attention.

Van had no one to talk to about this except the anonymous women she sometimes typed to on fertility and pregnancy message boards. She had grown apart from her college and law school friends, most of whom had moved to other states. When they talked or e-mailed they mainly discussed work, or kids, or people they knew. Besides, everyone else seemed to have no problem having children. Baby pictures popped up regularly in Van's e-mail, and she was always expected to write back about how cute and adorable they were. She didn't know how to break past all that bright chatter into real intimacy, the tell-everything best friendship she hadn't known since middle school. And anyway, it seemed that half the women she'd known in law school were becoming stay-at-home moms; their discussions of playdates and schools were edging Van out of correspondence. The one exception might have been Jen, but Van had been too ashamed of leaving the Center to maintain much of a friendship. Jen had a flat, unvarnished way of delivering her opinions that made the prospect of facing her in person or talking about her job in Ann Arbor seem unbearable.

It would have been a perfect time to have a sister she could count on, but Van couldn't imagine confiding in Linny, who could cook for entire families but surely wouldn't know about wanting a child of her own. Van never told her about the pregnancy and D&C, and of course talking to their father was out of the question. As far as they knew, Van and Miles had never even tried.


The law offices of Gertz & Zarou, located near a shopping mall fifteen minutes from the Birch Crest Hills subdivision, occupied half a floor of a squat building called Executive Plaza. Gertz & Zarou had contracts with the university and engineering firms around southeast Michigan, and the five lawyers handled employer-based H-1B work visas and permanent residency and naturalization applications. The hours were predictable and slow, with trips every two weeks to the Immigration field office in Detroit, not far from the International Center that Van now avoided. *She's basically a glorified paralegal*, she had imagined

Miles describing her job. He used to say that she did good things for little profit, though once he had added to a group of friends, "Van's a fighter. It's that Napoleonic complex put to good use."

That February night Miles left, Van had stayed late at her office. She had been working on getting Sunil Gupta, an H-1B at GM, a spousal visa for his new wife, and wanted to put the application in the mail first thing on Monday morning. An H-1B visa could only extend up to six years; after that, the visa holder had to leave the U.S. for at least a year in order to reapply, or he could stay in the States and ask his employer to sponsor his application for permanent residency. Because Sunil had been living and working in Michigan for nearly five years—like most of her clients, he was an engineer—he was eligible to begin applying for permanent residency. That's when Van advised him to get married as soon as possible, for while he still held an H-1B visa, he could get his wife to the U.S. in a matter of months. If he became a permanent resident while still a bachelor he would have to wait three or four years, maybe more, for a permanent resident spousal application to go through.

It didn't make much sense, Van admitted to her clients. But H-1Bs were considered temporary workers, while permanent residents were considered immigrants. It was a lot easier to get into the U.S. as a temporary worker, even if that person was hoping all along to become a permanent resident. For years the process of transforming an H-1B from temporary worker into permanent resident had been a standard procedure, overseen by lawyers like Van who kept careful track of each round of paperwork, each shift in forms and rules.

Each spring the U.S. set out a fixed number of H-1B visas,

available to whomever applied first. In many years the number ran well over a hundred thousand, but it was clear to Van that under the Department of Homeland Security, the process was going to get tougher and the number of visas would soon shrink. She always felt relieved to see clients through to approval, and was not surprised when the ones she met looked dazed, flushed with the joy of having won a kind of lottery. Still, their stay in the U.S. remained tenuous, dependent on whatever company had hired and sponsored them. An H-1B could never leave his employer without losing his visa, and his wife (Van had almost never dealt with a female H-1B) couldn't legally work.

Van hadn't yet encountered a company unwilling to sponsor their H-1Bs' applications for residency—the need for engineers was that strong. At that point, Van would place ads for each applicant's job. The goal was to show that the need for the immigrant existed, that no U.S. citizen out there was able to do the job. The immigrant's very presence in America had to be justified. So the advertisements went out for sixty days in the *Detroit Free Press* and journals like *Mechanical Engineering*. Typically this time would pass without a single response, allowing Van to prove that the would-be immigrant in question was a necessary one. After that, there was just the permanent residency application itself, with the fingerprinting and questions, the fees, and all the waiting time. Van never did feel that she'd completed a case until an immigrant's actual "permanent resident alien" notice—the sought-after status of green card, those two words still used, revered, meaning legitimacy, safety—arrived in the mail.

This waiting, this paperwork, this explaining and reexplaining—these made up Van's job now. She hadn't argued in court since Vijay Sastri's case, and perhaps never would again. But she was more cautious than ever.

So that Saturday in February, she double-checked the Gupta file. Sunil had shown Van pictures of his recent wedding: him riding an elephant; the couple holding hands against a backdrop of yellow brocade drapes. Sunil's bride, Madhu, wore a brilliant fuchsia dress, her neck and arms shining with gold. Something about her expression—the wide, uncertain eyes offset by the almost coy turn of her lips—kept Van's gaze. Madhu was only twenty-two, ten years younger than Sunil. Was she ready to leave her entire family for Michigan, to join this man she hardly knew at all? Their marriage had been arranged, Sunil had told Van, and Madhu, meeting him for the first time in Mumbai, had giggled uncontrollably. As Van looked over their paperwork she wished she knew more stories about what her parents' life had been like in Vietnam. Her father rarely talked about it. Her mother had mentioned vague snippets, still images: Van's father forgetting his shoes at a friend's house and walking home barefoot without realizing it; the color of a freshly opened papaya at an outdoor market. When Van pictured her parents in their early-married days, she liked to imagine them holding hands. Walking to a café in Saigon, sitting cross-legged on the ship out of Saigon, waiting in the noisy barracks at Camp Pendleton—surely, Van thought, they had held on to each other then. She hoped Sunil would hold tight to Madhu's hand.

It was past seven when Van drove home through a flurry of snow, resolving to talk to Miles about going to China and Vietnam. They had planned a trip a couple years back, but a case at Miles's firm had delayed it until the possibility dwindled away.

Then it seemed like every time Van suggested they renew the plans, Miles would sigh about his workload. It almost reminded her of the excuses she, Linny, and her father had made when Mrs. Luong had talked about visiting Vietnam. She had gone back twice, fewer than most of her friends, but Mr. Luong complained that airfare was too high for two people, and that he couldn't leave his studio when he was about to make a breakthrough. He kept that going for years, sometimes mentioning his concerns about flight safety. Then he moved into the basement, and that was that. And though Mrs. Luong had often asked Van and Linny if they wanted to see Vietnam, neither ever committed to it. Such a plan made Van feel nervous, foreign; she didn't like the thought of being looked over by all her unknown relatives. Her mother had died before Van had ever seriously considered a visit.

Now was the time, Van decided. She and Miles. Her mother would have liked that. They would see Saigon and Hanoi, Shanghai and Beijing. They would talk about their families' different stories of immigration. They would eat lychees, buy silk scarves, and try out their rusty Mandarin and Vietnamese. Maybe somehow it would all be the next step toward a baby.

When Van got home she found Miles asleep on the living room sofa, one arm trailing over the side, fingertips touching the floor. Even in this uncharacteristic state he looked graceful. He must have been exhausted, not to hear the garage door opening and closing. Quietly Van knelt next to him, reaching out to stroke his fine hair until he woke up. But she tripped over herself and bumped her leg against the glass coffee table. A thin ceramic vase fell over. She was relieved it didn't break, though it did wake Miles.

"What are you doing?" he said, sitting up.

"Sorry." Van touched her right knee. She knew by morning she'd have an eye-shaped bruise. "Hey, the weather's getting kind of bad out there."

"I thought it wasn't supposed to storm tonight." Miles checked his watch. "You were working pretty late."

"I lost track of time. There's this case I'm working on—"

"Deportation?"

She drew back at this. Miles knew they didn't handle deportations at Gertz & Zarou. Vijay Sastri was still a sensitive subject between them, something neither of them brought up.

Miles said, "I'm starving."

"There are some leftovers in the fridge."

"I don't feel like leftovers." He stood up and Van followed him to the kitchen. He picked up the jacket he had left on a barstool and opened the door to the mudroom. "I'm going to pick up something from Saigon Garden."

Van felt a sudden wave of panic. "I'll come with you." For an uneasy moment she was back in their last year of law school, unable to figure out how much he wanted her around. In those days, when Miles talked about going to a party, Van would tentatively ask, "Am I invited too?" To which Miles would say, "Do you want to be?" or simply, "If you want." He claimed that she was implicitly invited to everything, but Van didn't feel that was so. She needed proof; she needed to hear it from him. So she would keep asking him—"Do *you* want me to go?"—until Miles grew exasperated. There were nights Van found herself literally sitting at home waiting by the phone, though she would never have admitted that to anyone. When Miles did finally call and ask what she was doing she would always say she was work-ing. Her one constant. Even if she had been watching *Beverly Hills, 90210* reruns, or sitting with unopened casebooks and a cup of tepid tea.

"I'll only be a few minutes," Miles said. "You like the basil chicken and green beans, right?" He pressed the garage door button.

Van waited out the grinding sound of the door rising. Cold air blew into the kitchen. "Why don't we just eat here? I can make some pasta." She could see that Miles was distracted. His mind was already ahead of the moment, ahead of her. "I mean, it's late," she said lamely.

"I'll be right back." He extended an arm, a fluttery wave that didn't touch her. Van watched him get in the dark red Land Cruiser he had bought two years ago; she had inherited his old Infiniti sedan. From the driver's seat he waved at her. *Go inside*, he mouthed. And Van did.


By midnight she was telling herself to calm down. She stood at their bedroom window watching the snow flurries harden into ice. And Miles was out there, driving into a ditch, the big car tumbling over and over, trapping him inside.

He wasn't answering his cell phone. She didn't leave a mes-sage, though he would see that she'd called. She would have called Saigon Garden, if they were still open, and for a wild mo-ment even considered calling the police. She had, she realized, no one else to call.

Linny, she suddenly thought, was precisely the person she

couldn't call at a time like this. In middle school she used to say, *Take a chill pill* whenever Van got anxious about something— laundry that Linny hadn't done; rowdy friends that Linny had invited over. Van could still hear the high notes of her sister's laugh, thick with derision. *God, you're so uptight.*

No one would have said such a thing to Miles. As unalike as he and Linny were, they both possessed a genetic gift of self-confidence that had bypassed Van. They both seemed to trust that things would work out no matter what.

It occurred to Van that she didn't know where either of them was at that moment.

Outside, the streetlights cast an accusatory glow on the garbage bins still at the curb. They had been there since Thursday; surely the watchful neighbors didn't approve. A strange feeling made Van shiver: Miles had never before neglected to bring the bins inside.

Van had drifted off on the TV room sofa when she heard the garage door opening. It was past one a.m. She hurried to the back door, feeling guilty for falling asleep and forgetting about Miles. Of course he hadn't crashed or skidded off a road. He was a careful driver, something she'd mentioned to her friends when they complained about how their husbands drove too close to other cars, too fast for comfort. Miles wasn't like them.

"Where have you been?" She tried not to sound demanding.

All the kitchen lights were on, too bright. Miles walked into the house without taking off his shoes. He had his coat on and his hair was wet. He looked like he had been traipsing around in the snow.

"I was driving," he said.

He would not look at her and in a rush of fear she said, "What happened?" She approached slowly, reaching for him.

He stepped back. Van stopped. Her arms were still in mid-air, floating appendages that she had to return to her side. She knew that Miles was going to say something she didn't want to hear. He said, "I don't think I want to live with you anymore."

For years, probably for the rest of her life, she would have to know this. The exact sentence. The blindness of the moment, like falling in a dream and waking just before impact.

A long minute passed in which Van stared at him, disbelieving. Miles kept his head lowered.

"But we're married." It was the only thing she could think to say. They were married. That was the parameter, the barrier. The fact. The image of Sunil and Madhu reappeared, their hands entwined.

"I don't think I want that either." Like he was turning down a new cable channel. Like saying no thanks to something at a buffet.

He said, "I thought I should tell you."

"You're telling me."

"I'm telling you what I've been thinking for a long time."

Van let the house go silent. She closed her eyes and asked it to help her out. *Tell Miles this is* ours. She wanted to feel the snow falling on the roof, ice crystallizing on the windows. The difference between outdoors and indoors was stark—it was everything. If only Miles had not left the house. If only she had made him stay.

But through the silence came Miles: "I have to go."

"No." Her eyes opened. "You never told me anything."

"I'm sorry."

"You were thinking all these things and planning all these things and you never said a word."

"I wasn't planning. I just needed to think, Van. I just needed to *think*." His voice gave out. He was crying. He was actually weeping into the sleeve of his coat.

Van could feel herself beginning to crumple, something inside her folding in on itself.

"Are you—" She couldn't finish the thought: *Are you with someone else?*

"I'm alone, if that's what you're asking," Miles said.

Van felt a sense of relief at that. If there wasn't someone else, then everything would be all right. He would recover; he would have to recover.

He made a halting move toward the stairs. "I'm going to get some things." He walked around her.

Van fought the urge to go after him. It would only egg him on, she decided. He wanted another fight. Now, when the Gupta case was taking up her time—that would be a classic moment to begin one. Hadn't he always wanted her attention most when she was busiest with work? Even in the law library he used to graze her arm with his, toy with her hair. On her notes he'd scribble, *Hey, babe, let's go back to my place.*

When Miles came downstairs with a duffel bag, he headed straight to the back door, and with a pulse of panic Van saw that he actually meant to leave without saying another word.

"Good-bye, then," she called out.

Miles paused. His hair was still shiny with melted snow, his face a shadow. "I know what you're thinking. You think I'm going to come back here tomorrow and we'll just keep on the way we've been. But I'm not going to. We need to separate for a while."

The words were terrible, but Van kept herself steady. She watched him close the door, listened to the sound of his car backing out of the driveway, accelerating into the falling snow. She could stand there for hours, she believed, waiting for his return. Yes, she could wait. She would call his bluff.

And now here she stood, almost two months later, looking at the end of April, the almost-spring that had brought nothing she could call progress. In March the U.S. had invaded Iraq, which had generated fresh waves of anti–Middle Eastern fear throughout southeast Michigan. Van imagined her former colleagues calling emergency meetings at the International Center; she imagined her former clients keeping themselves, as much as possible, tucked inside their homes. They too would be closing every blind, double-checking all the doors. Van remembered how it had been after September 11, when mosques around Detroit had been vandalized, windows smashed. On the front door of the Center someone spray-painted the word *Terrorists*. One of the lawyers found a sign taped to her home mailbox saying *Camel jockeys go home*. Her husband wrote on it in large letters: *We're Sikh you idiots*.

March had also seen the Department of Homeland Security's official takeover of Immigration, dissolving the INS into ICE: Immigration and Customs Enforcement. The new rules and paperwork had brought chaos to Gertz & Zarou, as it called all future H-1Bs into question. Though Van felt more isolated than ever, removed from the real action in Detroit, she threw herself into sorting out the new messes as her only way to keep her mind off Miles.

She had only heard from him in the form of e-mails—sent, she knew, so he could avoid talking to her directly. His messages were brief: he needed more time—he thanked her, in fact, for giving him more time—and reminded her that she didn't have to worry about the bills, which were paid automatically. He said he would be in touch later. *I hope you're doing okay*, was the last thing he had written. Ever since that day she had driven around trying to track him down, Van had often considered staking out his office and trailing him after work. But the fear of being caught held her back; she didn't want to be that exposed, her heart made so visible to the person who could crush it. If this was a test, then she had to pretend to embody the strength that Miles had always valued.

She had assumed that if she held out he would come back and they would resume their life where they had paused it. But his e-mails, combined with her upcoming trip to Wrightville, illuminated the question that had grown within her, expanding like the daylight minutes as she checked the security alarm, the locks on the windows: What would she be like, and how would she feel, if and when Miles did come back? It was the first time she considered that as a real question, the first time she didn't have a clear answer.


Since Miles had been gone, Van had failed to stay the course of tidiness he had directed. He hated messes, dirty dishes on a table, papers cluttering the counters. Maintaining neatness had always been work for Van, though she tried to conceal that. She liked that Miles thought of her as disciplined. In his absence Van's own entropy, which she blamed her father for instilling in her, started creeping back. She let the junk mail pile up. She kept unwashed dishes in the sink. Once or twice a week she ordered an extra-large sausage-and-mushroom pizza to eat over the next few days. The boxes accumulated in the garage, overflowing the recycling bins that Van kept forgetting to bring out to the curb. Somehow, the less she cleaned, the smaller and safer the house seemed to feel.

The bedroom too was slowly becoming a different space. Van dropped towels on the floor, left dresser drawers half open. The bed did not get made. The show pillows with their square shams were piled on the corner chaise, and the silk drapes that were supposed to frame the plantation shutters no longer held their even pleats. Van's habit of eating cookies and crackers while walking around the house reappeared, resulting in a sprinkling of crumbs that got mashed underfoot. They reminded her of how, before Miles chose her, she hadn't even owned a vacuum cleaner. Instead she'd found at a garage sale one of those push-around sweepers favored by low-end restaurants. Of course, she had thrown the thing out before Miles had ever discovered it. He had, for their new house, purchased a fancy Miele. Pale and sleek, purring gently, it was nothing like the roar of the Luongs' ancient Sears monster, a hulking machine with all of the attachments jutting out unused. The Miele glided, flattened under beds.

But it also highlighted a problem: the carpets themselves. They should have gone with all hardwood on the second floor,

Miles said, not six months after moving in. "I don't know what I was thinking," he kept repeating. He seemed genuinely distressed about it, even embarrassed. Van, who loved the muffled comfort of her bare feet on carpet, who had championed the carpet in the first place, pointed out that it was cozy in the winter. "Rugs," Miles retorted. "That's what rugs are for." He declared his intention to have the carpet torn out and hardwoods laid down, but the plans evaporated after the disaster with Vijay Sastri.

That they had worried about the floors when Vijay was being evicted from the country—Van had not pointed out that juxtaposition to Miles. He had developed a habit of teasing her about her work, calling her Ms. Self-Righteous, Esq. or Madam Do-Good. He reminded her lightly, just once or twice, that he brought in the real money. Van didn't object when he veered conversations away from politics toward subjects like house design. In spite of his eye toward modernism, he talked of paying homage to his roots, which meant teak tables from his family's ancestral province in China and a Mission cabinet from San Francisco, where he was born and where his great-grandfather had landed at the edge of the gold rush.

Van had often envied Miles's fourth-generation status. It meant no questioning of origins, an ability to laugh full-on if someone told him to go back to his own country. It also meant his parents and his grandparents all spoke perfect English. They traveled and behaved, Van couldn't help thinking, like any white upper-middle-class family, so in tune with their affluence that they never hesitated to wave down a waiter or step into a posh boutique. Miles thought of the Midwest as an ironic space, had often pointed out the times Van slipped back into a phrase like "Where's it at?" Those Michigan, middle-of-the-country linguistics offered an endless source of amusement, in the same way that every new group of college freshmen had to marvel over "pop" versus "soda."

No, the Ohs were not at all midwesterners, and Miles meant for the house in Ann Arbor to prove it, from the Spanish tiles in the downstairs powder room to the antique French sideboard that was a nod to the semester he spent in Aix as an undergrad. To Van the furnishings never felt even, the centuries and countries pushing up against each other. But she praised whatever her husband praised. He talked of bathroom faucets and patio furniture. He circled furniture in catalogs and tabbed magazines with Post-it notes, seeming to know just how to go about attaining beautiful order in every room.

A *Design Within Reach* catalog still lay open on his office desk. The pale slate-blue walls complemented the clean lines of glass and stainless steel bookcases. Van surveyed all of it from the doorway where she stood, procrastinating instead of preparing to go to Wrightville for her father's citizenship party. For a while she had been avoiding this part of the house, for Miles's office was next to the guest room they were going to turn into a nursery. Van had already painted it the color of an opened avocado, a shade that she thought of as childhood green. She realized that Miles had probably told his parents everything by now. They were probably calling all the aunts and cousins, heating up the phone lines with speculation. She could imagine Miles's mother saying to her, *If only you'd had a baby.* She had never let up pestering them about it, even after Miles had told her about the almost-pregnancy. At their last Christmas gathering Mrs. Oh had scolded Van, saying, "As soon as you hit thirty, you're pretty much going to be asking for complications. What are you waiting for?"

Van had started wondering if Miles had insinuated that their lack of a child was somehow Van's fault. "You have to do things you don't always feel in the mood to do," Mrs. Oh went on, making Van squirm. "You have to make sacrifices to be a mother." Miles's birth had been difficult and Mrs. Oh had nearly died; the doctor had said she could not risk having more children, though she had wanted three or four. She planned to make it up, she told Van, with grandchildren.

Nearly every time Van drove to meet a client at the battered old INS building—in her mind she still called it that, not the Citizenship and Immigration Services building or Department of Homeland Security building—in downtown Detroit, just at the edge of the city between the bridge to Belle Isle and the Ambassador Bridge to Ontario, Van couldn't help thinking of her own family, half first-generation, half second. She felt the most lonely then, unsheltered, far removed from her father and sister, the loss of her mother seeming to pour in through the car windows. Van had never yet visited Linny in Chicago, and Linny had only been to Ann Arbor twice. As with their father, both times were occasioned by a visit to someone else in the Detroit suburbs. From the way Linny had gazed around the living room, looking up at all the recessed lights, it was clear she didn't understand the way Van and Miles lived.

There was no way, Van thought, that her sister would understand what it meant to almost have a child. To stand in Miles's office and look at his desk, his books, his Aeron chair.

There was no way her sister would understand these kinds of emptiness.

Van hovered over Miles's desk, wondering why he had left the catalog open to this page: a dining room table laid with square plates. Had he wanted a new table? Had he been dissatisfied with the way she set it for guests? What message had he wanted to convey to Van? She remembered how, in recent months, he sometimes came home from work with increasing impatience. "Do you ever wonder why we bothered with law school?" he asked. He spent his weekends surfing the Web, typing long posts on home and garden message boards. He sometimes went antiquing by himself, coming back empty-handed save for the time he had scored an overpriced Saarinen table that ended up in the basement.

When Van finally opened the door to his office closet, she couldn't recall why she had waited so long to look through his things. Politeness? Fear of getting caught? It was still a transgression she knew he'd never forgive, but she barreled past that now.

The boxes and plastic containers stacked in the back of the closet were labeled: *Graduate School, Undergraduate, Art, Misc. Files.* She dragged out the one cardboard box that said *Stuff.* The old packing tape peeled back easily, and Van drew out envelopes full of photographs, their negatives spilling out. She found a pile of cards bound with a rubber band, and three spiral-bound journals, empty of writing. At the bottom of the box Van saw what she had been waiting for: the three framed women and Julie's black and white photographs. They looked more plaintive here, almost pretentious. They wouldn't even work in this house, Van decided with a surge of bitter pleasure. But the women were just how Van remembered them, their faces stilled and taunting, seeming to know something about Miles that Van could never grasp.

She had guessed, early on, what Julie had meant. The one who got away. She knew it in the way Miles had spoken of her—with a certain admiration and respect, wistfulness. They had known each other in high school and had both gone to Pomona. They had a shared history, as Miles said. Van had overlooked it, reminding herself that she was the one he married. Over the years the jealousy had faded somewhat, pushed into a closed-off compartment called The Past. She knew that Miles heard updates on Julie once or twice a year, probably by e-mail, but she was careful not to appear bothered by this. She refused to let Julie become a lingering specter in her marriage.

Van skimmed the old birthday greetings and postcards, looking for the names. There was an amiable note from Maya, dated four years ago from London. Diana had sent a birthday card with a big loopy heart drawn on it, and the scrawled words, *Love ya always!*

When Van touched a square envelope of tan recycled fibers she knew whose it was. Julie's handwriting was artsy-looking, of course, at once jaunty and studied—a lot, Van realized, like Miles's. It was addressed to his apartment on Packard Street, with a return address of San Francisco.

Miles had slit the envelope open cleanly with a letter opener. Van pulled out the card made of heavy card stock, letterpressed with a pattern of golden birds. But there was nothing inside it. No handwriting, no words. Van was certain—she felt it like a weight pushing her to the floor of the closet—that there had been a note in here once. A letter—a love letter? A farewell?

Whatever it was, Miles had kept it to, for, himself. It was that private, that important. Van knew her husband well enough to know that.

From the moment they had married, Van had carried a secret pride. She had felt safe from the rest of the world, privately pitying single women like her sister, who tended to complain about the lack of decent and available men. For Van, marriage had fulfilled its ancient promise. *I am claimed*, she sometimes whispered to herself. She never thought that Miles, who had spoken so firmly about the importance of commitment, would break his end of the bargain. Wasn't marriage a guarantee against the easy shifting of one's mind? *They all think that*, Van remembered a friend remarking about her family law practice. *They say, I never thought this would happen to me.*

Now Van saw evidence of Julie everywhere. The specter she had avoided had been there all along, seeping uncertainty into their days, slipping into that space created whenever Van and Miles turned away from each other in their sleep. The specter was there in all of the silences, the ones Van had wrongly regarded as the quietude of marriage. "Julie." Van spoke the name out loud, because no one was there to hear it. What she really meant was *Miles*.

The postmark on the envelope said August 1998, right before the start of their last year of law school. A few weeks later, Miles sat down next to Van on that bench near the library and began everything between them.

# 6

# Linny

Driving the teal-colored Corolla an ex-boyfriend had let her have for five hundred bucks, Linny listened to a retro hits CD she had bought at a gas station. The songs were by Taylor Dayne, En Vogue, Color Me Badd, all reminding her of high school, and the lazy summer days in between when she roamed Woodland Mall and sneaked away with boyfriends to make out anywhere they could—someone's basement, or the woods behind Egypt Lake Golf Club north of town. Often when Linny went back to Wrightville to check on her father she ended up running into people from high school. It flustered her to see them increasingly overweight, saddled with toddlers. They walked the aisles of Meijer, their shopping carts heaped with Stouffer's and cases of Diet Coke.

Many of her classmates had gotten married right after college and stayed in west Michigan. By now, edging toward age thirty, they had two or three kids. They knew mortgages and parent-teacher conferences and, like their parents before them, clipped coupons from the Sunday *Press* and watched Suzanne Geha report the Channel 8 news. Linny didn't want any of that, exactly, but she couldn't help feeling somewhat exposed in lacking such markers of a grown-up life. At such moments Linny clung to Chicago as her prize, the gloss of sophistication that would cover her undistinguished career, lack of college degree, and nonexistent photo of husband and kids. She took comfort in not having gained weight or wrinkles; she was the same size she'd been at age eighteen. Still, she allowed herself to wonder: If she could trade places and be Pren, would she? Would she drive to Michigan with a greater sense of ease?

The day before, at You Did It Dinners, preparing pans of cheesy stuffed chicken, Barbara had introduced a new possibility.

Linny had been chatting away about the two dads who frequented You Did It and were well known among the regular crowd of stay-at-home moms.

"It's a new micro-trend," Barbara declared. "We'll be seeing more of them. We should start stocking beer."

"Well, these guys aren't one hundred percent stay-at-home dads. They have freelance consulting businesses or something."

"Oh, I know. There are few men who truly stay at home. They all seem to have their own businesses on the side. Or they're trustafarians."

Linny laughed at this unexpected word from Barbara.

"My kids taught me that." Barbara smiled.

Deftly she slit a pocket into a chicken breast and stuffed it with spinach and goat cheese, tucking in a quivering slice of ham. "What would you say, Linny, if I told you I wanted you to handle just about everything here?" Barbara went on to propose bringing in another assistant, shifting Linny into Barbara's place while she herself opened a second branch of You Did It Dinners, in Chicago's Lincoln Square neighborhood.

The offer was so unexpected that Linny hardly knew where to look. "Thank you," she said finally. She meant the words. She had never been offered a promotion in anything. Had never stuck out a job this long.

But as Barbara continued describing her plan, Linny realized what it truly meant: she could no longer think of You Did It as a temporary job, a lark, which was how she still viewed it even though she'd been there for three years. The realization lifted her spirits and then sank her: these meals, the meals of so many families, would become her complete responsibility. She had never thought of herself doing this forever, literally catering to moms. People would ask her what she did for a living and she would have to say she managed You Did It Dinners, specializing in convenience for families on the go. It would no longer be a holding place for the next whatever-may-be.

In the last class Linny took in college, the day before she just stopped going back to campus, her merchandising professor had given a lecture on branding. All of the other students seemed eager to own their own businesses—or so they all said when they introduced themselves on the first day—and the professor often cited successful or unsuccessful brands. On that day she stressed the importance of a name. "Your business can rise and fall on the basis of its name," she said.

You Did It Dinners, the name, had always bothered Linny. It was an awkward phrase, a tripped-up string of words. Out loud, You Did It could be an accusation, a backing into a corner of guilt. It sounded like culpability. The many women and few men who paid to "do dinners," as Barbara called it, were paying partly for a feeling of accomplishment.

As she drove to west Michigan, Linny tried to reconcile herself to managing the You Did It kitchen. She saw herself in the same apron whites, monitoring moms with their pans of vegetables and cheese and their glasses of pinot grigio. She saw herself promoting new recipes and updating the website. A lot of people, like Van, would surely say that was progress. That was what work meant. But in the moment all Linny could feel was something closer to claustrophobia. Closer to fear.

Added to that was the worrying she'd nursed all week, after seeing Miles and that woman, Grace. Of course her name was Grace. Such a standard later-generation name. Girls named Grace were bright and ambitious, bought makeup at Clinique and suits at J. Crew. They were the kind of girls Van probably always wanted to be.

Linny had debated calling her sister but what would she say? They hardly knew how to talk to each other without nitpicking, falling back on insults; Van might think she was rubbing the sighting in her face. *Your husband is having an affair.* Could Linny say those words? Were they true? And—did Van know? A sick feeling roiled Linny's stomach when she realized that either yes or no seemed plausible. She was used to feeling sorry for her sister the wallflower. This new mixture of defensiveness and worry, a kind of tenderness, carried Linny back to her earliest memories, when Van was the treasured older sister to look up to. Van had always been the one who could be counted on to take care of business, make sure all of her bills got paid on time, in full. Or as their mother had said, "She keeps all her chickens in a row."

So it seemed especially awful that Linny couldn't stop picturing Grace and Miles together, fresh from their hotel room, arms entwining as they merged into a bright day of walking on Michigan Avenue. She allowed herself to push the scene, let Gary and Pren enter into view. The four of them could go to a museum together, or draw up chairs at a café where Linny would be fixing cappuccinos behind the counter.

Of course, she knew that her own deal with Gary had never been about permanence. Gary saw her as an opportunity, a break from his daily life. To Sasha, Linny had claimed the same for herself. Yet it had become nearly impossible not to wonder what it would be to live not in Gary's world but in Pren's.

Maybe Van and their mother, in their own ways, had known this kind of question too.

When Linny turned fifteen she moved beyond her Belinda Carlisle phase and her popped-collar shirts in favor of acid-washed denim jackets. Back then, Rich and Nancy Bao were still throwing parties nearly every Saturday at their almost-mansion in Wyandotte, a suburb that became home to a burgeoning Vietnamese community just south of Grand Rapids and twenty minutes west of where the Luongs had settled in Wrightville. Growing up, it had seemed improbable to Linny and Van that so many white people in Michigan had sponsored Vietnamese refugees, and that the Vietnamese had not only stayed but increased their numbers. Every winter their parents complained about the cold but they never thought about leaving; they were going to stay where they had landed.

When Linny looked back at that time she saw so much in

relative aspect to the Baos. Van was always old enough to stay at home alone, something she apparently cherished, though she never did anything more exciting than read, watch television, and eat microwaved popcorn. Linny preferred the parties, where she could hang out with kids her age and pretend, for a while, that the puffed-leather luxury of the Baos' house belonged to her.

From the moment Mr. Luong parked on the Baos' street, joining a line of cars that would stay there for many hours, a divide fell between her and her parents, children and adults, English and Vietnamese. While the parents played cards and drank and danced in the great room to Vietnamese music turned up so loud that neighbors complained, the children claimed the basement. The Baos had a ping-pong table, an air hockey table, two TVs with separate Nintendo systems, one for each of the Bao children, and dozens of board games. Some of the older kids staked out the laundry room, where they smuggled in nearly empty bottles of whiskey and vodka swiped from the tables upstairs. It was there that Linny had her first kiss and her first make-out sessions, under a blanket in a corner of the laundry room, with boys Americanized into Jimmy, Bobby, and Matthew. There, Linny first understood the wondrous, addictive rush of having power over a boy. She remembered looking down at—was it Alex Phan?—her shirt half unbuttoned, and feeling certain that he would agree to do almost anything if she let him undo the rest.

In the warm months the Baos set up two big grills on their backyard patio. The men would lounge out there, drinking beer and Courvoisier while they cooked beef and shrimp satay. In the kitchen the women fried *cha gio* and shrimp chips. Somehow all at once the food was brought to the dining room table, and everyone fell upon it. Eating was a confusion of paper plates and chopsticks, *nuoc mam* and Open Pit barbecue sauce, hoisin and sweet pickle relish.

It was during one of these summer evening parties that Linny began to believe that her father and Nancy Bao were having an affair. That night, Linny and a new kid, Tom Hanh, had been talking about the imminent start of tenth grade. Tom was by far the cutest boy at the party and even Lisa Bao, the princess of her parents' domain and the self-appointed fashion arbiter of the younger set, had praised his restraint in not going overboard with the New Wave look—spiky hair, white shirt, and baggy black pants—that all the Vietnamese boys were still sporting. Normally Linny viewed Lisa as her competition, but that summer Lisa had a steady boyfriend, and Linny threw her a smile from her seat on the sofa next to Tom Hanh. His family had been living in Wisconsin and he was shyer, more unassuming than the boys Linny usually favored. He didn't make one move, later, as they walked around the neighborhood.

Already the crickets of late summer were out, signaling to Linny an awareness of time: months gone. School ahead. The night wearing down. The Baos' subdivision of cavernous brick homes seemed far away from the Luongs' ranch house. Here, the creamy sidewalks seemed to be lit from underneath, reminding Linny of the video for "Billie Jean."

From down the street Linny could hear the crescendos of laughter and music. The faint strains of a Vietnamese cha-cha song switched suddenly to Depeche Mode, turned up. This was accompanied by a screeching wail and a succession of popping sounds—someone had brought fireworks to the party again.

"Gosh *damn it*," came a voice. Clear and male, and so close that Linny started.

Tom nudged her, nodding his head toward a tall, pale-haired man standing on the front steps of his dormered colonial. The lamps on either side of the front door illuminated the frown on his face. He was glaring at the Baos' house, hard, as though willing it to disappear. He muttered, "Damn noisy gooks."

Neither Linny nor Tom said a word, but as they crossed the street she realized that they were holding hands.

As they walked alongside the line of parked cars, Linny's mind skipped ahead to future phone calls with Tom, Saturday meet-ups at the mall. She wanted to suggest that they get some food and bring it outside, but she was distracted by the sight of her parents sitting in their tan-colored Cutlass, arguing. At least that's what it looked like. Only when Linny got closer did she realize that it wasn't her mother—it was Nancy Bao.

Linny didn't dare face Tom, to see what he was seeing. She hurried ahead to the Baos' front door and went straight to the dining room, where she pretended to be hungry for shrimp and vermicelli. She didn't even know Tom. What if he gossiped to everyone? Linny could just imagine Lisa in hysterics, the whole community in an uproar.

"Where should we eat?" Tom asked.

"I'm going downstairs," Linny said, turning away, already planning to ditch him for one of her friends.

She poured a cup of Dr Pepper and grabbed a napkin, ready to flee, when Nancy Bao appeared, the image of cheerfulness with her freshly permed hair and flowered halter sundress. She set a bucket of ice near the two-liter bottles of pop. "Enjoying the food, children?"

Her Vietnamese was silky and languid. Linny looked straight at her and said, "The shrimp and vermicelli dish is no good."

Linny could feel Tom staring at her but kept focused on Nancy Bao, who didn't stop smiling. She simply took up the platter of shrimp and walked to the kitchen, the back hem of her skirt swinging out.

After that Linny stopped going to the Vietnamese parties. She didn't want to face Tom again or Lisa Bao. It was easier to stay away, enmesh herself in her own group of friends from school. She wondered when she would hear word of a fight—her mother getting the news from one of her friends, waking up the neighborhood with her shouts. But nothing happened. Van, oblivious, seemed to spend all of her weekends reading or working on projects to beef up her future college applications, while Linny cruised the mall with Missy and Becca and Caitlin, popular girls from school. She started dating boys who had their own cars, who took her to Pietro's for pizza and then, in the darkness of the Studio 28 Theater, slipped their hands up her shirt.

She never said anything to Van about Nancy Bao, though she wanted to, sometimes, in the quiet minutes at the end of dusk, twilight descending, the time when Mrs. Luong liked to sit outside and "not think." Then, Linny might glance at her sister bent over a notebook and long to say, *I know something you don't know.* Or maybe, *I want you to think about this too.* When she studied, Van kept her hair in careless ponytails that seemed to accentuate the flat plane of her face. Her expression was serious, lost in some textbook history, stories of other people's lives. Linny often had the urge to snap her fingers under her sister's nose or yank her hair as she did when they were little and had fights. But she always let the chance to speak fall away. If Van preferred to stay in her own solitude, so be it.

For Linny, knowing about Nancy Bao meant seeing her

everywhere. Picking up the phone and hearing her breathy English: "Is your da-ddy home?" She envisioned clouds of Dior perfume, eyelids painted royal blue. Nancy would cover her face with foundation, crab to her mother, sulk to her husband, spend long afternoons perfecting her fingernails.

If Van was too preoccupied, too focused on the debate team to notice, surely Linny's mother was not. Linny wouldn't have dared to say anything to her, make the subject a soft fruit smashed open. But she believed that her mother must have known, and somehow this thought became almost more unbearable than the affair itself. If her mother spilled a glass of water on the table or forgot her purse at home, if she broke a teacup or left the milk out on the counter all night—Linny saw these as signals, a communication no one would answer.

In the middle of her tenth-grade year, Linny acquired her first real boyfriend, an eighteen-year-old senior whose parents had bought him a red Jeep. They spent hours after school driving around town and finding secluded places to make out, testing how far they dared to go. One day, stopped at a light on 28th Street, Linny saw her father and Nancy stepping out of a Chinese restaurant. The day was bright and cloudless and Nancy shaded her eyes. She wore yellow pumps and a dress patterned with overlapping squares of primary colors. Linny could see her magenta lipstick and thick black eyeliner, no doubt meant to widen her eyes. Nancy Bao tucked her fingers into Dinh Luong's arm as they walked to the Cutlass Supreme. As the light changed and Linny's boyfriend drove on, the last thing Linny thought she saw was her father unlocking the door for Nancy. He lifted the handle, opening the door just slightly before walking around to the driver's side, as if he were unwilling to open the door fully and wait for her to settle in. Linny craned her neck to see more, but only glimpsed the colors of Nancy's dress, disappearing.

Linny's father called as she was driving past the exit to South Haven, where she and her friends had spent so many warm days, lounging at the Lake Michigan beach, skipping school. Linny would spread out her towel, look out at that seemingly endless expanse of water, and pretend she was at the ocean.

"Where are you?"

"About an hour away."

"The ceremony starts at three o'clock," he said reproachfully.

"Plenty of time."

"Did you talk to Van?"

Linny felt that sick sensation again. "No. Why?"

"She isn't calling back. You should've drive here together."

"We don't live in the same place, Dad." Sometimes she wondered if he was actually aware of that. "I'm sure she's on her way."

"She didn't call back all this week." A loud crashing sound. *"Chet cha!"*

"Dad?"

"I dropped the Arm. I'm setting up the studio for the party so people see my work. A lot of old friends haven't seen me in so many years. Now they'll get to see my big announcement. You and Van will see it also. It's my new invention. So everyone has to be here."

Suddenly Linny asked, "The Baos?"

"Of course the Bao family. Listen, Linh, you call your sister.

Tell her to not be late. I have to fix this," he muttered. He hung up and Linny kept her cell phone in her hand. Without letting herself think about it, she dialed Van's number.

To her surprise, Van answered.

"Dad told you to call, right?"

"He said you haven't been calling him back."

"I'm tired of seeing his number." She sounded more annoyed than she usually got with their father. It was Linny who typically had less patience. "Tell him I already left."

Linny took a breath before asking, "Is Miles coming with you?"

"No, he's out of town."

"Where?"

"What do you care? I have to go."

"I just thought—" Linny stopped. She had no idea how to complete the sentence. She drove past a giant homemade billboard shaped like a cross that said *If you don't get right yer gonna get left.*

"I'll see you at the ceremony," Van said.

Linny tossed her phone on the passenger seat and paused the mix CD. It was a box set, the kind of thing she'd wanted to order for years, ever since the "Freedom Rock" commercials from the eighties. *Remember?* she imagined saying to Van. Back then, they both knew the commercial by heart, down to the succession of featured song snippets. They sat close to the screen and sang along: "I've been through the desert on a horse with no name . . . I've seen fire and I've seen rain . . . Sunshine go away today . . . We may never pass this way again . . ."

At such times, Linny could forget that she was the bad Asian daughter and Van was the good one. Van, who had kept up her Vietnamese, attended to her parents, and hardly ever talked back. She had taken Asian American Studies classes in college and sometimes talked about various immigration acts, which Linny pretended to ignore. Words like *awareness* and *heritage* nestled right into Van's vocabulary. Then she had gone on to law school, something their father deemed just as worthy as engineering or dentistry school. And she even married an Asian guy.

Linny's boyfriends had mostly been white or black, and she hadn't even finished college. Even in high school she had done everything half-assed, which she saw confirmed in the glances her mother's friends used to give her. The ones that said, *When is that girl going to shape up?* Linny hadn't even had the decency to consider working in a nail salon. *That* kind of Vietnamese girl, at least, did her part in keeping the community intact.

Linny had always imagined that Van's life was an exercise in discipline, a how-to kit in which all the directions were followed exactly. But now, having seen Miles in Chicago, having guessed at how much her sister might be concealing, Linny reconsidered.

Floating on that highway toward home, Linny felt barely rooted to her seat. She thought of ghosts, spirits, or whatever form her mother was supposed to be now, conjured whenever Linny wrote another recipe or wondered what her mother had thought, their first months in Michigan, when she couldn't find any decent rice in the stores. Linny had often tried to find comfort or guidance in the memory of her mother but she usually ended up answerless. She searched for threads in the sky in front of her, invisible webbing reaching to Chicago, Ann Arbor, Wrightville. She didn't know which line to tug first.

# 7

# Van

The day after Miles left, after Van had driven around Ann Arbor looking for him, after her father had called with the news of his citizenship, Van sat on the carpet-covered staircase in her house for five hours. The pile was thick and plush, just as in an advertisement, and she had a notion that if she did not stir from her spot, then she would be okay, like riding out a storm. Eventually she fell asleep, spread across three steps, rolling in and out of consciousness so that the waking world seemed a half-lucid dream. When she finally got up, aiming for the sofa in the TV room, she was almost glad to feel an ache in her body, distracting her from the absence in the house. It didn't last long enough.

She called in sick to Gertz & Zarou that week, something she never would have dared before. She slept in a position of waiting, preparing to spring up at any moment if the garage door should rise. At the very least, she didn't want to leave the house in case he returned. She tried to think of the days as a countdown, even if she didn't know when the count would be over.

But by the end of the week, Van became restless. She turned off the incessant television that had seeped into her nightmares, mixing laugh-track sitcoms with visions of Miles and Sunil, elephants and motorcycles, a swirl of gold and jade bracelets. She awoke thinking that Miles was testing her. Perhaps he wanted her to come after him. Didn't he say she should have more initiative, more assertiveness? Perhaps he was waiting for *her*.

The thought compelled her to get up and shower, shave her legs, and wash her hair with the botanical shampoo Miles favored. Afterward, wrapped in a towel, she tiptoed to the top of the stairs, listening in case he had come home. Then she went to her closet to find something to wear. Miles always liked her in fitted suits and solid-color dresses. His praise words were *elegant* and *stylish*. Van pulled out the burgundy cashmere turtleneck he had bought her last year. Moving quickly through the racks at Neiman Marcus, he'd plucked the sweater as if from the air, resolving it out of nothing but his will. The neck of the sweater was slightly cowled, and the fabric fit smoothly over Van's narrow shoulders. She paired it with gabardine dress pants Miles had also chosen for her that day. They'd had them hemmed in the store, and Van remembered the way Miles watched her as she looked at herself, standing almost tall on the dais, facing the three-way mirror. He had leaned against an opposite wall as if he liked what he was seeing. The seamstress, taking pins out of her mouth, had spoken not to Van but to Miles about when the pants would be ready.

Van realized that she must have dropped off the pants at the cleaners last week. Some of Miles's clothes had gone too. A feeling of dread washed over her to think of him reclaiming his shirts and leaving her pants behind. What would the woman at the cleaners think? Van made a note to pick up all of the clothes herself first, make Miles return to *her* in order to get them.

She put on black wool pants instead and grabbed a pair of

trouser socks from a drawer. She would wear the black pumps Miles had also bought for her, from the intimidating shoe department at Saks, where Van never went herself. She had been so shocked by the price that she hung on to the years-old Naturalizers he had wanted to toss out, keeping them in her car to change into before work.

Like her sister and mother, Van was slim, small, and short. Mostly short. That was the primary adjective people used to describe her. In a crowd of white students, white lawyers, it was easy to identify her as the short Asian girl. Linny had said it was possible to slip past that; she had a way of dressing to perfect advantage, knowing exactly what worked for her figure. She spoke of how certain prints "overwhelmed" a short girl, and how certain styles had a lengthening effect. Van saw how clothes could transform her sister but didn't believe they could have as much of an effect on her. Miles preferred suits because they lent her the strongest guise of authority. *Of course*, he had laughed, *someone could also think you're a little girl playing dress-up*. The words stung Van, got to the core of her fear of being unseen, interrupted, dismissed. She couldn't shake the way Miles said, *Come on, Van. It's a joke. Learn to laugh at yourself.* It was a phrase he had invoked repeatedly in recent months. *Don't you know how to take a joke?* He didn't know he was echoing Linny in her teenage years, part of the barbs she and Van had traded.

In the bathroom Van applied a light coating of lipstick, blush, and powder. That was all the makeup she ever wore. All of Linny's complicated accoutrements—the weapon-shaped eyelash curler, pots of shimmer, a box full of different-sized brushes—seemed foreign to Van. She didn't know how Linny could paint herself up so unselfconsciously. Wasn't she afraid of appearing effortful? Even on her wedding day, Van had worn minimal makeup. Besides, Miles had always said he liked the natural look; women who wore too much makeup were probably hiding insecurities.

There wasn't much to be done about her hair either. It hung limply at her shoulders, plain and unmistakably Vietnamese. It had been this way since high school and, except for the occasional ponytail or bun, she'd never seen a reason to do anything different. This was the body Miles had fallen in love with, after all. Linny, who never failed to offer unasked-for advice on Van's hair and wardrobe, could know nothing about that. As Van hurried down to the garage, she thought of what Linny had said after she'd met Miles. "He's nice. Maybe a little too nice. You can tell he really wants to be cool. He's friendly but calculating, just like a lawyer." When Van got mad, Linny said, "Hey, I'm just being honest."

That was Linny's typical defense, and she got away with it too, because she happened to be beautiful. It was an all-encompassing answer. An acceptance and definition. Matt Staven, Van's prom date and Model UN partner, had said, *Your sister is really something*. Her first boyfriend in college saw a picture of Linny and exclaimed, *That's your* sister? Beauty was Linny's distinguishing characteristic and it satisfied people. They needed to know nothing more. Van was the one who had to prove herself, raise her hand to deliver answers, get the grades.

As a teenager she would sometimes confront herself in the mirror, asking: *Am I jealous?* Sometimes it was yes, sometimes no. She could see how she was the imperfect amateur portrait of Linny. The resemblance was clear, the effort commendable,

but the lines just didn't match. There was a faltering, a funda-
mental lack. It wasn't unfair so much as an unchangeable fact.
Van even had moments of pride when she considered what her
sister possessed. She imagined it was what mothers felt while
shooing their daughters onto a beauty pageant stage. Linny
smiled and it seemed a bestowal. Surely the world opened up
for women like her.

Van remembered a song blaring out of Linny's high school
boom box: *I've got the brains, you've got the looks, let's make lots of
money.* Linny sunning herself in the yard, listening to WKLQ. It
was mid-June, the end of Van's junior year, and she was studying for the SAT while Mrs. Luong rolled out *cha gio* for a party
that night.

"That's a funny song," their mother said. She tilted her head
a little, listening to the chorus coming in through the window.
"You and Linny are like that. That's why you have to stick together. Make money and save money. Together."

Van glanced up, irritated, from the vocabulary words she
was memorizing. "It's just a stupid song."

"You go to the same college," Mrs. Luong said, a grim order.

"No way. I'm not going to end up at some fourth-tier school."

"Same college," she insisted. "Stick together!"

Linny came into the kitchen for a can of Sprite. She was
barefoot, almost naked but for a pink string bikini, another item
"borrowed from a friend" so Mrs. Luong couldn't throw it out.

Mrs. Luong still glared at the bikini but Linny appeased her
with, "I'll help you with the rest in a minute. The bean cakes
too."

Van concentrated on the vocabulary words, pausing to

repeat *concatenate* to herself. She thought, *There is no way in the world we will go to the same college.* Her mother arranged a *cha gio* roll on a platter.

Soon, college pamphlets and applications would fill up the mailbox. Fees waived. Honors programs touted. All for Van.

Linny's feet slapped on linoleum, the screen door slamming shut.

Van closed her eyes. *In one year I'll be free. I'll never come back.*


Driving toward Miles's law office in Ann Arbor, those polished black pumps already pinching her toes, Van banished her family from her mind. If things worked out, if Miles returned, no one would have to know that he'd ever left. He had married Van for a reason. He had chosen her above all the prettier, flirtier, taller women surrounding him in law school. But as she headed downtown her heart seemed to grow heavy with worry. It was like the old days, dating Miles, when she never quite knew where she stood. Her sometimes breathless anxiety as she climbed the steps to his apartment. Would he smile? Would he be glad to see her? Or would he turn her away gently, saying *I really need to work tonight*.

Volker, Voss, and Williams occupied a brick-and-mirrored-glass building surrounded by greenery and Japanese maples. Every aspect of the landscape seemed to anticipate the clients' expectations of marble and mahogany, low voices commingled with the sense of importance that pervaded the office. It was nothing like Gertz & Zarou. At Volker, the clients were wealthy and white, and owned German luxury cars or gigantic SUVs. At

Van's office the clients were Indian and Chinese; they slipped into the waiting room with as little noise as possible, sat with their hands in their laps.

Miles's secretary, an early-twenty-something woman whose mother was also a secretary in the firm, tilted her head smilingly when Van walked in.

"Hi, Mrs. Oh," she called out. "I didn't know you'd be stopping by."

"Nice to see you, Holly." To Van's relief her voice sounded normal. She was always startled to be called by Miles's last name, because she had not changed hers when they married. He had claimed to approve, calling it independent, but asked for a compromise: she would keep her name legally, but be known socially as Mrs. Oh, and she would change it for real once they had a child. "Is my husband here?"

"He's in a meeting but it should be over in a little while. Want to wait?"

"Yes. I think I will." Van sank into a modernist silver-trimmed leather chair. As she crossed her legs her pants hiked up, revealing the trouser socks she had put on earlier. Van realized that they were dark brown, not black as she'd thought, and they looked silly against her black pants and shoes. Van uncrossed her legs and tried to draw them underneath the chair. At that moment two women walked by, obviously an associate and her client. The lawyer wore a pencil skirt, black hose, and stacked heels; the client swished by in wide-legged trousers. No matter what she wore or how good she might feel about herself, the sight of a pulled-together tall woman could always make Van feel like a short little stump.

"So, how have you been?" Holly asked from her desk. "I haven't seen you since the Christmas party."

Van had missed the first half of the party due to traffic coming back from the immigration office in Detroit, and she remembered the dread she had felt at an impending argument with Miles, who hated it when she was late for events. But he hadn't seemed to register her timing. When she arrived at the restaurant, wearing a red dress and realizing that none of the other associates had dressed festively, Miles had simply waved at her from a conversation he was having in a far corner of the room. It was a gesture of hello, she thought at the time, rather than an invitation. But she'd joined them anyway, stepping into her role as the spouse.

"I'm doing fine," Van said. "How have you been?"

"Well, *great*, actually." Holly grinned, then lifted her left hand to smooth a lock of blond hair. The gesture was so deliberate that Van understood: the girl was wearing an engagement ring, a large one that gleamed flatly in the office light. "I don't know if Miles told you," she began.

"You're engaged!" Van blurted. "How fun! How great! Congratulations! Who's the lucky guy?"

"You know Kevin Anders?"

"Of course." Van smiled, but she was secretly shocked. Holly was barely twenty-five. Kevin was a partner at the firm, gym-fit to make up for his advancement beyond middle age. He had once declared he would never get married, sparking rumors that he was gay, and Miles had told Van that all the single women in the building were aiming to find out the truth.

"It's only been a couple of weeks," Holly gushed. "But I still can't believe it. When you and Miles got engaged, did you spend hours looking at your ring or what?"

"Can I see it?"

Holly's left hand shot out and Van rose from her chair to get a better look. The diamond was thick and oval-shaped, with baguettes on either side.

"I wanted gold," Holly said, "but Kevin said platinum was better."

Van lifted her own left hand, where her plain diamond solitaire circled her finger above the channel-set wedding band Miles had selected. She was standing there, her hand almost close enough to Holly's to bear a comparison, when she heard Miles saying her name.

She blushed, Miles staring at her with an expression of uncertainty bordering on amusement. She could have been a comic moment at a zoo exhibition, or an audacious child. Still, his face, softened since that terrible Saturday night, gave Van hope. Holly piped up, "I was just telling your wife my news."

"It is very good news," Miles said, starting toward his office.

When he had shut the door behind them and sat down at his desk, Van remained standing. The room was clean and noncommittal, with recessed lights, stern Berber carpeting, and cherry-stained furniture. A bold white orchid, no doubt a client gift, perched on a filing cabinet, and on the desk one picture frame faced him. Back when he first took this job Van had framed some of his college art photographs so he could hang them in his new office, but he had never even moved them from their box.

He gestured to one of the chairs in front of his desk but Van would not be treated like one of his clients.

"I knew you'd come here," he said.

This deflated her, and for a moment she felt like a stalker. A predictable one at that. "Then why didn't you call?"

"If I had wanted to talk I would have called." Miles spoke evenly. He was no longer the sensitive man weeping into his coat sleeve. He was straight-faced, prepared. His tie glowed iridescently, changing from silver to blue and back again.

"I think you owe me an explanation." The words emerged from Van as though she knew what to say. She didn't. It was only later that she realized that she'd taken her cue from movies and television shows, probably reaching all the way back to the evening soaps her mother had favored.

He leaned back in his leather chair, looking altogether too relaxed. "I wish you'd sit down."

"No thanks."

"Van, all I know is what I've known for a long time. I just didn't realize it until I did. So let's face reality for once. Do you honestly think our marriage is okay?"

She blushed again, feeling as though she'd been called out in a law school lecture. "I don't think it's not okay."

"Well, it's obvious we're not on the same track. Our minds aren't aligned."

"Aligned," Van repeated.

"When we first got together, we were a real couple. You had ambition. Potential was everywhere. And now, as you well know, Van, it isn't."

A wave of panic rose inside her, and she fought to keep her voice in control. "You didn't even want me to work at the International Center. You persuaded me to quit."

"Don't be ridiculous. You can't blame me for your mistakes and failures, Van."

"You did. You said—"

"We've both said a lot and most of it is a lot of nothing. We go right past each other. This isn't just about work. Van. Stop being so literal. It's about character, personalities."

"In what way?"

"Shh," he said. "Please keep your voice down. I have to work. This is my workplace. I'm meeting clients all day."

"You want me out of here."

"In a word, yes."

In the few days Miles had been gone Van had cried only once in the shower and only once while watching TV. It was a strange thing with crying: by herself she could contain it; in the presence of another person she lost control. As a girl, if she was yelled at she would burst into instant, hyperventilating sobs. Even bad customer service could make her throat swell. She'd always been careful to maintain composure around Miles, but she knew he could see that she was on the verge.

"Don't cry, Van." It was a weary command. He stood up and said it again, more gently. "Van," he repeated.

He walked over to her and, hesitating, patted her on the shoulder. "I'll tell you though—it's nice to hear you actively disagreeing with me. Not just going along."

*I thought you* wanted *me to go along,* she almost said, but stopped herself. Was she supposed to agree or disagree with what he just said? Van found herself grabbing at Miles's hands. His face, his eyes were inscrutable—had they always been? She had never understood how characters in books could discern entire ranges of emotion and understanding in someone else's eyes. Miles's steady gaze told her nothing more than what his words said. He let her hang on for a moment before drawing himself away. "Now's not the time for this," he said quietly. "Get yourself together." And then, as if to reward her, he put his arms around her.

"We'll talk soon. I have to come by the house to get some more things."

She focused on the picture frame on his desk. "When?"

"Whenever I can. I'll call you."

"Where are you staying?"

"Don't worry about it. Here." He went back to his desk, opened a drawer, and set forth a box of Kleenex. "You have to go now."

She looked around helplessly. "This isn't right."

"It's okay. We're going to be fine. Just go home now." He spoke so tenderly that Van held on to the phrase *we're going to be fine*. It was her lifeboat. "Don't make a scene, okay?"

When Van left the office she moved quickly, letting her hair hang in her face to avoid seeing young Holly's diamond ring.

It was only in the car, starting back home, that Van remembered something she had meant to do. *Just keep going,* she told herself, but the need to know was too strong: she did a U-turn and drove back to the maroon-and-glass building of Volker, Voss, and Williams. This time Van ignored Holly and headed straight to Miles's office. He was standing at an open filing cabinet, briefcase on his desk. "What are you doing back here?" he demanded.

At his tone of trespass, the slight emphasis on *you*, Van stopped. She realized that she should feel ashamed. Ordinarily, she would. She would have felt like the desperate, needy girl who didn't know when to walk away, take no for an answer. Now Van felt angry. It came on suddenly, like a boost of adrenaline in the last minute of a timed debate. It was anger, finally, that made her reach out to Miles's desk. Her hand grasped the one picture frame sitting there and flipped it around. Van let out a breath she'd been holding. All that time, she had been expecting to see Julie.

Up until Linny was eight years old, the Luongs lived in an apartment complex near a freeway and a construction site that turned out to be a correctional facility. Linny remembered waiting at the school bus stop, which was right next to the city bus stop, and watching the prison go up in rounds, studded with tiny window slits. Often in the mornings she, Van, and their mother would wait at their stops together. Linny always hoped that her mother's bus would carry her off to her sewing job at Roger's Department Store before the pencil-yellow school bus loaded with their classmates rumbled up to the curb. Back in the apartment Mr. Luong would be dawdling, or sketching out some design idea, or convincing a friend to give him a ride to whatever tiling or construction job he might have lined up for the day. The work was too easy for him, he said; he had studied civil engineering in Vietnam (no degree, Mrs. Luong sniffed).

Linny's mother often said they would have been able to buy a house sooner if he hadn't spent so much time "being the bum" with his inventions. Van was seven when their mother said she was old enough to be in charge, and accepted the full-time job at Roger's. When Linny had recalled this, the night of

Van and Miles's rehearsal dinner, Miles had been shocked, exclaiming that he couldn't imagine leaving a seven- and a six-year-old home alone. Van had laughed it off, but Linny had wondered then what else Van had never told him.

Van had managed the two of them well, Linny thought. They would ride the school bus home together and Van would fish out the key to their apartment from the zippered inside pocket their mother had sewn into all of her jackets. Then they'd spend the rest of the day reading and watching television, snacking on crackers and apples and chocolate mints, whatever was in the kitchen, until Mrs. Luong returned. Those early evening hours between Linny and Van made up the closest years of their sisterhood, when they pretended to live in the apartment by themselves. Linny was Laverne and Van was Shirley, both of them sassy and in control, just back from shifts at the beer factory.

Two years later, Mrs. Luong's scrupulous savings allowed the family to move out of the apartment and into the little ranch house in Wrightville. That was when Mr. Luong started cutting back to part-time construction work, something his wife resented at every step. "Your father," she would say to the girls, "he always prefers the fake work."

But he had invented the Luong Arm in that apartment by the freeway. Linny believed she could trace it back to the way she and Van used to climb on the kitchen counters to reach boxes of cookies or graham crackers. She recalled one day in particular—her father sitting at the kitchen table, staring at the Oriental Market wall calendar beside the refrigerator—when Linny slipped into the room to get some Halloween candy. She was seven then, and she boosted herself onto the counter with one hand while her other hand opened a cupboard and located the bag of sweets. When she turned around her father was looking at her with a shining interest he rarely had. A few months later, at dinner, he presented the prototype of the Luong Arm, demonstrating it by grasping a bag of chips from the top shelf of a cupboard.

When he wasn't around, Linny and Van practiced using the Luong Arm and Linny boasted that she had given him the idea. "No you didn't," Van said. "He got the idea from *me*." When they finally worked up the nerve to ask him, he simply said, "It was my idea."

Linny's mother never used the Luong Arm. She tolerated her husband's talk about it, mostly meeting his enthusiasm with nods and silence. But she raised her voice when he spent money on infomercial items that he called research and she called a waste of money. She had been especially furious when, that Christmas, he gave her a Tidie Drier, a contraption that somehow promised to fast-dry her hair as well as her hand-washed underclothes. He said he was on the lookout for the next big thing in sewing machines too, but Mrs. Luong told him to leave her out of his plans. Long before they occupied two different floors of the same house, they had each retreated to their own work.

Roger's was going out of business now, done in at last by the shopping malls, and Linny sometimes wondered where all of the Vietnamese ladies who'd worked there would end up. Before Mrs. Luong died, she had considered leaving Roger's to work at her friend's nail salon. *Don't do it*, Van had urged her. *It's just too stereotypical, even worse than sewing.* Linny had to agree. But their mother had said, *It's a good job. Don't be so stupid.*

After her death, Linny and Van both worried about what their father would do to get by. He received a minor life insurance sum, but they suspected, in one of their rare longer phone conversations, that he'd soon spent most of that on his inventions or drinking and playing cards. He had never been one to submit to steady work, even though, as he'd bragged, he was the best person around for setting complicated tile patterns just right. He also refused to talk about money matters. When Van decided she was going to send him monthly checks, Linny said that was good since she couldn't afford it herself. She made a joke about how it was the duty of the oldest to take care of the parents. *What else am I here for?* Van had thrown back sarcastically, sounding a lot like their mother.

On the day of his citizenship ceremony, Dinh Luong sat alone in the ivory-paneled auditorium of the Gerald R. Ford Museum. He wasn't truly alone—surrounded by families, other ethnic-looking people also about to take the oath—but to Linny he seemed to be set apart, nearly invisible. As though he were still hovering over his studio desk in the basement or laying out pieces of tile before grouting. When Linny was a girl she would feel nearly abandoned by that faraway look on his face, and would sometimes barrage her father with questions about his work just to make him come back to life.

When he saw her he called out in Vietnamese, "Where's your sister?"

"I don't know," Linny said, instantly irritated. She hurried past a South Indian family to get to the seats her father had saved with an umbrella. The auditorium, its high ceiling rippled with lights trained on the wide wooden stage, reminded Linny of her high school's production of *Our Town*.

"But she's never late." He looked uneasy in a gold-buttoned navy blue sport jacket Linny recognized from years ago. He tapped his knee with the program, his eyes searching the auditorium. "A lot of people will be coming to the party tomorrow, so you have to cook a lot of food. Van has to help clean," he added, which Linny knew meant, *You and your sister need to clean the entire house.* "You know, your ma never thought I'd be a citizen."

He invoked her so rarely that Linny felt cautious. "How do you know?"

"Listen," he said, changing the subject, "did you know there's a song called 'Short People Are No Reason to Live'? One of my friends play it for me."

"It's *got* no reason."

"What?"

"The song. It goes, 'Short people got no reason to live.'"

"You know this?"

"I heard it on a TV show."

Her father was astounded. "They play it on TV? This is the trouble we are in. This is the trouble!"

"I don't think the song is for *real*."

"I heard it myself. What do I say to you and Van all the years ago, and even now? I say you have to fight them back. This is why you listen to me."

Before he could keep going, a middle-aged blond woman walked onto the stage. She introduced herself as Janine, a local-chapter ambassador from the Daughters of the American Revolution, there to lead them all in singing "The Star-Spangled Banner." A rustle of fabric and the bounce of auditorium chairs as everyone stood up. Janine, facing the U.S. flag and the state of Michigan flag beside her, launched into it.

Her bombs were bursting in air when Van appeared at the end of the row of red seats. She scooted by, ducking under people's voices.

"Hey." Linny couldn't stop herself from glancing her sister over head to toe. Van wore a cardigan-and-slacks uniform, straight out of a Talbots catalog. It fit in better in this town than her own vividly printed wrap dress.

Van said, "Traffic."

The word, reminding Linny of Gary, sent an unexpected shiver through her. What would Van say if she knew about him? But the anthem was over and Linny clapped, watching her hands blur together in their movement.


The circuit court judge presiding over the ceremony had a comb-over and a wide face like a baseball mitt. "Today," he said, opening his arms, "America embraces you. America welcomes you to her shores. You have come from far and wide to pledge allegiance to this country, forsaking all other nations. You will find that this is indeed the land of freedom, the land of hopes, and the land of dreams. From Plymouth Rock, to the plains of Nebraska, to the miracle of the Grand Canyon, to the beaches of California, you will find the glory and the spirit of all that is this great land of America."

Linny didn't remember any of this speech-making from her

mother's naturalization ceremony twenty years ago. It had taken place in a courtroom, just a small group of mostly Vietnamese who, like her mother, were among the first wave of refugees to reach for citizenship. Thuy Luong had thought it a matter of pride and duty, since her husband refused to apply, and because she thought it would give Linny and Van an extra sense of security; she didn't want her daughters to be alone as Americans. Linny remembered feeling special when her mother told her that she and Van were already citizens just by being born in the States.

She also remembered that some of the people in the courtroom had wept, and how that had made her think of a school history lesson on Ellis Island. Her teacher's description of huddled masses yearning to be free and the wonderful giant melting pot of America seemed out of place here. Somehow Linny understood: that moment, her mother, the Vietnamese voices—these made up a different kind of island.

Her father, at the time, hadn't wanted to hear anything about it. "You think it's so special being the normalized citizen," he had said, as if it were a taunt. "Why not all people in America have to take the tests?"

Linny's mother called him jealous. When she cast her first vote, for the 1984 presidential election, she brought Linny and Van with her. "The three of us can do this, but your ba cannot," she had explained. "And it's all because we're citizens." Her mother had tugged Linny close as if to emphasize the divide between them and her father.

When Mr. Luong's patent for the Luong Arm got rejected—Van had insisted he hadn't filled out the forms correctly—he claimed it was because he wasn't a citizen. "So become one,"

Mrs. Luong had said. But in his stubborn way, he had clung to the opposite, taking it as a challenge. It had taken him this long to uncurl that resolve.

In the Ford auditorium Van whispered, "Look who's here."

"Who?"

"The Oortsemas." She nodded to the far left, several rows forward.

"I wonder why."

"For Dad, I guess."

Dirk and Paula Oortsema had been Mr. and Mrs. Luong's sponsors back in 1975. They had said they decided to help bring refugees to Michigan after their pastor gave a series of moving sermons about the plight of the Oriental boat people. Dirk Oortsema steered Mr. Luong toward carpentry jobs and ESL classes, while Paula Oortsema gave Mrs. Luong baby clothes and formula and showed her how to cook tuna noodle casserole. Linny's mother had often said she had tried to forget those first few months. Everything had seemed too sharp—the cold, the language, the confusion of all those aisles in the grocery store. She had wished for dullness.

The Luongs found some comfort in a community center life skills class, where they learned how to open a bank account, cash a check, apply for jobs, and read bus maps. It was also there that the Luongs found their new friends, including Rich and Nancy Bao. But there was still so much they didn't know. When they first got a car, procured through Mrs. Luong's shrewd Vietnamese bargaining skills and hoarded savings, they hadn't known they needed a scraper for winter days. When a storm left a coating of ice on the windshield, Mr. Luong decided it would melt more quickly if he tossed boiled water on the glass. It had burst like gunfire. Linny didn't remember that but her mother had insisted it was true, telling the story only when Linny's father wasn't around.

In Linny's first memory of the Oortsemas, she and Van were given matching white leatherette Bibles. Dirk and Paula liked to stop by every month or so, and they always had little gifts or candy for the girls. "Hi, there, Din," Dirk Oortsema would say at the apartment door, his barrel-shaped body blocking out the light. "How you doing, buddy?"

Paula took Linny and Van aside, kneeling down and holding their hands. "Girls," she said, "would you like to go to *Sunday school*?" Her voice made it sound like she was offering up Disney Land.

But even Van wasn't convinced by the idea of school on a Sunday, and they never did end up going. The Oortsemas didn't force the issue, though every once in a while Paula would say, "I just want what's best for my girls." She had been successful, at least, in introducing the gifts of Christmas to the household.

"Nice people," Mrs. Luong always said about the Oortsemas. "They try very hard. Nice people."

Linny said, "I'm not her girl, but she can bring me presents."

Perhaps because the Oortsemas had three boys, Paula doted on Linny and Van. She liked to bring them barrettes and hair ribbons, and clothes donated by her church. Only she didn't call them donations. She called them "presents from church." Mrs. Luong always smiled when she accepted the clothes, but later Linny would see them tossed into bags. Her parents weren't quite willing to throw such things away, since that seemed wasteful, so they just stuffed them into closets for years. Van refused to sift through the bags, but Linny dug through with a will, searching for anything that she thought her friends would like, or anything with a brand-name label. She made the clothes over into her own, enough so that even her parents forgot that they had ever belonged to anyone else.

In the auditorium Linny said, "I guess it's nice of the Oortsemas to be here. I haven't seen them since the funeral."

"I have. They came over to meet Miles once. Dad invited them."

"Really?"

The judge asked the candidates for naturalization to stand up and raise their right hand. Mr. Luong stared straight ahead while repeating the oath of citizenship, promising to renounce allegiance to other nations, support and defend the Constitution, and take these obligations freely, without any mental reservation.

Linny remembered gazing up at her mother, squinting at the overhead lights. Mrs. Luong's face had seemed expressionless as she spoke the words.

Her father repeated them loudly, as if in competition with the others standing near him.

"And now," the judge said, smiling, "I pronounce you to be citizens, with all of the rights and obligations contained therein, of the United States of America."

The audience applauded, and someone in the back let out a loud whistle. "If you'll please take your seats," the judge called out, "we will now have each individual citizen come to the stage and be presented with a certificate of naturalization."

There were over forty new citizens and the judge announced their names in no particular order. "Haruki Watanabe of Japan!

Feyza Sercan of Turkey! Kim Hyoun of Korea! Henrick Van der Berg of the Netherlands!" Each person shook the judge's hand and crossed the stage to where other volunteers from the Daughters of the American Revolution handed them miniature plastic American flags.

Van muttered, "This is unbelievable."

"It's like a pageant," Linny said with a laugh.

"Manjit Singh of India! Dinh Luong of Vietnam!"

He bolted out of his seat. On stage he shook the judge's hand, then threw out a big grin to the audience, as if he were on a game show. The judge towered over him, actually bending down a little, which made Linny cringe. But her father didn't seem to notice. Suddenly she understood that he was looking to the back of the room. He was smiling at someone in particular. She turned around, scanning the faces.

Van nudged her, for their father had moved on to shake hands with the DAR women, waving his plastic American flag. He took his sweet time exiting the stage, still smiling, and Linny swiveled around again, this time aiming for the back row of the audience, where Nancy Bao was waiting.

# 9

# Van

When Dinh Luong declined to attend his wife's citizenship ceremony, he said, "You don't need me there for you to be normalized." It was dinnertime, and he slurped at his bowl of *pho*, using chopsticks to push the noodles into his mouth. For years he said *normalized* instead of *naturalized*, and Van didn't know if he meant it as a joke.

"Shameful!" Thuy Luong said in Vietnamese. "How will it look? Bad enough that you're not getting your own citizenship. You have to face up to this the same as the rest of us. This is the way things have to be."

It was not a new argument between them. Van played with the corner of her vinyl place mat, curling the corner like a book page and watching it slowly lie flat again. Linny, seven years old, kept her focus on an episode of *Gilligan's Island*.

"Afraid of the test," Mrs. Luong baited him.

Instead of answering, her husband dipped his chopsticks into her soup bowl, taking a piece of beef. Mrs. Luong turned to her daughters. "Who was the first president of the United States?" she asked in English. "Van, answer."

"George Washington."

"Correct." Her mother returned to Vietnamese. "So simple. That's all it takes to be a citizen in this country."

Mr. Luong replied, "What is the Sixth Amendment?"

Van and Linny didn't know. They shrank from their father's sharp gaze. Van's mother pretended not to hear the question. On the TV, the Skipper was scaring Gilligan out of his rope hammock.

"Nobody knows, huh?" Van's father smiled triumphantly. "They asked Sem that question. He failed the exam. You know what we are? No one. We have no citizenship. Refugees aren't belonging anywhere."

He stood up from the table. "In America, we don't belong until we make them see it. It's not a piece of paper with *citizen* on it."

Van's mother had heard it all before. She was flexing her fingers, stretching them out. Often in the evening she asked her daughters to massage her hands. She would change into a comfortable tunic and flowy pants as soon as she got home, then lie on the sofa and hold out her hands. "Just for a minute," she'd plead, closing her eyes with a sigh.

The three of them, Van, Linny, and her mother, knew Mr. Luong wanted only to return to what he called his real work. He had promised them, too many times to count, a future of riches, thickets of hundred-dollar bills falling forth from his inventions. This was when they were still in the two-bedroom apartment, where he had claimed the girls' room as his work space. For a while Van and Linny had slept there surrounded by his papers and tools but soon got edged out to the living room sofa bed, which Van made and unmade for them every day. Linny slept easily, but Van would sometimes stare out the window, keeping track of the construction on the prison. Late into the night Van could hear her father humming Vietnamese folk songs, his voice filled with hope.

"Why now?" Van had asked when he called to say he wanted to apply for citizenship. This was nearly three years ago, the fall of 2000, not long after she and Miles had moved into their new house. Their days then had seemed to promise order and contentment. When her father called Van had been sitting in front of her laptop in the TV room, waiting for Miles to return from work so they could go out to dinner.

"Basically, my inventions have to be made in the USA. I was talking to my friend Jerry. He's this big American guy, works at this company here—"

"But they're already made in the USA because you live in the USA."

"I mean *really* made in the USA. Jerry said permanent resident is not enough anymore. People want to know you're for real. So I have to prove it."

"So you need to be seen as legitimate," Van supplied, channel-surfing with the sound on mute.

"Legitimate," her father repeated the word. "That's it."

Van couldn't help saying, "After all this time it's your friend Jerry who convinces you." How many times had she presented similar arguments to her father and he had waved them away? She felt a buzz of meanness come over, a hardness that reminded her, as such moments always did, of law school. "Well, U.S. citizenship definitely confers legitimacy."

She expected her father to snap at her. Maybe say, *You help-*

*ing or not?* Or even, *I don't need your talk.* Instead, her father said, "Why you the lawyer, Van? What for?"

She should have guessed he would lob something at her out of nowhere, make her remember her place. It had been this way since she was a child: he would change direction on her, make her sorry to have spoken. And it always worked. For years now she had wanted to ask if he realized how much she did for him, that she had even gone to law school at Michigan just so she could be closer to home. But she'd never yet had the nerve to say it.

When she was in eighth grade he had made her go to the local library to find out how to apply for a U.S. patent for the Luong Arm. The process appeared to be more intricate than a green card application, and a librarian had directed her to the Detroit Public Library, one of the few places in the state that housed a complete directory of patents.

"See, you have to make sure the patent you want isn't just overlapping with one they've already given," Van had tried to explain to her father.

"So call and you ask," he'd said.

"I can't. You have to go look in the directory. There are millions and millions of patents."

He actually drove her to the Detroit library that summer, dropped her off while he visited an old friend from the refugee camp who now lived in Hamtramck. Van had looked helplessly at the huge binders stamped *United States Patent and Trademark Office*, with lists, descriptions, and photos of inventions dating back to 1790. At last two kind librarians showed Van how to get an application form mailed to her father, then helped her comb through the directories. As far as they could figure out in the few hours Van was there, no patent seemed to match exactly the one he wanted for the Luong Arm, which was a good sign. But the application process was really complicated, Van said again to her father. The librarians had told her it was very difficult to get a patent, and that most people were rejected the first time they tried. Her father would have to submit notes, sketches, and pictures of the prototype. And the application fee was several hundred dollars. Somehow, though, probably after a good night gambling with his friends, he managed to mail in the application and fee. When it came back to him, a rejection due to insufficient information, he had been enraged. *It's because I'm not a normalized American*, he had said. But Van was sure he had probably just ignored half of the application instructions. Since then, though, he had refused to reapply for the patent and, until now, had refused citizenship.

With two clicks Van had a naturalization application open on her computer screen. "All right," she said to her father, falling back on her role as the obedient daughter. "We'll make you a citizen."

In the auditorium of the Gerald R. Ford Museum Linny laughed when she said, "It's like a pageant."

Van wondered, *Who is the winner?* Out loud she said, "It's not funny."

After the ceremony ended and everyone was filing toward the glassed-in lobby, Van said, "You have to live here at least five years as a permanent resident, and most people are here for years before that on a visa. Citizenship isn't something that happens in a snap. It takes years, and money. Who do you think paid Dad's application fee? And that judge! Acting like all these people just got here. 'Welcome to America!' God!"

When Linny looked at her Van fell silent. She was not the kind of person to talk so loudly, and she felt overheated in her wool cardigan, disheveled next to her sister's sleek wrap dress. But Linny cast her gaze beyond her, raising an eyebrow. "Look."

Their father was talking to Nancy Bao, whom Van had spoken to a few years back but hadn't seen since Mrs. Luong's funeral. Nancy had the same tight skin and close-cropped permed hair, though the features of her face seemed to have spread out a little. "So what?"

"So, what is she even doing here?"

They watched their father and Nancy receive sugar cookies from the DAR ladies. Their father had always bent himself solicitously toward Nancy, as though she were some sort of patron he was hosting. A Vietnamese host had to do just about anything—go into debt for lobsters and crab, if need be—to make a guest happy. Mr. Luong had never behaved that way toward his wife, Van couldn't help thinking. Was that what Linny was so agitated about?

The museum lobby echoed with non-English chatter, jarring Van from her one memory of her visit here in grade school. Growing up near Gerald Ford's hometown she'd learned a lot about him, recognizing him as a real-life symbol of their tall, conservative city. And she had been fascinated by the idea of seeing his White House china transplanted here. But there were only a few place settings, so the table was pushed against a mirror to make it seem twice its length and fullness. Van had disdained the trickery, and ever after when she drove past the triangular museum building, itself half covered in mirrors, she remembered the half-sized table and felt vaguely cheated.

"Hiya lawyer lady," a voice boomed out. It was Na Dau, Nancy's younger brother. Nancy had sponsored him a few years back and Van had helped her file the application. She had met Na only the previous Christmas when her father's truck broke down at a friend's party and Van had had to retrieve him. Na had been sitting on the front porch, drunk, singing nonsense words to the tune of "Jingle Bells." Nancy, when she'd called Van about Na's application, had admitted he was kind of a troublemaker. He was wild, Van's father said. You wouldn't know he was over forty, and none of the Baos knew how to handle him.

But now Na stood primly in a starched button-down, as though he'd just come from an office job.

"Remember me? It's Na Dau. This a nice day for your ba," he said, adding proudly, "I say to my sister, one day I be here too."

Van introduced him to Linny, who asked him how long he'd been in the States.

"Almost four year. Nancy got me work sometimes at one of Rich's stores." He shrugged. "I got dreams that look bigger. That's why I talk to your ba about his inventings."

"You're interested in inventing things?" Van asked.

"I have many, many interests," Na answered earnestly. "I have many plans. Rich has the money but I have the bigger ideas."

Mr. Luong and Nancy Bao came up to them and Linny beat Van to congratulating their father.

He still had the little American flag in his hands. "That was good, huh? I'm the normalized citizen now." He spoke with the voice of someone who'd gotten away with something. "Now they say I'm legitimate. The proof is right here." He held up his certificate of naturalization.

"This is a good thing, Dad," Van said.

"It's good for my business too."

"We'll celebrate at the party," Nancy said. The fabric buttons of her pink jacket were limned with sequins that flashed when she tightened her grip on her handbag. She nodded at Van and Linny, then told Na in Vietnamese that it was time to go.

"Okay, big sister," Na replied.

"See you tomorrow," Nancy said. She led Na away, but he turned back to Van for a moment.

"I want to say thank you."

She was unnerved by the intensity of his gaze. "For what?"

"For you helping bring me here."

Nancy gave a patient smile but touched her brother's arm.

"I go," he agreed, shrugging.

As they left, the movement of Na's back reminded Van of how her clients, from both the International Center and Gertz & Zarou, bore a similar uncertainty in their bodies. Their very way of walking seemed to reveal the commingling of hope and caution they held—a longing to belong and the fear that they never could. Van was, in fact, at that moment in the lobby, surrounded by people she could have helped.

She wondered if her father ever had these kinds of thoughts. But all he said then was, "Don't forget to get extra beer for tomorrow."

"I know," Linny answered.

"Are you cooking enough food? We need a *lot* of fish and shrimp."

Just like that the celebratory moment was over. The buoyancy he'd had onstage disappeared, and he was back to being the same Asian father, requiring his daughters to bend around his commands.

"Are you going home now?" Van asked.

"Not sure." Which meant no. He fixed a sudden sharp eye on her. "What's wrong with you?"

"Nothing," Van replied. "I'm tired. I want to go home."

"I'll see you later then," her father said, beginning to edge away. He had that familiar look of distraction on his face that meant he had already left the scene. He was at a friend's house, playing cards; he was getting a bowl of *pho* at another friend's restaurant; he was planning to settle back into the cave of his studio.

"Well, congratulations," Linny called after him.

"Let's go," Van said. She was already walking away, trying to avoid Dirk and Paula Oortsema, who were chatting with the judge. "I want to get out of here."

Before heading home Linny insisted on Van accompanying her to Meijer to pick up groceries for the next day's party. In the fluorescent aisles Van followed along like a schoolkid while Linny scrutinized vegetables and tossed handfuls of shallots into the cart.

"I wonder how bad the house will be," Linny said. "Maybe we should get some cleaning supplies just in case."

After their mother died Van and Linny had taken responsibility for maintaining the house, which they were sure their father would have just let disintegrate. Often, when Van checked on him, she found the dining table covered with old newspapers and catalogs, the bathroom untouched from the last time she'd been there, the laundry chute clogged with towels. Sometimes when her father ran out of them he would use sheets to dry himself off. It was hard to compete with his chaos. But there were times, too, when the kitchen would look unexpectedly tidy. In the living room the credenza and the urn that held Thuy Luong's ashes would be freshly dusted and polished.

At the checkout Van paid for the groceries, blinking at the conveyer belt full of things she never bought—mint and cilantro, peanuts to crush and sprinkle on hoisin, disposable chopsticks to supplement the well-worn plastic ones their mother had collected over the years. Van didn't know how to make Vietnamese food, something that always surprised people. As if she had to know how to cook *pho* just because she was Vietnamese. Van's mother had tried to teach her to prepare a few dishes, back when Van was in high school, but she'd always begged off, preferring to study or read or watch TV. In Ann Arbor, Miles had liked taking on the role of household chef. He had a penchant for fine cookware and authentic ethnic food; he liked to buy hardcover cookbooks and bring home expensive olive oils and balsamic vinegars from Zingerman's.

"How do you know how to make all of this stuff?" Van asked Linny.

"Mom taught me. I brought a bunch of ingredients from an Asian store in Chicago."

"Oh." Why was it startling to think that, all those years ago, Linny really had paid attention to what their mother had been cooking?

Linny always drove too fast, so her car was already parked

outside the house by the time Van arrived. At nine years old, seeing it for the first time, she had been enchanted by the squat ranch with its brown siding and picture window. It had looked beautiful, large, and most importantly, theirs alone. There would be no more of the crying baby in the apartment to the right of them, no more of the couple who shouted beneath their feet. Sometimes in that apartment Van could hear someone snoring and not know where it came from. This house, their house, on Garland Street in Wrightville, Michigan, had a maple tree in the back, a garage, a sunny yard to play in. But as Van grew up and went to school she understood what it meant to live in such a place. She learned *working class, middle class, blue collar.* The house seemed smaller every time she returned from college, and never more so than when she brought Miles here to meet her father. She would never forget that day because he had, without telling her, invited Dirk and Paula Oortsema, whom she hadn't seen since her mother died.

"Our girl is getting married!" Paula had exclaimed, and Van had returned her hug stiffly. She had never felt comfortable around the Oortsemas, too aware that they were, in a sense, her parents' benefactors. Plus, her parents had always had a habit of behaving in an overly deferential manner toward them. With Miles there her father seemed to be especially, well, *first-generation.*

"We keep track of all our kids, all our families," Dirk had said proudly to Miles. "They've done good, every last one."

"Thanks to you," Mr. Luong had said. "Or we still be in the camp! Miles, where you think Van would be? You get married in the refugee camp!"

By the time Van walked into the house Linny had already

cleared the dining table free of their father's papers and had started on the kitchen. The house was actually neater than Van had expected. The usual cobwebs hadn't formed near the windows, and the living room television's old remote control had a fresh application of packing tape to secure the battery cover. There were three TVs in the house, including the portable one in the kitchen and the mammoth set in the basement. There had been many times when all three played at once, her mother, sister, and father all tuning in to separate vistas.

Over the years Linny had tried to make some cosmetic improvements to the house with a new coat of paint here, a few throw pillows there. But it would have taken a drastic renovation to alter the basic elements of each room. None of the appliances had even been changed since the Luongs had moved in. Only after Van had lived in her house in Ann Arbor did she understand: a house required a daily battle against deterioration.

In the living room the credenza that Van's mother had splurged on, carefully polishing its maple surface each month, displayed the family's Buddha statue. He sat flanked by candles, incense, and a few pieces of fruit, while the cabinets held Van and Linny's old board games and books. Van would never forget how her mother had said to her, *My ashes and your ba's will sit here too someday*. Van had said, *That's creepy, Mom*. But here her mother was after all, nine years now, her ashes in a ceramic urn, her photograph in a gold-tinted frame. Van bowed three times to her mother and Buddha, keeping her hands clasped together. Growing up, she had seen her mother pay such respect to Buddha but never did it herself until she had to, on the day of her mother's funeral.

Bringing her overnight bag to her room, Van stopped in the

hallway to look at the pencil marks on the wall that recorded their heights. It was something she did every time she went home. Her mother's last mark, four-eleven-and-a-half, was dated a year before her death. Every time Van saw this she had an urge to darken the notations, to make them more permanent, but she was afraid of ruining her father's small, fine script.

After she and Linny had both moved out of the house their father had consolidated their rooms so he could use Linny's for storing shipping boxes and remnants of tile and carpet. Van, home for Christmas break her second year of college, had been shocked to see her room set up with two twin beds. All of Linny's old posters, torn on every corner from years of tape, lay on the beds in such a way that the stars of Culture Club and Depeche Mode looked frozen in repose. Linny had been angry, but it couldn't be changed. So Van and Linny ended up sharing a room whenever they visited their father at the same time.

The bedroom still had the same window blinds and the patterned green carpet that, Van realized, must have been nearly twenty years old. She and Linny had been thrilled to have their own rooms, even though that turned out to be the very thing, Van realized later, that drove them away from each other, dissolving the times in the apartment when they had pretended to be twins, secret agents, partners in crime like Charlie's Angels. "You can be the famous Trung sisters," their mother had told them, explaining how once, in ancient times, two sisters rebelled against Chinese rule in Vietnam and became queens of the land.

"How did they do it?" Van had asked.

"Through skill," their mother had answered. "They had martial arts skill, and swords skills, and they had the support of the people. They rode on elephants into battles and they were the most famous queens in the world."

Van and Linny had been enchanted by the story, and often pretended to brandish swords around the apartment. Later, in high school, Van accused her mother of lying to them. "You always said the Trung sisters were so great, but they only ruled for three years. I looked it up. There's hardly anything about them." They were nothing like the British queens whose dates and accomplishments she'd memorized in history classes.

"What difference is it? They're Hai Ba Trung. They're legends." Her mother, working on some extra sewing at the machine she'd set on the kitchen table, spoke in a way that revealed her disgust at Van's ignorance.

"But they committed suicide. They threw themselves into a river."

"They had no choice. They lost power and the Chinese were going to kill them. The important thing is they controlled everything themselves, right until the end."

Linny, eavesdropping from the living room where she was watching a game show, shouted out, "Who cares!"

Van's father, walking into the kitchen from his studio, said, "Hai Ba Trung did something, at least. What you two do?"

Moving into that house had given them all more space, more doors to close between them. There, Van and Linny had drifted into their own separate identities. Van kept her bedroom walls blank except for the Van Gogh print of "Starry Night" she had bought in middle school because it had seemed so cultured to do so. Linny decorated her room with rock star posters and photos of her friends, tucked movie ticket stubs around the edge of the mirror she set on top of her dresser.

In the top drawer of her own dresser Van kept the jade bracelet she had worn in elementary and middle school. All the Vietnamese girls were supposed to start wearing them at a young age, so their wrists could keep growing to fit the bracelets, make the stones irremovable. Van had pried hers off in ninth grade, when it kept clanging against the desk in her keyboarding class. Linny had discarded hers too. Only Mrs. Luong had kept hers on. She'd been cremated with it, even, and Van had wondered what happened to the jade in such fire, if it too burned into ash indistinguishable from the matter of the body.

Van took up her bracelet now and tried to slide it over her left hand. When it would not go past her wedding set she removed her rings. She knew she shouldn't be trying to do this; the bracelets had to be carefully forced, the hand and wrist soaking in warm soapy water. But still she pushed. The jade bore down on her knuckles until all at once it settled around her wrist, leaving red marks on her hand.

Van lay on her bed, rolling onto the sunken-in part of the mattress. The pillow smelled like stale sunshine on dust. She told herself not to wonder where Miles was but her mind rebelled, taking her back to that photo frame sitting on his office desk. She could see her hand reaching out, grasping the frame to see what it contained, expecting to find a picture of Julie. But the frame had held nothing. Maybe he had removed a photo of Van; maybe the frame was supposed to be some kind of self-conscious symbol for Miles, who had his moments of believing in ritual. Van didn't ask—she was only relieved not to see someone else in her place. Miles shook his head to express his disappointment in her behavior. *What are you doing?* he said, volunteering no information about the missing picture. Then some gust of fear and blame, of deep chagrin, pushed her out of his office, sent her retreating back to her car.

It was dark when Van woke up, surprised that she'd fallen asleep. In the kitchen Linny was mixing *cha gio* filling with her hands; they were shiny with the shrimp and pork, fish sauce and mung bean threads. Near her the portable television was broadcasting *Forrest Gump*. The fluorescent light overhead gave everything a greenish tinge, making the yellow countertops glow.

"Is Dad home yet?"

Linny made a little laughing sound. "What do you think?" With her head down, her hands in the plastic bowl, she looked so much like their mother that Van had to look away.

She opened the refrigerator door. "I'm hungry."

"I got some sushi rolls from the deli at Meijer. Kind of gross but I knew I wouldn't have time to make anything."

*You mean* I *got the sushi*, Van stopped herself from saying. With Linny she was always the one who paid.

"Might be scary, but it's probably better than frozen pizza," Linny continued.

Van didn't offer up that frozen pizza had become one of her mainstays. She pulled out the plastic trays of tuna and salmon rolls, bringing them to the table. How many times had she sat here, in the same chair? That same flowered plastic tablecloth—probably fused to the table by now. That same rooster-shaped napkin holder—empty. And that same knobby brass chandelier that Linny always said she wanted to replace. Years ago, their mother had enlisted Linny's help to paint over the silver and orange wallpaper, and with every return home Van saw more and more glints of metallic peeking through. Miles had noticed too, of course; he hadn't approved of painting over wallpaper but the vintage print interested him.

"Are you going to help me roll these?" Linny called out, referring to the *cha gio*.

"If you need me to." The sushi rolls tasted flavorless to Van. She doused them with extra soy sauce and wasabi, watching Forrest Gump's depressing New Year's Eve with Lieutenant Dan. After a while she stored the rest of the rolls in the refrigerator and headed downstairs to her father's studio.

The basement had been spruced up since she'd seen it last winter. Her father had added icicle Christmas lights around the ceiling to look like a lit-up wallpaper border. The TV area was home to a new standing lamp and potted plants, probably fresh for the party. The futon was made up into a sofa decorated with Linny's dot-print throw pillows. A zebra-print rug covered the original shag carpet that was exactly the color of burnt sienna from Van and Linny's shared Crayola box. Van knew she should feel glad for her father and these small signs of progress, but it pained her to see the buckets of new geraniums, the futon cover tucked in tight. The feeling wasn't exactly new, but deepened, tinged with what haunted her: even more than the rest of the house, the basement belonged to someone who lived alone.

His studio, shielded by a curtain, revealed the side of her father Van knew better: disorganized, unfinished. A dismantled Luong Arm lay on a table near the old binder that Van had given her father, back in grade school, to help him organize his notes. She had also included a compilation of "Famous Short People" and added on to it over the years, her print steadying and maturing with each notation.

Queen Elizabeth I (about 5'3")
Elizabeth Taylor (5'3", probably shorter)
Alexander Pope (4'6")
Danny DeVito (5')
Charlie Chaplin (5'4½")
Edith Piaf (4'8")
Honoré de Balzac (5'3")
Dolly Parton (5')
Sammy Davis, Jr. (5'3")
Pablo Picasso (5'4")
Tom Cruise (5'6"?? probably shorter)

Van had actually searched the local library for these facts, pinned them down with an earnestness she almost couldn't believe, looking back now. How plainly she had tried to gain her father's favor, like someone trying to keep an insider joke going for years as a way to force a friendship. The binder was just another layer in her father's piles of paperwork, sketches, blueprints, and general plans. He had, at least, created a new sign, *Luong Inventions* announced in inkjet calligraphy along one wall, replacing the handwritten banner he'd had for years. Van spied another curtain, narrow and black like a magician's cape, hanging over the back wall. She lifted it to see three simple shelves, nothing on them.

"Hey," Linny said from the foot of the stairs. "What's behind that curtain?"

"Just some shelves." Van showed her, then let the fabric fall.

Linny walked toward the desk, hugging her elbows. "It's too cold down here."

"He's improved some things."

"When did you start wearing that?" She looked at the jade bracelet on Van's left wrist.

"Just now."

"Where are your rings?"

Van panicked for half a second until she remembered. "I took them off to get the bracelet on."

The light in their father's basement was part fluorescent, part halogen, part Christmas twinkle, and the combination made Van uncertain of what she saw on her sister's face. Was it caution? Once upon a time, long ago, she could read every expression of Linny's, from the look she had right before she burst into tears, to the bravado she used to mask fear. Once, for a brief time, Linny had been the little sister who merely wanted to hold Van's hand and go along with any game Van wanted to play. How had she gone from mimicking and adoring Van's every gesture and liking, to this—watching and judging, as if waiting for her to make mistakes? Linny had always wanted to stride ahead, Van supposed. She had always wanted to be the one looking down, looking back, gathering together all the recipes that Van had never bothered to learn.

Still, Van wished she *could* talk to her sister. Tell her. Tell someone.

"Van," Linny started to say.

"What?"

A pause. "Are you going to help me with the party?"

"I said I would." Clasping her hands together, her right covering her left, Van headed back up the stairs.

# 10

# Linny

Rich and Nancy Bao were drinking whiskey and soda in the living room. Nancy had a weird way of laughing—instead of throwing her head back she dipped it toward her neck, creating a momentary double chin. Rich Bao looked bigger than ever; his belly seemed to begin at his shoulders and bow outward. Linny remembered him as casual, always in flip-flops and loose-fitting short-sleeve button-downs. Tonight he was oddly preppy, the collars of a red polo shirt peeking out from under a butter-colored cable-knit sweater. He held his drink with three bulbous fingers. When he took a sip his mouth opened wide and flat.

Linny didn't know how to think of him outside the context in which she grew up: Rich as his own first name. When Mrs. Luong first learned the phrase *got taken to the cleaners* it became her enduring wisecrack about the Baos. For years, Linny had wondered if her mother had known about Nancy; she would probably always wonder.

Linny had friends whose families laid out every particle of their past for inspection. These friends, always white, with politically progressive, hip parents, weren't afraid to talk about former relationships and flings, joke about all the feuds and mistakes that made up a family history. It made Linny a little awed to witness such open conversations. It embarrassed her to admit the mystery of her own family, the Asian stereotypes they kept reinforcing by saying so little to each other, and the secrets they locked inside those silences. *Us Vietnamese*, Linny's mother had once said. *If we tell you a story, it'll never be the same way twice.*

The Baos had brought bottles of cognac and champagne, a giant sheet cake, and Na Dau (Linny and Van used to make fun of how so many Vietnamese names rhymed: Bao and Dau, Huong and Cuong, Lam and Nam). Na was not the stoop-shouldered guy he'd been at the citizenship ceremony. Now one of his hands held a drink while his other tried to slide broadly over Linny's shoulder. Nancy, who usually maintained a chilly demeanor, playing the role of doyenne, had to tell Na to act nice. "He's drunk," she said apologetically.

Linny guessed that Na was drunk a lot. No doubt he was the indulged boy who didn't have to worry about finding a job since his sister would always support him. Linny had avoided the Vietnamese get-togethers for years but she knew the central covenant hadn't changed: family as community, community as family. Even if Nancy couldn't stand her brother she would never stop giving him money.

"Where you live?" Na asked after Linny drew away from him. When she answered he pretended to stagger back, impressed. "Big-city girlie, huh? Maybe I visit you in Chicago." He inflected it the way recent Vietnamese immigrants always did: *shee-cah-GO*. It reminded Linny of how distant the city felt whenever she visited her father, as if she'd never established her own life in Chicago at all. Barbara and You Did It, Gary and

Pren, Sasha and the salon—in her father's house, they could seem not quite real. The feeling was both comforting and suffocating.

"You like me visiting you?" Na persisted. "You and me have fun."

Nancy snapped at him in Vietnamese to go away. Na complied, giggling to himself, aiming toward Rich and his friends while casting a backward wink at Linny.

"Don't pay attention," Nancy said. Her dark lipstick had half rubbed off onto her plastic cup. Linny thought of how strange it was to have known her from a distance these nearly thirty years since 1975. In this living room, standing only a few feet away from Mrs. Luong's ashes, Linny reminded herself that her mother had been dead for nine of those years. If after all this time there was still something between her father and Nancy Bao, then maybe Linny would have to accept that.

"Na told me he's only been here a few years," Linny said. She meant it to be polite conversation but it ended up sounding like an accusation.

"He's still learning and adjusting." Nancy sounded defensive. "I guess you don't remember when he arrived. You and your sister do not come home very much."

Linny almost snapped at her, *I check on my dad every couple of months*. Or, *What do* you *know?* But instead she just excused herself to check on the food.

The Baos' cake—the kind Linny couldn't stand, with Criscoed buttercream frosting, too sweet, institutional-tasting, decorated with balloons floating around the word *Congratulations*—occupied one corner of the dining table. The rest was covered with all of the food Linny had spent the day cooking: *cha gio*; summer rolls stuffed with shrimp, herbs, and vermicelli; beef and chicken satay; shrimp chips; pickled vegetable salad; asparagus with oyster mushrooms; snapper steamed with ginger and soy sauce. Linny had enlisted her sister's help but Van was slow at mincing and chopping and had too many questions, seeming not to know basic things like how to mix *nuoc mam* sauce or how long to cook the vermicelli. She was skittish of the wok of roiling oil that fried the *cha gio*.

The house filled up with people Linny hadn't seen since her mother's funeral, when her parents' friends had drifted through for two days, lighting incense and bowing, offering trays of food. A few die-hard women still wore *ao dais*, but most had switched to bright pant suits and dresses, their husbands in olive sport coats. They all paused in the living room to pay their respects to Mrs. Luong. The photograph of her was an Olan Mills portrait, her face set against a heathered blue background, smiling at something slightly off to the side of the camera. Linny remembered exactly when that photo was taken: it had been her last year of high school, when her mother had insisted on tagging along when Linny went to get her senior pictures taken. Even then Linny had thought it an odd ritual: all the seniors had professional photos done, trading them with friends and choosing the best one for the yearbook. Some of the girls in her class had multiple photo shoots in outdoor locations. They perched on fallen trees in an apple orchard and leaned against a stone fence in a pasture. A lot of the guy jocks posed with their varsity jackets, holding footballs or baseball bats like trophies. The Luongs couldn't afford more than the basic head shot at Olan Mills, so Linny compensated by wearing low-cut shirts and extra makeup. Her mother, glancing at the studio's advertisement for Glamour Shots, had made that little throaty noise of reproach.

"In a few years you will laugh at this," she had warned Linny, and of course she was right.

When the proofs came back Linny found pictures of her mother among her own poses. The photographer had taken them while Linny had changed outfits. When her mother ordered an eight-by-ten photo of herself, Linny had laughed. She had no way of knowing, at age seventeen, that that same photo would accompany her mother's ashes forever.

At Mr. Luong's citizenship party the old Vietnamese friends were careful not to set plates or cups on the credenza. Linny replenished the *cha gio* while Van did the dutiful daughter thing, bringing drinks and napkins around and hanging up coats. Van greeted people—*Chao Ba, Chao Co, Chao Ong*—with a deferential manner. Once again, Linny thought, the good Asian daughter. Her parents' friends had always nodded with approval at Van's modesty while their sharp voices targeted the girls who showed too much skin.

Earlier, getting ready for the party, Van had spurned Linny's suggestions on what to wear. "What difference does it make?" she had said, seemingly determined to preserve her khaki pants and plain crewneck sweater.

They were in Van's old bedroom, the one their father had made into Linny's as well, looking into the same floor-length mirror that still hung on the back of the door. "Maybe you could just not hem your pants so much," Linny said.

"I didn't get these hemmed. They came in exactly my size. They're ankle-length."

"You should learn how to hem things yourself. It's so easy,

and a lot cheaper." Van had resisted learning it, had even gotten special permission to skip the required home ec class in middle school so she could take Latin instead.

"I don't have time for that."

"The pants are also too big," Linny said. Couldn't Van see how easy it was, really, to look a little taller, better, more at ease in the world? "I'm not trying to be mean. They're weirdly baggy around the thighs. And when your pants are too short you end up looking too short. You need a nice long pant and a nice heel. The hem of the pants should come down almost to the floor without touching it. This would make you look taller." She refrained from commenting on Van's shoes, which were probably made by some comfort brand. Linny depended on high heels. Without them she felt diminutive—a step away from being a little girl or a doddering old Asian woman.

Van hesitated; Linny could see that. Looking too short was her one sartorial sore spot. But finally she said, "Everyone's short here, tonight."

Now Linny noticed again the sad bagginess of Van's pants and how they seemed to weigh her down. *Stand up straight*, she wished she could say, the way their mother used to command them. Walking past the girls as they watched television, Mrs. Luong would shout out, "Posture!" Linny noticed, too, that Van was wearing her wedding rings again, gleaming above that jade bracelet. The jade bothered Linny, as if Van were somehow trying to arm herself with jewelry. Did she know about that woman in Chicago, that Grace? How could Linny ever bring it up? They didn't talk the way true sisters did; their conversations barely ventured beyond the mundane, the argumentative. They had gone from sharing a sofa bed, clothes, toys, a whole imagined universe, to where they were now, with such swiftness that Linny couldn't track how they had changed.

Yet she remembered pretending to be the Trung sisters, fashioning swords out of wrapping-paper tubes. She remembered running the length of the Baos' basement, holding their arms up to stop their jade bracelets from sliding off. Linny's was a mottled red, Van's a bright sea green. In middle school Linny had coaxed hers off for good in the school bathroom during lunch. She didn't know why, exactly, except that the weight of it, the insistent feel of the cool stone knocking against her wrist, felt almost like a trap.

Linny discovered that her father had invited the Oortsemas to the party when Dirk and Paula stepped into the kitchen just as Linny was filling a bowl with pickled vegetables.

"Linny!" they exclaimed, folding her into hugs. They handed her a blue tin of Danish butter cookies that she and Van used to love. "It's just been too long," Paula sighed. She was round and soft, her eyes crinkling up as she reached out to touch Linny's hair. "Look at you—so pretty."

"Did you make all this food?" Dirk asked. Even hunched as he was, his body was huge in the small house. "I heard you were a good cook."

Linny wondered where he'd heard this. "It's nice of you to stop by. Can I get you something to eat?"

"We just wanted to congratulate your dad again. Such an accomplishment." Paula gazed around the kitchen—maybe thinking, as Linny often did, that it was so preserved in its late seventies style as to be borderline fashionable again. "Tell me, Linny. When can we get together and talk? I've always thought we should be in better touch, especially ever since your mother died. You know I'm always here for you girls. Dirk too. We like to stay close with the people we've sponsored."

*You didn't sponsor me*, Linny wanted to say. Before she could come up with a suitable response, Van appeared in view long enough for Paula to snatch her up. "You two just get more and more adorable," she declared. "Where is that charming husband of yours?"

Van sounded neutral when she replied, "He couldn't get away from work."

"Well, I want to see both of you again soon. Now, what's this I hear"—Paula lowered her voice—"about some good news you might have?" She winked.

Linny was stunned for a moment, but the quick grimace crossing Van's face revealed the truth. "There's no news," she said. "I hope my dad didn't tell you there was."

"It's my fault," Dirk apologized. "I thought I heard someone say that just now. I've been trying to learn the Vietnamese language all these years and I guess I haven't improved much."

Linny could see her sister forcing a smile. "Don't worry—I'll be sure to keep you updated." She excused herself by saying she needed to get a few drinks for people in the living room.

Before Paula left she grabbed Linny's hands and said, "You're going to call me, okay?" Linny nodded, but she had no intention of calling. Her mother had always emphasized the Oortsemas' generosity, using *sponsor* as if it were a synonym for *friend*. "But I was born here," Linny always countered. "She didn't sponsor *me*." "It's the same," her mother had insisted. Because of this, Linny had never gotten past the uncomfortable feeling that she owed the Oortsemas something.

It was strange to think that when her parents left Vietnam they had been younger than Linny was now. They couldn't have known they would end up seeking a community in the cold isolation of Michigan, living in this ranch house with the three little rectangular windows in the front door that always struck Linny as undefinably sad. They couldn't have guessed how many years Thuy Luong had left. The difference between them and Linny, their lives and choices, seemed vaster than any years could explain. She never could imagine, really, what it must have been like for her parents to start over in a new country, with a new language and new children to balance. What had they known about America then, beyond the well-worn promise of opportunity? And why had her mother seemed to figure out how to manage, but her father could not? For as long as Linny knew her, Mrs. Luong had had the same routine of working at Roger's, doing some extra sewing at home and on the side, visiting with friends on the weekends. She had memorized the bus schedule right away and always had the fare ready in her pocket. When they finally got a car, she was the one who remembered to check the gas gauge and get the oil changed. She was the one who insisted on keeping the car in the garage in the winter, to avoid all that shoveling and scraping of snow. By comparison Mr. Luong always seemed a step behind, not knowing what time it was, never able to say a quick no to telemarketers. Because he skipped so many of the language classes that his wife took, he never learned to speak English the way she did. No wonder he often seemed irrationally angry, unable to make the world, the town, the very household, bend exactly to his wishes. Linny had always guessed that her father invented products as a way to invent himself in a new land. But why did it seem he was doomed to stay in that dark studio, working away mainly for himself? When he emerged it was to be heard, finally, by the only people who would listen to him—his wife and daughters—who, too, turned away. Maybe it was inevitable that he had to seek out his friends' parties and gambling, living out whatever recklessness of his youth that war and escape had truncated.

While the Baos held court in the living room, Mr. Luong stayed in the basement with some friends, a group of them laughing through the Vietnamese music floating up the stairs. He sounded happy, already drunk, and Linny told herself to relax a little. Why not let him celebrate, and even celebrate with him?

She was pouring herself a vodka and cranberry when she saw the person she'd wondered would stop by: Tom Hanh. The last time she had seen him he had been lighting a stick of incense and offering a prayer for Mrs. Luong. Linny had barely said hi to him then.

Tom headed straight over to her. She could tell that neither of them knew whether to hug or shake hands or what, so they just looked at each other.

"Are your folks here?" she asked, casting for conversation.

"They're visiting my brother in LA. I promised them I'd come here to represent the family."

He was so close to what she remembered—the laid-back gait, quick smile, eyes that put people at ease—from when they were fifteen. They fell into talk about his family and from there he followed her easily to the kitchen and helped her transfer a fresh batch of *cha gio* into a colander lined with paper towels.

"My mom said you were living in Chicago."

"Yeah."

"You got away to the golden city. I'm still just here."

Linny plucked rolls of crisp *cha gio* out of the oil, using chopsticks as her mother had. "Do you want to leave?"

"I sort of let myself get settled. Oldest son, parents still live here—you know. And I'm a dentist now. Typical Vietnamese career path. I fell for the whole thing."

They laughed. It was true that, in high school, all the Vietnamese families seemed to push pharmacy, engineering, or dentistry careers on their children. Families won bragging rights over this, over whose children and grandchildren could get themselves into the most sensible, dependable, reliable practice.

"How about you? I heard Van was a lawyer."

"Yeah, she is. I'm a cook, kind of."

"Kind of?" The spring rolls were still too hot, but Tom picked one up with his fingertips and took a bite. Steam puffed out, a tendril of mung bean noodle curling from the fried lumpia wrapper. "These are your mom's," he said. "I remember them."

"You do?"

"She brought them to some of the parties. They're the best. They used to make my mom jealous."

Linny was suddenly nervous, recalling the image of her father and Nancy Bao in that old Cutlass. She opened a cupboard and pretended to look for something, seeing instead the same melamine tumblers, printed with fading orange slices, that her mother had bought years ago. "Are you still going to all those parties? I mean, are people still throwing them every weekend?"

"It's tame now compared to what it was. The community

has changed a lot. It's bigger, but I know fewer and fewer people. A lot of my parents' friends have left for California or Florida or even back to Vietnam. People are spreading out to farther-away burbs here too. I live in downtown Grand Rapids, in one of those conversion buildings." Just yesterday Linny had wondered, while driving past the once-abandoned furniture warehouses from the late 1800s, who was buying all those new lofts and condos.

A woman shrieked Tom's name. The voice, and the woman bearing it, were immediately recognizable: Lisa Bao herself, grown and high-heeled, hugging Tom Hanh in the Luongs' kitchen. Linny was next, enveloped in Lisa's perfume and brassily dyed and highlighted hair.

"Oh my god, I almost didn't even come to this party!" she said. "I haven't seen you *forever*. Where've you been at? You've never even met my husband." Lisa pointed toward a heavier-set Vietnamese guy with spiky hair, a gold and diamond watch flashing at his wrist as he poked through the bottles of liquor near the buffet.

Then Lisa gave Linny her full attention, lowering and raising her eyes to take in Linny's outfit, hair, makeup, shoes. It happened in an instant and was what Linny called the Asian Once-over—the assessing look so many Asian American girls had to give each other upon meeting or passing on a street. A way of gauging cred and territory, Linny thought, as if to determine which of them was going to be the alpha Asian girl. Whenever Linny got the Asian Once-over she gave it right back.

"I didn't know you'd gotten married," she lied, although her father had informed her of the news six years ago.

"You missed it. It was a huge wedding at the Amway Hotel.

Tom was there, weren't you?" Lisa gave him a smile. She preened, smoothing down her shiny camisole over dark-wash jeans. "Of course, that was ages ago. What are *you* up to, Linny? Is it you or your sister who's a lawyer?"

"That's Van. I work at a catering business. As a cook." She decided to keep it vague. No need to reveal the truth of cheesy bean enchiladas and sausage manicotti.

"You need to meet my two boys," Lisa declared. "Nick and Landon. They're playing outside." Linny looked out the kitchen window. In the backyard, a small band of children ran around as if in a game of old-fashioned tag, while another group sat with their Game Boys on the teak bench Mrs. Luong had placed near the maple tree. "There they are, in the Pistons jerseys. Nick is five and Landon is four. My boys are obsessed with basketball. The doctor says they're both on track, so we're starting the medication soon."

"Are they all right?"

"They're doing the growth hormone medications. Didn't your dad tell you? He's so hilarious about it. A journalist at the *Press* is covering the whole thing for a series of articles. It's kind of like reality TV, but in a newspaper. Growth hormones are the new Lasik."

Mr. Luong interrupted the moment, coming up the stairway to the kitchen. His voice, fueled by alcohol, boomed as he greeted Tom and Lisa, slapping Tom on the shoulder and telling Lisa he wanted to talk to her about her boys. Lisa threw Linny a conspiratorial rolling of her eyes, and in Lisa's face she understood: people thought her father was ridiculous. It didn't help that he'd paired dress pants with a short-sleeve shirt printed with bluebirds. But he was all smiles, his face bright red. He started walking through the house, clanging a glass with a chopstick. "Attention! Listen up!" he yelled out in Vietnamese. "I have an announcement!"

Someone in the crowd said, "Are you going to be a grandfather?" and Linny cringed for her sister.

Ignoring the question, Mr. Luong went on to say something that Linny strained to understand. "Yesterday I became a true American citizen" was what she thought she heard, but couldn't piece out the rest except the word *American* a few more times.

"Now," he said, switching suddenly to English. "Please go downstairs to my studio, please!"

"I better go check on my boys," Lisa said. She gave Linny a big I'm-a-confident-Asian-American-girl smile. "It's *so* nice to see you again! Don't forget to go say hi to my husband."

Linny waited for the rest of the party to file into the basement. She and Tom took places near the foot of the staircase, on a step so she could see her father standing proudly in front of his office desk, a metal behemoth from Steelcase that could by now be called vintage. Behind him were the curtain-covered shelves Linny and Van had peeked at the night before. Mr. Luong had managed to tidy up his work space—probably he just shoved all the papers under the futon—and the printed sign of Luong Inventions, canopied with Christmas lights, looked almost business-like.

He started speaking in Vietnamese again, stepping away from the desk to show off the new and improved Luong Arm and the Luong Eye. Failing to catch his words, Linny glanced over the crowd. Her father's friends hadn't changed that much over the years. Sure, they were grayer-haired as he was, and most had potbellies, but they still drank their favorite Courvoisier or

Hennessy V.S.O.P. and laughed too loudly, as if their status depended on it. There was Phuong Trinh, whom her father had said still worked second shift at a napkin factory, and who was as languid-limbed as ever. Linny had never seen anyone smoke a cigarette with such slow movements, as if each drag cost him something. Co Ngoc, her mother's best friend who still ran the same nail salon where Linny's mother had collapsed, maintained a posture bolstered by years of meditation. And Rich and Nancy Bao still looked like they owned the place, any place. Nancy's sharp face had widened slightly, but her permed hair would forever be dyed black. Off to the side, Van stood with a couple of their mother's old sewing friends from Roger's. She had her arms firmly crossed, a stance Linny recalled her mother having whenever she got mad at Mr. Luong.

Linny's father positioned himself at the curtained-off shelves. With a guttural proclamation—something like the Vietnamese version of "Aha!"—he yanked away the curtain to reveal the three dark varnished shelves bearing one of Van's school dictionaries, a small alarm clock, and a new picture frame that still contained the stock image of a woman smiling in a field of wildflowers.

Linny leaned toward Tom. "What's he doing?"

"He said we have to watch closely."

Mr. Luong stepped around the desk to join the audience. He fished a remote control from his pocket, aimed it at the shelves, and began to laugh when, with a mechanical whirring sound, they slowly began to move. The shelves jutted out like planks on a halved Ferris wheel, lowering and rising, returning to lie flush against the wall.

Mr. Luong faced his audience, his friends, his party. "This," he said, projecting his voice, "is my new invention, the Luong Wall."

Everyone began to clap but he held up a hand. He declared something then that Linny didn't understand except for the word *television*. Linny was embarrassed to have to ask Tom to translate. Before he could explain, a man at the front of the group—Na Dau—started shouting rah-rah sounds, pumping both fists in the air. Then the rest of the crowd clapped and whistled, her father grinning and laughing, loving it all. He stretched out his arms as if to embrace all the cheers of his friends.

Looking around the room again, Linny caught her sister's eye. Van seemed troubled and for a moment Linny considered crossing the space between them. But Tom was there, leading her back up the stairs, and as they stepped into the kitchen he let his hand rest for a moment on Linny's shoulder. He said, translating before she even had to ask, "Your dad's auditioning for a reality TV show, next month, in Detroit."

Past eleven, Linny and Tom headed out to the backyard, where Mrs. Luong had once maintained a garden of herbs, vegetables, and flowers—nothing too showy—until incipient arthritis from years of sewing began catching up to her. Now only perennials wavered up through thickets of weeds, bordering the teak bench she had purchased on clearance. Mrs. Luong had loved to sit there, counting down the minutes of twilight.

The bench looked now like a kind of plea against abandonment, probably one of the last things Mrs. Luong had done for the yard before she died. Linny and Tom sat there now, sipping beers beneath the black branches of the maple tree that she and Van had climbed when they were kids. She would almost climb it again, except that it was too cold. In Michigan, the end of April always felt more like winter than spring. The whole month was a tease, usually delivering a last blast of snow before giving in to the warming months.

Inside the house, the party had just begun winding down. It would move on, Linny knew, to someone else's place, someone else's stash of alcohol and cards. Before bringing Tom outside, Linny had set out the last of the plates of orange slices, pineapple, and moon cakes and hidden the rest of the Courvoisier from Na Dau. She waved good-bye to Lisa with her growing boys and Rolexed husband. Mr. Luong had been holding court in the living room while Van fetched and gathered drink cups, keeping her head down.

Linny kept bringing the conversation back to the reality TV show. "Do I really want to see my dad on a reality show? Does anybody?"

"He might be good on TV."

"You mean because he's strange? Nonsensical? A clown?"

"I get the sense that your dad could be absentminded or brilliant or both. In any case, he's not a fool."

"Or he's just faking it."

"Well, this party was a good idea. When I heard about it I figured it would be about the only time I'd get to see you again, until the traditional wedding invitation came in the mail."

"Not likely." As Linny spoke, a little beeping noise emanated from the cell phone in her pocket. She knew it would be Gary, because she was still ignoring his voice mails. Let him worry, she decided. Let him wonder if she was ever coming back. At that moment she couldn't have felt more far away from him.

"When we were fifteen," Tom said, "you just disappeared. Why? I've always wanted to know."

Linny could revive the exact feeling she'd had back then, how her sense of humiliation, even fear, had clouded everything for her. "I guess it was stupid," she admitted. "It was about my dad and Nancy Bao."

"What do you mean?"

"The way they were in the car, when we were taking a walk. They were together. You didn't see?" Tom looked so mystified that Linny almost wanted to laugh. "I thought you saw them. It was weird—it was a big deal to me. I didn't know how to handle it."

But Tom had had no idea. He hadn't been looking at anything but Linny.

"I still don't know the whole story," she said, meaning her father and Nancy.

"Are you sure there is one?"

And Linny wasn't. Somehow, as she sat beside him, the events beyond the yard seemed unable to consume her the way they often did when she was alone in her apartment in Chicago. Why had she always marked such a delineation between past and present, the apartment and the house, Wrightville and Chicago, with her mother and without?

In high school she had fantasized about traveling the world and, if she returned to visit Wrightville at all, doing so with style and righteous contempt for the provincial folks left behind. After Mrs. Luong died, home started to seem like merely a protected space for her father, the one arena where everyone would accommodate him. No wonder he no more wanted to leave it than Linny wanted to stay.

Of all the guys Linny had known or been with, only Tom could sit so easily under this maple tree. Its leaves and branches held lifetimes of glances, taking in all the staring-up that Linny, her mother, and sister had done. Tom had been raised in the suburban Midwest too, a place where no one on the coasts expected Asians to be. As a fifteen-year-old, Linny hadn't understood. As a twenty-seven-year-old, Linny knew: she didn't have to explain all the allusions and worries to Tom. She didn't even have to explain her family, her father, the history they both saw from a second-generation perspective.

When Linny's parents first started looking for a house they could afford, her father had insisted on being in Wyandotte, near the Baos and his other friends. But Paula Oortsema convinced Linny's mother to buy the house on Garland Street, in the better school district Wrightville offered. They turned out to be the only Asians in the neighborhood, though one of Linny's friends from down the street had said that an Oriental family, the Chens, used to live around the corner. *Oriental* was the word everyone used back then, until suddenly it changed and Linny and Van, especially Van, had to keep correcting their parents. *You can't say Oriental anymore, Mom. You have to say Asian.* The one other nonwhite family in the neighborhood was black, and Linny and Van used to play with Candace, the girl their age, until the family moved away suddenly, their house looking abandoned overnight. In fact, families seemed to move away a lot. After Linny started taking classes at the community college and got her own apartment, the neighborhood seemed quieter, more stagnant, whenever she came home. Now her father was surrounded by retirees and widows; at night the familiar flashes of television shows illuminated the houses.

Maybe if the Luongs had moved a little farther west of town, into the heart of where the other Vietnamese families had settled in Wyandotte, things would have been different. Where Tom and Lisa had immersed themselves in the Vietnamese community, Linny and Van had become outsiders. It started with Linny becoming best friends with the popular girls at school, and with Van shying away from the Vietnamese parties so she could stay home with her books and TV. Had they even known what choice they were making? One day Linny was a Vietnamese girl with a jade bracelet, the next day she was trying on clothes at the mall, standing on tiptoes to try to match her tall blond friends. She lost her grasp of Vietnamese as easily as she did the valences and chemical elements she was supposed to memorize in school. It happened so quickly she could hardly recall what it had felt like to know any other language but English. And the less she knew, the more she stayed away. She became, in the words of Mrs. Luong complaining on the phone to her friends, "just like a white girl."

With Tom, Linny realized that so much of this was already known between them. She didn't have to work the flirtations she'd exerted with every other guy. Tom didn't flirt with her, either; he talked. When they heard whoops and shouts coming from the front lawn, Tom read her mind by wondering if anyone had brought illegal fireworks to set off.

Around midnight Linny walked him toward where he'd parked down the block. They had exchanged e-mail addresses and numbers, agreed to trade a home-cooked dinner for a dental checkup. She almost held his hand but too many people stood in the front yard saying good-byes. The streetlamp gave everything away, and already Linny could spy a few women glancing at them, assessing, storing, and building the next day's gossip. No doubt Tom Hanh was talked about for still being a bachelor, the target of endless setups.

He didn't give Linny a kiss good-night and she didn't angle for it. She sensed that they both agreed: in this crowd, it was better just to give a little wave and say they would see each other soon. Linny turned around and headed back to the house quickly so she wouldn't have to watch him leave. It always gave her a pang of misplaced regret to see people drive off and that wasn't how she wanted to think about Tom. She wanted to stay up a while longer, take in the last of the party's merriment.

Just inside the living room, Van was bidding good night to Co Ngoc.

"When you're going to come to my store?" Co Ngoc stretched out an arm to include Linny in the question. "Why I do not see you two in so long? You two girls need to come over. I'll take care of you, no charge." She caught Linny's hands to inspect them, then grabbed at Van's. "Better than this one here—no nail polish!"

"She's never worn nail polish," Linny said. It seemed almost a source of pride for Van, who steadfastly avoided all Vietnamese nail shops. Linny hadn't been in Co Ngoc's salon in years, since the time she had stopped by to collect her mother's acrylic-blend cardigan and favorite teapot. After that it had been easy to avoid the place, tucked into one of the many strip malls off South Division Street, and Linny could imagine that the puce-pink walls and diagonal squares of white linoleum, limned with dark grout, had remained exactly the same. Only the calendars, free from the Vietnamese grocery stores, would change.

"Come over to my store," Co Ngoc said again to Van. Co Ngoc was about the age Mrs. Luong would have been, which was fifty-one that year. Her face bore that contradiction of soft-cheeked youthfulness and elderly stateliness that so many Viet-namese women had. "Bring your husband too. He work so hard for you. He a good husband. Your ma would be so proud."

Van kept a smile going but pulled her hands away. Linny, feeling an unexpected rush of protectiveness toward her sister, ushered Co Ngoc to the front door. Out on the sidewalk Mr. Luong stood around laughing with a group of friends, his voice ringing out above the others. The only times Linny heard him sound so confident were when he was drunk or when he was excited by an invention breakthrough—even if the latter was followed by disappointment, like the time his declaration of developing shoes with adjustable heels resulted in a row of mangled pumps in his studio. Opening the front screen door for Co Ngoc, Linny glanced back at Van with an impulse to say, *Remember how mad Mom was when Dad ruined two pairs of her shoes trying to figure out that invention?* He never did make progress with it. But Van just stood in the middle of the living room, staring straight ahead of her at the picture window, which must have been throwing back her own reflection. Framed there, with the credenza and all it held stilled behind her, she looked like someone who was merely waiting to see who else would come and who else would go.

# 11

# Van

At one o'clock in the morning Van and Linny cleaned the house. Their father and his friends had sped off an hour before, leaving the living room looking like a bunch of frat boys had blown through. Van found balled-up napkins behind the couch, plastic cups of flattened beer balanced on the television set. She was annoyed, though not surprised, that her father had left without saying good-bye or acknowledging the work she and Linny had done for the party. It reminded Van of how often she had felt uninvited around him, cast out from his thoughts. Why else had she worked so hard to capture his attention? She was the one who had organized his notes, had tried (and failed) to help him get a patent for the Luong Arm. It shamed Van to admit that she'd had years of lawyering to help him get that patent, and hadn't yet done a thing.

Linny, on the other hand, seemed untroubled, skimming around the edges of the house, sipping whiskey, picking at the platters of food while wrapping them in foil. The remainders of the sheet cake she simply tossed in the trash.

"It's so weird seeing everyone after all these years," she said.

She got chatty when she drank. "They all look so old but exactly the same too. Sometimes I forget that time doesn't stop just because we're not at home anymore. I don't know why so many of them stayed."

"Where else are they supposed to go? They've made this place their home. You make it sound like *we've* just landed here from London or Paris." Van got what Linny meant, though. In high school they had shared an unspoken solidarity in declining to attend any more Vietnamese parties. And they had both fled after graduating.

When Van and Miles got engaged, they decided against inviting all of the Luongs' old friends and acquaintances to the wedding, a move that would have wounded her mother deeply but only vaguely bothered her father, who, as the man in the family, didn't have to worry so much about keeping up appearances. Visiting at holidays, Van and Miles rarely stayed longer than forty-eight hours. To Miles, the monthly checks Van sent her father balanced out all the extra time they spent with the Ohs in San Francisco.

For all of her supposed involvement in the immigrant community of Detroit, Van had practically opted out of the Vietnamese one in west Michigan. Linny had too, but she didn't seem to feel bad about it. She wasn't bothered by the sense of being on the sidelines, of having let membership dues lapse. Van was the one who felt out of bounds. She was looking in, not knowing how to get back, or if she even wanted to get back, to where she thought she was supposed to be.

But all she said was, "I think Mom would have been happy that Dad finally got his citizenship."

"Sure. Not that it changes anything."

"It's an added layer of security that we take for granted."

"Yeah, that's what Mom always said."

"She did?" Van didn't recall this.

"She was anxious about it. Remember when she gave us photocopies of her naturalization certificate in case hers got lost or ruined? I still have mine, even."

And suddenly the memory floated back: Mrs. Luong handing Van a black and white sheet of paper that said *United States Certificate of Naturalization*. Van had humored her mother by sticking the copy on a pile of school papers that, somewhere along the line, had gotten thrown out.

"What do you think about the TV show?" Linny asked suddenly.

"It's just an audition."

"Dad seems to think it's a done deal."

"Well, that's a problem. We're both going to have to go, you know." At Linny's look of incredulity Van added, "Can you imagine him trying to navigate a TV show audition by himself?"

"You act like he's helpless."

"He doesn't even know how to use a computer. He spends his time exactly the same way he did twenty years ago. A little tiling and carpentry work, fussing around in the basement, hanging out with his friends. Do you know what I saw on TV, almost two months ago? This infomercial where one of the featured products was basically a Luong Arm."

"You're kidding." Linny started laughing.

"It wasn't even as sophisticated as Dad's version. And it

was being pitched as an accessory—the rest of the infomercial was for products for people who are housebound. *Don't* tell Dad."

"Like I would. Why are you watching infomercials?"

"It was late at night," Van answered, self-conscious. In fact it had been nearly dawn, sometime in that first week after Miles had left. Van had been mortified to see a primitive version of the Luong Arm on the screen, modeled by a feeble-looking old lady in a recliner, trying to reach a pair of slippers. The only consolation was how much better-looking, even more useful, the Luong Arm seemed by comparison. "Anyway," she said, "I think we should go to the audition."

"I don't want to drive all the way from Chicago just to take care of him. You do it, if you want to."

Van brought a heap of oil-stained paper plates to the kitchen. She felt the old arguments rising again between her and Linny and she wanted to say something to keep them at bay.

Linny had the refrigerator open, trying to make the leftovers fit. She shifted the subject by saying, "I wonder what Dad's friends really think of him. Do they think he's weird or pitiful?"

Van had thought this herself, at times hating to see the comparison between her father and Rich Bao, whose Polo clothes and sweeping McMansion made Mr. Luong look—she hated to admit it—*fobby*.

"That stupid bitch Lisa Bao was making fun of the TV show right to my face. Did you see her? Carrying a Louis Vuitton logo bag, of course. And she's giving her kids growth hormones. Did you know that?"

"She told me, but those kids didn't look that small." Van

brought a bag of pop cans to the back door of the kitchen, wondering how long they would sit in the garage. When she and Linny were kids they would collect as many cans as possible and take them to Meijer for the ten-cent deposits. The numbers would add up fast, until soon the girls had ten dollars to split between them.

"They're normal. She just wants them to look like big white-bread American guys."

"Good god. Does Dad know?" Van had thrown him into near hysterics the time she'd showed him a *New York Times* article about a gruesome height surgery that was gaining popularity in some parts of China. The article had described how patients elected to have their leg bones broken and stretched in order to become a couple of inches taller, though many of them ended up never walking again.

"He already knows. She told me he tries to lecture her about it. She thinks it's hilarious."

Van could picture her father trying to persuade Lisa not to do such a thing to her sons. She knew just what his reaction would be. Her father had always believed in the ingenuity and triumph of short people—he believed in inventiveness, his own inventions. He said it wasn't about being tall; it was about being smart. And he, Dinh Luong of Luong Inventions, would offer the gift of cleverness to all the short ones out there. He would equal the playing field.

Dawdling in the kitchen, Van was relieved to have averted an argument with Linny. They almost never sustained this kind of gossip without bickering. So Van went along as her sister assessed Nancy Bao's hair, Co Ngoc's pestering, and Na Dau's drunken antics. Gathering stray bean sprouts from the floor,

Van realized that she hadn't thought about Miles in at least half an hour. That was a record, so far.

*You're kind of a different person around him,* Linny had said once in that half-pensive, half-blunt way she had. No doubt she meant that Van was even more reserved, which was true. Van's family had seemed a lonely crew compared to the dozens of cousins, aunts, and uncles Miles claimed and visited along the West Coast. Not that he had ever been less than polite and kind to her father. Still, Van had always been fearful of possible judgment and ridicule. Miles had come close, several times, to witnessing what she often felt to be her fraudulent Vietnamese identity. Like the time they had flown to California to attend one of his cousin's weddings in Irvine. Miles had wanted to drive to Little Saigon and eat some really great *pho*. Van, who had never before been to Little Saigon, had felt lost in the on-slaught of strip malls and Vietnamese signs; she had no idea where to eat. The sidewalks teemed with the most confident-looking Vietnamese kids she'd ever seen. Girls had big gold hoops swinging from their earlobes, their shirts revealing tawny midriffs and surprisingly curvy figures. They carried patent leather bags and clopped along on wedge heels higher than Linny's. And so many of the guys were downright gangster-looking, with slick-backed hair, neck tattoos, and the white sleeveless tees that she had heard people refer to, odiously, as "wifebeaters." These were Vietnamese who had the look of ownership and swagger, far removed from the pale population Van had grown up with in small-town Michigan. Eventually Van and Miles found themselves in a café where the waitress seemed amused by Van's halting Vietnamese. *You use words kind of like my grandma*, she had said in English, meaning that Van's language was too formal. She had missed the years of updates and slang, the immersion she never knew in a Little Saigon.

In her father's house without Miles, Van's family seemed like an old habit she had secretly returned to. Sometimes when Van conjured an image of her father she saw him standing in the cold at the bus stop, waiting to get to the grocery store. They had all done that together, before they had a car. Back then, the winters seemed especially unrelenting with their stone-colored cap of sky, the empty trees that could hide nothing. Van would draw a knit hat over her ears while Linny had a fake fur muff that she stuck out in front of her. Their mother, holding tight to her purse, made sure the girls stood far enough from the curb to avoid being splashed with slush. Their father had always stood a little to the side, anxious, staring down the street as if willing the bus to arrive more quickly. He said so little to them that, once they were on the bus, Van would wonder if other people could tell he was her father. Sometimes the only thing that seemed to bind him to the family was his very face, his hair, his Vietnameseness a mark of identity that all of them had to bear.

That night when Van and Linny climbed into their opposite twin beds Linny said, "I saw Dad with Nancy Bao once. When I was fifteen. It was at a party. I saw them—in the car."

"How drunk are you?"

"A little. Not too much." Linny stretched out her arms. She'd thrown on an old T-shirt printed with the state of Michigan motto—*If You Seek a Pleasant Peninsula Look About You*—and the near-fluorescent print shone faintly in the dark. "She used to call sometimes after that. You probably didn't notice. Then it all stopped, sometime before my senior year. I remember one day thinking about her and realizing the phone hadn't rung and Dad hadn't answered in his weird way in a while. I bet you didn't know, huh?"

"I'm not sure." The scenario was unsettling but not completely surprising. "What about Mom?"

"I don't know. Tom says he's never had anyone gossip to him about it, but that could be a generational thing."

"Who's Tom?"

"Tom Hanh. He's a dentist now? He said whenever the patients are Vietnamese they like to talk and talk. But then again, he's splitting the community's business with a bunch of other guys. So maybe the big gossips are getting their teeth fixed somewhere else."

"I have no idea who Tom Hanh is."

"Van, you even talked with him tonight. He's from the old school parties."

Van had not tried to retain the faces she'd spoken to, or who'd spoken to her, over the course of the party. She'd spent most of her time trying to dodge questions about Miles and when she was going to have a baby. That took enough of her attention. Her parents' friends were tenacious in their demands to know why she wasn't pregnant yet. They had no compunction about asking after her fertility, or squeezing her arm to help them decide if she'd gained weight. She got only a few minutes of respite when her father gave his speech in his studio. There she had been able to stand by herself, pretending to listen, letting her father's voice fade into the dimness of the basement. It was a way to gain a little peace: zone out, drift off, put her mind anywhere else but where she was.

It figured that Linny had been off having a great time, reigning over the kitchen so as not to have to chat with the elders. Tom Hanh—of course. He must have been that cute guy she'd noticed Lisa talking to. Linny wouldn't have bothered otherwise. Of course they had spent the evening together. No matter where Linny went, even at home, she could find a guy.

"What about Mom?" Van repeated.

"I think she *must* have known."

"It doesn't really make sense, though. Dad's never seemed interested in anything besides his inventions and parties. And watching action movies."

"Well, what do we know? It's not like we know him." As if sensing Van being taken aback, Linny went on, "Have you ever even had a real conversation with him? I haven't. He's an Asian father. No real talk. That's how it is. Anyway, I thought this whole Nancy Bao thing was ancient history until she showed up at the citizenship thing yesterday."

"What about Rich Bao?"

"God, who knows? Maybe they had some sort of arrangement, which is gross to think about."

"Maybe you're wrong. Maybe you didn't see what you thought."

"No way. It was very clear."

"You were fifteen."

"I know what I saw. I know Dad and Nancy Bao talked to each other on the phone. And then it all just stopped."

Van still wasn't convinced. She didn't say any more but Linny noisily turned over on her mattress and said, "You can think whatever you want. You weren't there."

That night Van listened to her sister breathe for a long time before falling asleep herself. Linny never seemed to have a problem with insomnia. Same with Miles. Van could fall into naps just fine during the day but nights gave her anxiety. She could stare at the ceiling for hours, flipping the pillow over and over. How many times had she watched Miles sleep, the wall of his back silhouetted by the glow from the streetlights? She would slip out of bed to walk the house and check the window locks, finally collapsing on the sofa with the television volume on low.

In her old bedroom with Linny, Van thought about how fast it all seemed to go, those growing-up years. *You weren't there.* She had missed a lot, she knew, buried so deliberately in her books, lost in the library or school projects. Tuning everything out with the noise of television shows. Which was what she'd wanted at the time, constantly pushing toward college. She had wanted to be on her own, and she thought Linny had too. Hadn't they shared that feeling more than anything, that wish to be free? But free from what exactly? Van had a sense that she herself had reached back somehow as if with a blurring tool to swirl all of those years together, leaving a final impression of something like guilt, forgetfulness. And every return to this house, to this room, left her awake in the dark by herself.

Yet in the morning she knew she would get up, unsure of how she had ever fallen asleep; she would dress and brush her hair while looking in that same full-length mirror tacked onto the back of the door. In middle school and high school Van used to approach the mirror thinking she might suddenly be pleased with what she saw. It took years for the lesson to be learned, for such optimism to be tempered. The mirror, unlike the teachers who favored her for her discipline and grades, would never give her an easy pass. No grade inflation there. The reflection was accurate, telling her she was the same plain, short girl she had always been.

Van believed she wouldn't care so much about being short, wouldn't continue thinking about it still, if the subject hadn't always consumed her father. But it was the one thing he liked to talk about, the one thing she could get him to talk about. His pronouncements at the dinner table—about how short people were discriminated against, and how short people had to work extra hard to get good salaries and respect—well, these did seep into Van's thoughts.

*There's a core insecurity about you*, Miles had told her once. This was weeks before their wedding, when a sentence like that could both shatter Van and make her determined to be the opposite. *I'm not criticizing*, he added. *I'm just curious about where it comes from*. Van didn't say what she really thought: Didn't he think she'd tried to figure that out a thousand times already? She'd blamed her height, and being Asian in a mostly white, conservative town in the Midwest, and sometimes called it a shyness coded into her genes. Van had never explained to Miles, or to anyone, how exhausting it was to work against the sense of inadequacy that arose whenever she felt on display—whether it was on the Model UN team or in the courtroom. She had been standing on her tiptoes for most of her life.

There were times, of course, when she did forget about herself altogether, when no one else reminded her of her place in the world. That was why she only liked going to theaters that had stadium seating. It figured that the movies Miles always wanted to see were in the old-fashioned indie art houses where the barely graduated rows forced Van to strain her neck around the tall person who inevitably sat in front of her.

In college Van's favorite job had been at the university fund-drive office. Everyone else loathed the work, and the turnover was high because people couldn't handle the rejection of rude responses and phones slammed down. But Van got bonuses for completing more transactions than anyone else. Each call she made to coax a donation seemed a game. She was allowed to identify herself as Vanessa, and she knew that the people on the other side of the line, if they talked to her, would never know who she was. They couldn't see her; they couldn't perceive her race, her height, or anything about her. She relished being a disembodied voice.

Her mother had expressed a similar thought, once, about sewing at Roger's, where she and the other seamstresses worked in one large room above the floors of shopping. Van had only been there a few times but would never forget the sound of the sewing machines, all the individual buzzes adding up to a roar, and the black-haired heads of Vietnamese women bent over hundreds of yards of accumulated fabric. "It's nice to be up here, out of the way," Mrs. Luong once said. "Most people shopping don't even know we're here." Hearing this, Van had felt both understanding and aversion. She knew well that secret feeling of being tucked away, unseen. But she hated that her mother had known it too.

When Dinh Luong came into the kitchen the next morning Van couldn't tell if he'd just woken up or if he'd been out all night. He was wearing the tan windbreaker he'd owned for as long as Van could recall, and the same clothes from the party. He'd slept in his clothes before. He even made a point to do this sometimes, claiming it was easier to get up in the morning when already dressed.

Looking a little dazed, probably hung over, he walked past Linny at the kitchen sink and sat down at the table where Van was starting to eat a bowl of cornflakes, the only cereal her father kept in the house. "Problem with Na," he declared. The skin under his eyes looked like dark putty, his hair an oily mess. Van wondered, as she had so many times, what he and his friends did with all their time—what did they talk about when they were drinking and playing cards?

"Problem with what?"

"Na Dau," he said impatiently. "Nancy Bao's brother. From the party. He's in trouble." He explained that Na had gotten pulled over, after leaving the party, and arrested for drunk driv-ing. "Rich Bao just go to get him out of jail."

Van's body felt heavy with the morning. She was instantly ir-ritated with her father, his friends, the same old ways. Wouldn't they ever learn? "It was only a matter of time before this hap-pened, Dad. I've told you a hundred times that you and your friends need to be careful. You should be thankful this didn't happen to *you*."

"This is not about me, it's Na."

"Well, he was drinking at your party. And drunk driving is drunk driving. You can't do it. It's dangerous, not just to you but to everyone."

Her father put up a hand to stop her. "I already heard it be-fore. What all I want to know is: how much trouble is it for Na?"

"Is this his first offense? Is it an Operating-while-Intoxicated or what?"

"I don't know. I'm asking about the green card."

"If it's a basic OWI, then he should be okay, I think. There'll be a fine, maybe some community service, probation."

"Rich is asking about the green card."

"He probably won't have to worry too much. DHS doesn't look kindly on drunk driving, but as long as it's a first-time OWI he should be okay. Besides, Na's from Vietnam." Van was more alert now, answering these questions.

"What does all of that mean?" Linny asked from where she was washing dishes by hand, the old dishwasher having died years ago. "What's DHS?"

"Department of Homeland Security."

"What happened to the INS?"

"I don't know what news you haven't been paying attention to, Linny, but DHS just absorbed Immigration. It's all part of controlling the threat of terror and tightening the reins on civil rights."

"What you mean," their father interrupted, "about the part about Vietnam?"

Van explained how Vietnam was one of the few countries that wouldn't accept deportees from the United States. She was certain she had mentioned this to him before, during one of her warnings about how he needed to be careful not to drink and drive. It had become a chronic problem for guys in his generation, in the community.

Linny asked, "They can deport people for getting DUIs?"

"Even if they're permanent residents."

"Jesus."

But Mr. Luong was cheered. "But it's okay for Na. It's good."

"I wouldn't say it's *good*. Na can't get deported but he could be detained. He still needs to be careful. *You* need to be careful. Plus, if you haven't been in the U.S. for seven years, at least five of them as a permanent resident, then you don't have as much protection."

But already Van could see that her father was losing interest. He tapped his fingers on the table, his mind clearly moving on to some other place. "I already told Rich Bao you help just in case. And if they can't deport to Vietnam, then it's all right."

"Help with what?"

"You be his lawyer. I already told him if there's trouble, you're going to fix it." Somehow he managed to sound both casual and stern, his words a directive. Then he stood up from the table.

"Hold on," Van said. "If Rich Bao wants to retain a lawyer he should get someone here in town, in Grand Rapids."

"You already the lawyer. You helped him before."

"That was completely different."

"He better pony up the cash," Linny put in.

Mr. Luong didn't look Van in the eye. His hands ran along the edge of the table as if considering how to wear it down. Then he produced a crumpled piece of paper from his pocket and dropped it next to Van's bowl of soggy cereal. "That's Na's cell phone number. He call you if there's more trouble."

The discussion was over. That was how her father worked: the beginning and end of conversations were always his to decide. As he retreated to his basement studio he didn't say thank you to Van, who knew better by then not to expect the words anyway. He had probably never once in his life said thank you to his wife or children. Or the word *sorry*. That was something you didn't hear from an Asian dad, Van thought, remembering the time she was in middle school and he had screamed at her for leaving papers on the dining table, smacking the back of her head for good measure. Later, just before her bedtime, he had walked into her room and silently handed her a twenty-dollar bill.

Linny asked, "What did you do for Na before?"

"I helped Nancy file the paperwork to sponsor him a few years back."

"He looked out of control last night. I bet the Baos have to take care of him all the time."

Van picked up the slip of paper with Na's cell phone number scratched onto it with her father's calligraphic handwriting. "Dad and his friends are crazy. It's a miracle they haven't all been picked up for drunk driving. I used to worry about it constantly. And Mom refused to say anything to him."

"He went ballistic once when I hid his keys." Linny swished a soapy sponge around an ancient Pyrex pan as she said, "I didn't know you ever helped Nancy Bao."

Van shrugged. She didn't tell her that over the years she'd filed dozens of applications for her father's friends. Some of the fees she never got and ended up having to pay herself. Miles gave her a hard time about that but Van always argued the word *community*. Sometimes *obligation*. What Linny didn't seem to feel any measure of, tying her to this place.

Yet why then did Linny seem to belong in this house more than she did? Van never remembered where all of the dishes and foil and utensils were kept but Linny never forgot. Linny knew exactly how to work the old rice cooker, and didn't even use a measuring cup to pour in the rice. Just yesterday she was sharpening knives on the bottom of a ceramic coffee cup, the way their mother used to do. The knives had flashed in Linny's hands, singing a note that sounded like preparation. It had sparked jealousy in Van to see how deftly her sister cooked their mother's Vietnamese dishes.

When Van brought her cereal bowl to the kitchen sink Linny said, "So even if Na fucks up royally he can't get deported."

"No, but as I said, he could be detained. And Vietnam could change its policy. There are stories all the time about immigrants who get deported even though they've lived here for years and years. If you don't have citizenship, then you don't have full protection. Especially these days. For Na, it's probable that nothing will happen. If this is his first offense he'll get a fine and probation, community service, and that's that. But he could get handed over to DHS afterward. Or if nothing happens now, then later on down the line it could trip up a future citizenship application." Van was aware that her voice sounded like she knew what she was talking about, as if she hadn't been out of the real game for over a year now. Here too she was on the sidelines, reading newspaper articles about Immigration and Customs Enforcement—ICE, the acronym too fitting—starting to wait at jails, show up at immigrants' homes, or raid factories in border towns. In Michigan, ICE was building its own detention centers in Battle Creek and Monroe County. If those filled up, then picked-up immigrants could be sent to one of the new for-profit detention centers beginning to crop up around the country. But she didn't mention any of this to Linny, who'd never asked much about Van's job, who didn't know a thing about the day-to-day paperwork at Gertz & Zarou. Neither her father nor Linny had ever heard about Vijay Sastri, the pregnancy that never took, why she had stopped working at the International Center.

"That's pretty insane," Linny said. "I didn't know all of this was going on."

"It's a tough time to be an immigrant."

"I guess it's a good thing Dad got his citizenship. Is this what you've been doing all this time? Helping people not get deported?"

Van picked up a dish towel to start drying pans. "Not really."

Linny looked at her as though reading her and it made Van nervous. She'd never been very good at masking her feelings in her face. Miles said that, and it was true.

The door to the basement opened and Mr. Luong appeared again, wearing a fleece jacket over his windbreaker. He had shaved his face and combed down his thinning hair. "You girls driving back today?"

Van nodded and her father said, "I call you about the details of the TV show so you can go see it." At the very mention of it his humor changed, lighting up in a smile. He clapped his hands and let them fly apart, waving away the previous talk of Na Dau. "What do you think? Pretty great, isn't it?"

"Sure, Dad."

"Linh—what do you think?"

Linny barely turned from the sink to say, "Yeah, Dad. It's great." Years of their standard responses, of telling their father what he wanted to hear.

"I tell everyone about that song."

"What song?" Van asked.

He started singing, "*Short people are no reason to live.*"

Linny laughed but Van corrected him. "*Got* no reason. Anyway, isn't that song supposed to be ironic? The guy who wrote it is pretty short himself, isn't he?"

"Really?"

Her father's interest made Van feel eager, like she should keep talking to keep him in the room. "Randy Newman—that's the guy's name." She remembered then that she'd heard he wasn't short at all. But her father didn't need to know that.

"I never hear of him. Only the song. Did you know one out of ten infocommercials is successful? The TV show is a good way to go because then people really see. They *watch*. You saw the Luong Wall, didn't you? Great name, huh? It's the big three with the Arm, the Eye, and now the Wall."

"Very nice," Van answered, though the very word *wall* made Van think of boundaries, the Berlin Wall, the Great Wall of China, the tightening border between the U.S. and Mexico, between the U.S. and everywhere else.

"Yeah," Linny chimed in.

Their father fished his car keys from his pocket, signaling the end of the conversation. Outside, his truck was parked at the curb instead of in the driveway, as if his wife might still come back home in her own secondhand vehicle and hem him in. When Van thought of winter in Michigan she thought of her father's truck at the curb, covered in snow. While the engine ran, he scraped ice from his windshield, the sound echoing back into the house.

"Tell Miles I say hi," he said as he headed out the kitchen door. "Tell him to help you look after Na." And then he was gone.

Van saw her sister staring at her, reading her again. A vague shift seemed to be happening, and Van didn't know how to stop it. I'm *the older sister*, she wanted to insist to someone. I'm *the one who worries, not the other way around*.

It was Linny who made Van talk, after all, by asking, "What is up with you?"

Van felt the morning draining away and she knew: What use was there? Linny would have to know. Her father would have to know. The realization was one that struck her as irreversible: by telling the truth, she was committing herself to it, to the story she never wanted to create. She was creating fact by admitting herself to it.

Van sat back down in her old place at the table. On the long-ago days the four of them ate meals together, they always took the same seats. Her mother, closest to the kitchen, would ferry plates of lime wedges and bottles of hot sauce back and forth. When Van and Miles visited at holidays, he would sit in Mrs. Luong's chair.

Van said, "Miles left."

Linny didn't move, didn't flinch. Van, for once, met her sister's gaze and was relieved not to see the pity or smugness she'd braced herself for. "When?"

"February."

"February!" Now Linny was really shocked. "Jesus, Van." She tossed the dish sponge on the counter. "I have to tell you something."

Van had a sudden, wild thought that her sister was going to say, *He left you for me*. She truly almost expected those words to tumble out of Linny's mouth, so much that she was not at all prepared for what Linny said:

"I saw him with someone. In Chicago, last week. They were at a hotel."

Van had the sensation of falling down all over again, that same inward crumpling feeling she had felt when Miles had first stood in the thrown light from the entryway and said, *I don't want to live with you anymore.*

"I was at the hotel bar and I ran into them. I saw them get into an elevator together. She's a lawyer."

Van tried to speak slowly. "How do you know they were together?"

Linny looked amazed. "I saw them. I even met her. Her name is Grace. She gave me the Asian Once-over. Are you listening? I'm sorry."

Van couldn't bear those two words, couldn't bear the idea of a name. *Don't say Grace*, she wanted to say. Instead, she said, "That's circumstantial at best. You don't know what they were doing there. They could be working together."

"They were in a hotel bar, on a Saturday, together. In Chicago. They were getting in an elevator that was going up to the hotel rooms."

Van got up from the table as if it would stop Linny's bluntness, prevent her from seeing what Van was feeling. She remembered the image of the photo frame, its blankness. How he had removed her as if from his entire line of vision.

"Look, I don't know what I'm supposed to say here," Linny said. Her voice softened at the end.

"There's not necessarily anything to say. Separations are very common." It helped to remind herself of that fact.

"What are you guys doing about money?"

"We share bank accounts. It's still all the same."

"Aren't you afraid he'll drain them and leave with you nothing?"

Van shook her head. "He would never do that."

"But it's been more than two months. Where's he been?"

"He's just taking some time," Van said, avoiding an answer. The words were smooth, rehearsed-seeming, but they didn't soothe her. She may as well have said, *He's on vacation from our marriage.* "I need to get going anyway," she said. The thought seemed to impel her to action, made her hurry down the hallway, until suddenly she couldn't wait to get out of there, before Linny could say anything more, before her father got back from wherever he had gone. In the old bedroom she stuffed her clothes into her bag. She didn't bother to brush her teeth or make the bed. Why stay? She should have left hours ago. She never should have told Linny the truth. Now Linny wouldn't let it go. She'd bring it up forever, demanding answers, spilling forth information Van didn't want to hear.

When Van carried her bag out to the living room she found Linny sitting at the table, her arms flat on the surface like she was waiting for a palm reading.

"Don't go saying anything to Dad," Van said.

"I won't. But—"

"I have to go," Van insisted. "I guess we can figure out Detroit later." She pushed herself out the front door so quickly that she forgot to glance back at the credenza, to bid good-bye to her mother, as she'd always done in the past. For a moment Van hesitated on the front stoop, but then kept going to her car. She didn't want to go back and face her sister. It seemed like a long time had passed since last night, when they had cleaned the house together. The audition in Detroit was four weeks away—enough time, maybe, to let their conversation about Miles descend into the realm of the unbroachable.

Van backed the old Infiniti away from the spot where it had been sandwiched between Linny's Corolla and their father's truck. She wondered where he'd gone—to his friends, or even, as Linny perhaps believed, to Nancy Bao? All the way back to Ann Arbor, driving I-96, U.S. 131, M-22, and the windier roads leading to her subdivision, Van's mind whirled around the faces and words of Miles, her father, her sister. Of Na Dau, whose number lay somewhere in her bag. She could guess what he'd say when she called, fulfilling her father's directive. He would have the same questions that so many of Van's clients had: *What will happen? What should I do?* And sometimes: *Where will I go?* And Van would have to try to provide the answer.

# 12

# Linny

As much as she and Van had argued over the years, Linny always hated to see Van leave ahead of her. One thing they agreed on during their visits home was that they wanted to stay as little amount of time as possible. They both only returned at all because they worried about their father being alone in the stale air of that house. Besides, they might never see him otherwise. He had never visited Linny in Chicago and as far as she knew had only stopped in Ann Arbor once, on his way back from a friend's house in Detroit. Linny couldn't imagine her father in Chicago, anyway. He sometimes talked about Saigon and its uncontrolled traffic of mopeds and bicycles, but for twenty-eight years now his life had been bound by strip malls, suburbs, and a mid-sized midwestern city whose downtown he never even had to see. And when he was away from his studio he grew anxious. Van had complained about how he'd paced around her house trying to fix or improve things—the hinges on a cabinet, the way the kitchen faucet worked—that weren't broken. She'd said outright to Linny that she didn't want the sole responsibility of taking care of him just because she was older. When Linny had defended herself, pointing out the times she'd driven back home just to check on him, Van shot back, "Who do you think has been paying the mortgage?" It was her handy fallback: *I give money, therefore I'm a good daughter.*

So whenever they came back for obligatory Thanksgiving and Christmas holidays they tended to leave at the same time, saying tandem good-byes. Linny was a faster driver, so Van always ended up following her to the freeway entrance, where Linny took the westbound exit and Van took the eastbound. Through the rearview mirror Linny could keep Van in sight all the way there, but she never did. She sped into the left lane and in a minute Van fell behind. From there it would be weeks, or longer, before they spoke to each other again.

Van had also had the advantage of Miles as an excuse. "My family" was all he had to say, and then they were out of there. There had been the one uncomfortable Thanksgiving when the three of them had carpooled to meet Mr. Luong at a friend's house half an hour north of Wrightville. Miles's one comment about the distance made Linny understand how annoyed he was, in spite of his veneer of pleasantness, his mild-mannered tone, to have to go out of his way. The three of them had spoken little during the drive. From the backseat Linny couldn't make out the few murmurs that passed between Van and Miles. They hardly seemed to glance at each other.

When Van drove away the morning after their father's party, Linny remembered the echoey sense of emptiness she'd felt around the house when Van first went off to college. Linny hadn't realized how much she would miss having her—anyone—around to help diffuse the tension between their parents. In her senior year of high school Linny spent as many days as possible at her friends'—anything to get out of the house.

Three weeks before her high school graduation Linny had come home to see Van's car parked in front of the house. It had been unusually warm that day, a burst of almost-summer that had drawn Linny and her friends to the Lake Michigan beachfront forty minutes away. Linny could still smell the sand on herself when she walked inside. Van, sitting in the living room with her father, looked up at her with swollen eyes. Their father stood up, keys in hand. He said they should go to the hospital now, where Mrs. Luong, her body, was waiting. Just like that, he said it. *Your ma died at Co Ngoc's.* She'd been dead for hours by then, after collapsing on the floor of the nail salon. *She had so strange look on her face*, Co Ngoc said later. *Then she just fallen down.* It had all happened while Linny had been at the beach tossing around a volleyball and showing off her bandeau bikini.

Later, no one spoke of her father's return to the upstairs part of the house, just as they didn't speak of leaving Vietnam and whatever distant relatives they had remaining there. After Linny moved out she sometimes stopped by when her father wasn't around, slipping juice and eggs and apples into the refrigerator. He didn't mention these things, or seem to notice the magically washed towels and dishes. Sometimes when Linny found the house unexpectedly clean, fresh vacuum marks in the carpet, she realized Van had been there before her.

On this morning, alone after Van's hasty departure, a feeling of Sunday solitude settling into the empty house, Linny went to the living room to light a candle and a stick of incense

for her mother. She'd always referred to her parents as "vague
Buddhists"—they participated in a few of the traditions, like this
one, but they seldom visited one of the three temples in town.
Her mother's death had been Linny and Van's first real glimpse
into Buddhist rituals. The day after her death, Linny's father
told her to get some white scarves to wear as headbands. Linny
had been confused, picturing the preppy headbands a few girls
in her school still wore.

Her father had mimicked tying a sash around his forehead.
"We have to wear them at the funeral."

"Why?"

"Because you're in mourning." He'd sounded exasperated at
having to explain.

"Where do I get these things?"

"I don't know. Make them."

So Linny had taken a white pillowcase from the hall closet
and cut it into strips, using her mother's sewing machine to finish the edges. Linny still remembered the feel of the cloth against
her forehead, and how Van had tied her own too tight so that
her hair puffed up over it. They only wore them a few minutes,
to light incense and bow three times, copying their father. A
few people took pictures, which ended up sitting in one of the
credenza drawers. Mr. Luong said he would burn the sashes
after the ceremony but she never asked if he did.

Though Mr. Luong didn't speak much about his wife he
kept her credenza clean, usually remembering to set out a
piece of fruit as a symbolic offering. The one thing that made
Linny feel truly Vietnamese was this ritual of honoring the
dead. Linny lit two sticks of incense and bowed quickly. She
studied the photograph of her mother, though she was never

sure whether to keep her eyes open or shut. Mrs. Luong, head tilted, chin resting on one manicured hand, smiled back, wearing the same marbled jade bracelet she'd worn to the very end. She'd been cremated wearing it, because she'd meant it when she'd told the girls that jade was forever. *Wear it for good luck*, her mother had instructed them. Like all proper Vietnamese women, she had a collection of gold and jade necklaces and bracelets, supposed armors against whatever ills may come. It hadn't helped, Linny had thought bitterly when she opened her mother's jewelry box two days after the funeral.

Linny tried hard to conjure her mother now, to pretend that her ghostly presence had descended into the room. But her mind couldn't help circling back to Van, to their father. *Make them come back*, she silently pleaded.

But the incense burned out and Linny knew it was time to head back to Chicago. She didn't even need to leave a note of good-bye to her father. She just hoped he would remember the pyramid of oranges and grapes and the box of tea she had arranged on the credenza the day before; the spirit offering of fruit had to be retrieved before going bad. It was, as Linny's mother had said, a simple matter of respect.


The night before her mother died, Linny had gotten home late—it was a Saturday night—but not later than her father. As she tiptoed down the hallway Mrs. Luong called out to her from her room. Linny opened the door a sliver and saw her mother lying in bed, reading *Parade* magazine. She had a small stack of them near her, as though catching up on weeks of suburban recipes and articles on how celebrities balanced work and family.

"I thought you were asleep," Linny said.

"Not asleep. Just resting. I heard you just getting home so late." Mrs. Luong shook her head. "I don't like that boyfriend. He's not serious and he's not Vietnamese. If you end up getting in trouble—"

Linny sighed loudly. She didn't want to hear another lecture about this, and said so.

Her mother flattened her lips. "Come in here for a minute."

Reluctantly Linny went into the room. Her mother, wearing an old Detroit Lions T-shirt, looked so much younger than her years that people often assumed they were sisters. Mrs. Luong looked smaller than Linny, almost frail. Her feet made a minor bump halfway down the bedcovers.

"When's the last time you hear from Van?"

Linny shrugged.

Her mother dropped the magazine, which was turned to the "Ask Marilyn" section. Marilyn had a genius IQ and offered puzzle answers and general advice to the masses. "Look at your sister. She goes to college, and boom! We never see her again. You and Van are not the same."

Linny laughed at the idea. She perched on the bed in a way that made her feel like a caregiver to a patient. In the days and weeks following, that feeling bothered Linny, stayed with her. Had she known something was even then rising in her mother?

In the small room the rust-colored carpet seemed to glow against the walls that they had painted lavender. The mini-blinds were tinted cocoa on one side and pink on the other. The room seemed hurriedly feminine, as though they'd been in a rush to add colors and floral prints and banish the presence of Mr. Luong.

"Sometimes with Van you can't tell her anything because she's judging. She is smart, but at the same time she's not so smart. Both you girls have the problem of too much pride." Linny had rolled her eyes at this, though later it would bother her enough to consider telling Van about the conversation.

Mrs. Luong picked up another *Parade*. On the cover an actress clutched an Oscar to her chest. "When I met your ba my sister had a big crush on him. She was a waitress at a canteen he used to go to with his friends, and she would come home and tell me about him. Your ba and his friends were working on the thinking side of the war—the intelligence, right? Well, I tell you—not too intelligent. So, your Co Hoa like him a lot and finally one day I go to work with her to see him. We started talking, and boom! It was just like that. Hoa was so mad! She still tells me sometimes when I call her on the long-distance. But she met someone else anyway."

"I never heard this story before." Linny was taken aback by the rush of her mother's words, the volume of information. She had rarely stopped to picture her parents young and dating.

"You never asked."

That much was true. She and Van seldom inquired about their parents' lives—nor did the parents volunteer much. Mrs. Luong had a sister and a brother still in Vietnam and Mr. Luong had an older sister, but they might as well have been characters in an obscure novel to Linny and Van.

"I'm going to Vietnam this winter," Mrs. Luong announced. It had been three years since her last visit. She had gone alone then as well as the time before that. Mr. Luong refused to go with her. He always had a reason—his business would suffer; he didn't have time; they couldn't afford two plane tickets. Since the early nineties when travel back became possible, it had become almost a competition among the Vietnamese to see who could make the most trips. Mrs. Luong and her friends had endless discussions over the cost of tickets, who got the best deals and the best seats, and which flight paths and airlines were superior. Mr. Luong had plenty of his own opinions on these matters even though he clearly had no interest in going back.

"You come to Vietnam with me."

At that Linny fell silent, as she always did when her mother brought up the topic. Like their father, she and Van cited excuses. School, Van would say, and underachieving Linny would agree. Also work, and needing to earn more money. The truth, which Mrs. Luong surely knew, was that Vietnam seemed a scary unknown to Linny. It seemed more than a commitment; the idea of traveling there felt like heading to therapy to face some latent trauma.

Although Linny had urged her father to go to Vietnam with Mrs. Luong, she could understand his unwillingness. He was someone who talked about going forward into the future, and who avoided the past. Maybe he was afraid of looking like a failure back in his old neighborhood. Maybe he was afraid of seeing how un-Vietnamese he had become. After her first trip Linny's mother had said, "I didn't realize that I become so American."

To think that she and Van might have been born there, that they might have lived entirely different lives had their parents not fled the country—this hypothetical seemed to become more potent as Linny grew older. It stood in sharp contrast to their childhood of playgrounds and MTV. Linny had always felt relieved to be American, and the fact of her Vietnameseness often seemed accidental. She wondered if Van too felt that going to their parents' birthplace would only emphasize the distance between their generations. Linny couldn't even connect herself to the few photographs her parents kept of their families; she had never felt a tug of obligation toward them. It was strange to think of all the relatives she'd never met. They lived in a different language, a different *everything* that Linny was almost afraid to see, to face, to know. Going to Vietnam would mean she couldn't go back to not knowing.

"I go in December," Mrs. Luong said that night before she died. "You should come with me, and Van too if she wants."

"I don't know."

"You never even met your aunt and uncles. Or your grandmother. They always ask about you and Van."

Linny grimaced at the reprimand in her mother's voice. Deflecting, she said, "Well, what about Dad?"

Mrs. Luong scoffed at this. "He's not going. He has less reasons for it, anyway."

Mr. Luong's parents were long dead—his father sometime in the sixties and his mother a few years before the North Vietnamese troops marched into Saigon. His two brothers had both been killed in the war, and his sister, several years older, never married. He had never said much about any of them.

"Is his sister still in Saigon?"

"She was three years ago. She was still working at that orphanage. I didn't hear anything about her since then. She wanted

to be a nun, but I don't know if she did it. You know she con-
verted during the war."

"Will you see her when you go back this time?"

"Maybe. I don't know how much your ba talks to her. When
we left Vietnam, it was his decision. He didn't want to regret
anything. He didn't want to go back, ever. That's how he is."

This information was also new to Linny. "So it was really
Dad's decision to leave?"

"It was a time—you would not believe it. Everyone was afraid
of the future. Your ba, though, he said he would put his hope in
this new country. He seemed, what is it, certain when everyone
else was not. It was his decision, yes. I was scared to leave my
family. I didn't want to leave them. But your ba and I were married, and I had Van in my belly. So we went." She paused and
gave Linny a tired smile. "It's so long ago. No use being sorry
about it."

"But it sounds like you didn't want to go."

"Of course I'm glad to be here. America is America. Look at
you and Van. We're very lucky to be here—I know that. We
could have been killed any time along the way. We could have
left too late and sunk in a boat. We were very lucky, yes." But
there was wistfulness, a note of bittersweetness, in her voice.
"Your ba was different then. What he expected from America is
not what he got."

Linny said nothing, let her mother talk on. In the room it
could have been late afternoon or sunset; it could have been
hours since she'd stepped inside. Linny's mother talked, and
Linny heard her out. And she understood what her mother
had been complaining about all these years: her father had

always feared failure. Even escaping had come to seem like failure to him.

It hadn't been that way at first. All those times he stood in line for meals at Camp Pendleton and played card games through the hours of waiting, Mr. Luong had felt ready to see what would happen beyond the gates and barbed-wire fence. When Van was born in the camp, three months after they arrived, he told his wife he was proud of their daughter for being an automatic U.S. citizen, for anchoring them to this new country.

But then came, as her mother described it, a slow letdown. Linny could imagine that easily, for it brought to her own memories of childhood a kind of sharpness, like seeing a map in three-dimensions: the cobbling together of a community, the breath of relief just glimpsing another black-haired head in the aisles of the grocery store. It wasn't easy, her mother said, to ignore the people who crossed their arms at the sight of them and said, *I can't understand you. Speak English!* And perhaps Linny too made up part of that long fall into disappointment, in turning out not to be the boy her father had imagined having. Then, before Thuy Luong knew it, she was installed at a sewing machine at Roger's while her husband installed tile in houses around west Michigan. No wonder he had buried himself into Luong Inventions, as if such burrowing would dig a tunnel toward light, fame, his name aglow. He had been fascinated by the children's series of biographies on great inventors that Van brought home from the school library. Thomas Edison, Marie Curie, George Washington Carver—these people rose from obscurity and made people listen to what they could do.

Mrs. Luong didn't talk about the one thing Linny wondered about the most: What kind of love existed between her parents? Why did nothing ever seem quite clicked into place for their family—nothing like the laughter-filled get-togethers they all watched on evening sitcoms? Had the love between her parents dissipated like so much steam as they crossed the ocean, and so many hundreds of miles of land, only to end up in this cold climate, with no context to shape how they had begun? Or did their squabbles and resentments spring from realizing how leaving their country further cemented them to each other? For years they'd *had* to rely on each other for even the smallest errands, even just figuring out how to order a hamburger from a drive-through window. But while Mrs. Luong thought in terms of weeks and months, measuring the seasons, her husband couldn't stop his mind from wandering to the next big possibility. He looked to the distant future, when grand things would surely happen. Money would come, adulation would follow. It had been the only way, Linny guessed, to keep his inventions alive. She remembered, in fact, her father sometimes saying, "Tomorrow is another day," and not realizing until she saw *Gone with the Wind* in college that he'd probably lifted the line from the movie. It seemed an odd pairing, but perhaps Vivien Leigh had been short. Who knew? You could try to peer into his mind but he would never give a full answer.

Linny was glad that her last conversation with her mother had been meaningful, that she hadn't just fought with her over her clothes or boyfriends or said something sarcastic and teen-agey. But it bothered her too to think of that evening as a premonition, her mother somehow needing to sit Linny down and talk.

At the funeral, Linny told Van that their mother had planned to go to Vietnam again. "I didn't say I'd go," she admitted.

Upset, Van said, "She should have gone back one more time. I wish she had. Now it will always be too late."

"Would you have gone with her?"

At that Van looked away. "I don't know," she said, just as Linny had in response to the idea. "Maybe. One day."

In Chicago, one week after the party and back into the routine of You Did It Dinners, Linny stepped onto Milwaukee Avenue, squinted against the spring sunshine, and saw Gary. That was how she must have looked to him, halting as the door to her building clanged shut behind her. Gary leaned against his car—how had he even gotten a spot right in front?—keys in hand as if he'd just arrived. But Linny wondered how long he'd really been waiting, listening to NPR, keeping his eyes fixed on the door.

"You haven't returned my calls or e-mails." Gary was in a dark gray suit, his tie a long pattern of dizzying stripes.

Linny said, "You look like a gangster in a movie."

"Are you going to come over here or what? Or do you want the whole world to see?"

He walked up to her then, and even though Linny knew he was going to kiss her—like something out of a bad drama, she thought—her back was up. She felt like a camera was on her, affixing to digital permanence the image of Gary leaning his mouth toward hers. Anyone could drive up and see them.

It was with this feeling of exposure that Linny let Gary back in her apartment. They went straight to her bedroom this time, and even though she understood it to be a mistake—so much a mistake that she almost, perversely, wanted to lose herself in it—she didn't stop. She kept her eyes closed the whole time.

She didn't begin to feel clear-headed until Gary was half falling asleep and she got up to put her clothes back on. It was then that she felt, at last, what she'd been waiting to feel: the inward self-disgust; the wince. The embarrassment flooded her—the horrible humiliation of being here all over again with this guy. The room, the apartment, the day all seemed like glass. Clarity. For a long while a rueful feeling had been forming in her. It was not quite remorse, but close, jarred into place by her visit back home; by Van; by Tom Hanh; by what Linny knew now about Miles. And it crystallized in the space she recognized as that moment between now and the last time Gary had been in her apartment.

"You have to go. I'm supposed to be at Barbara's."

"Who's Barbara?"

"Barbara. At work."

"She can wait."

"Well, I can't. Don't you have to get going too?"

"I don't work on Saturdays."

"Then why are you wearing a suit?"

"Because sometimes I *do* work on Saturdays. Money can move anytime, you know." Gary grinned at her and his face seemed to her almost sickening. "Especially now that things are back to normal."

Linny put on the rest of her clothes. "Nothing is normal."

Gary sat up in the bed, stuffed a pillow behind his back. Linny used to reassure him that he looked younger than thirty-eight, but the truth was that the more she knew him, the older he looked to her. She had seen him too up close too often. "Are you really still upset?" he asked.

She went into the bathroom to retouch her makeup. She wished she could flee now without an explanation—a replay of that night in the sushi restaurant—but she was stuck until Gary left. That was another reason why she'd never liked guys staying over at her place.

"You need to go," she said again.

"We just kissed and made up." She knew he was trying to angle their situation to his point of view, defuse where necessary, then ratchet and demand. When they first met, shaking hands over one of the granite counters in his kitchen, he had seemed so agreeable, easygoing; nothing could shatter his feeling of being accomplished in the world. Linny had had moments of being intimidated by him, by the sneaking-up thought of wanting more than just Sundays and evenings in hotel rooms. How she had glanced around his kitchen and pictured, just once or twice, her own self there.

But that too seemed an impossibly long time ago from where she was now, standing in the doorway of her bedroom while Gary refused to budge from her bed. The old feeling of encroachment came over her again—she wanted to get him out of here, to negate the last half hour. For that was how things always ended for her: with a wince. That inward shiver, the desire to erase all evidence of where she'd been and with whom. Linny had always relied on that wince to keep her moving on, make sure she didn't become the needy, guy-directed girl that she had sometimes suspected her sister of being. Linny left guys before they could leave her, letting that pride her mother had said she had too much of propel her forward.

Gary, lying there in her bed, had no idea.

"I have to go work," was all Linny told him.

"Come here and let's talk." He patted the mattress, trying to use a winning voice that left Linny cold. Then, "I thought you were done playing hard to get. Didn't you say you liked having your freedom and independence? We agreed on this. These were the terms."

"This isn't a contract."

"I'm not ready for this to be done."

"I don't think you get to say."

All at once Gary threw back the covers and got out of bed. Linny stepped back, waiting to see what he was going to do. He paused a moment, as if considering possibilities, but simply reached for his shirt and got dressed. They ended up leaving the apartment together, walking down to the ground floor and out to Milwaukee.

"I'll see you again," Gary said just as Linny thought she would make it out of earshot, toward her car parked three blocks away. She couldn't tell if his statement was a wish or a warning. When she finally reached her Toyota and got in, she auto-locked the doors. Glancing in the mirrors, she drove toward Oak Park and the company kitchen she was supposed to be looking ahead to managing.

The parking lot behind You Did It Dinners was empty save for Barbara's car, and Linny had a sudden sense of dread, the kind she associated with job interviews or the ominous note of *See me* her teachers had sometimes scrawled at the top of her assignments. "Linny, I'm concerned," they would say, earnestly shaking their heads. "Your performance isn't up to par." Linny knew they were comparing her to Van, in whose star-student afterglow Linny had trailed. She could use it to her advantage only for so long. Teachers wanted to give her the benefit of the doubt, as if expecting her to wake up one morning and be the good model minority her sister was, but Linny refused to follow through.

Inside the You Did It building, she heard Barbara calling out her name. The tone confirmed Linny's worries: trouble. "Linny, come here for a minute," Barbara said. "Before you wash up, I want to talk to you."

Linny tightened her grip on her handbag as she approached Barbara, who wore a clean white You Did It apron. Her hair was tucked back in a bob-like net. The kitchen was quiet; stacks of disposable tinfoil pans and zippered plastic bags sat on the counter, soon to be filled, sealed, and labeled as chicken fiesta burritos, Hungarian goulash, zucchini lasagna. Later in the day, the weekend groups of moms—the work-out-of-the-home moms—would stream into the kitchen to make their two weeks of family meals.

Ordinarily Linny and Barbara would start the cooking together before the moms arrived, working across the counter from each other. They would discuss recipes, restaurants they'd tried, Barbara's kids, celebrity gossip, wending their way toward a few new dinner ideas. Whenever Linny threw out a suggestion that Barbara thought too upscale, Barbara reminded her, "We don't want people to think this is complicated. Keep your eye on our demographic."

But now she said, "Prentice Millen called me."

Linny felt herself blushing. No way to hide it. She looked down at the tiled floor, whose diagonal pattern always, immediately, brought to mind her father. He had opinions about flooring wherever they went, and in these past years had come to disdain the diagonal setting of square tiles. The brick pattern was the nicest, he had said.

"Do you not want to work here? Are you trying to get me to fire you?"

"I do want to work here."

"I thought I could trust you to have better judgment. I thought you were better than this, Linny. You were supposed to be my ideal employee."

"It was a huge mistake," Linny tried to explain, but she was thinking, *Was I an ideal employee?* Had Barbara viewed Linny the way people usually viewed Van? Her mind raced past to Gary, standing half clothed in her apartment, trying to get her to stay. Did he himself go to Pren, fling this secret into the air of some argument between them? Or could he not deny, finally, the suspicions that Pren had intuited? Linny could see them fighting in their bedroom, under the soft light cupped by a domed ceiling fixture. They would be on opposite sides of their big framed bed, speaking tensely, trying not to shout so the children wouldn't overhear, until Linny's own name spilled out. Then Gary would be running away, driving to Wicker Park, looking for absence and solace in Linny herself.

"You know," Barbara continued, "how much this kind of business depends on word-of-mouth." Her body seemed rooted to the floor, solid and white-clad, giving Linny nowhere else to face. There were times, like that one, when Barbara looked relentlessly American, that mix of European ancestry that conferred on her a kind of everyday comfort Linny could not access.

"I know. I'm sorry."

"It was incredibly awkward and embarrassing to get a phone call like that. Not to mention the business I could lose. I always thought my husband cheated on me," she said suddenly. "He said he didn't—even after the divorce he insisted that was the truth, but I always wondered. It's a terrible feeling all around, that kind of suspicion."

Linny simply stood there, exposed, small and punishable in a way that called back high school, after she'd skipped too many days of class and the principal threatened her with expulsion. *You've had too many chances*, he had said, and Linny wondered if Barbara was deciding the same thing.

"I'm just going to go," she offered.

Barbara picked up a pan filled with chopped peppers and gave them an unnecessary stir. She said, "One of my sons is in town, so he can help me out this weekend. You and I can talk next week."

Linny didn't ask when she should come back, or if she should at all. She didn't wait to find out more. She backed out of the kitchen and left, quickly, the way she had come in.

Out in the parking lot she sat in her car a few minutes, trying to figure out what to do. The leafy village of Oak Park was filled with strollers and bicycles, families going out for the first ice cream cones of the season. Linny thought of Gary, possibly lying in wait near her apartment building, wearing his aviator sunglasses. She wanted to be someplace where he couldn't find her. She thought of going to Sasha, but Saturday was Paolo Francesca's busiest day. She had a momentary urge to call Tom, but she knew better than to talk to him about this.

Linny's old impulse to escape surged back. Throw some clothes in a bag; leave a job without calling in to quit. The feeling kept her from being a pack rat, for she liked the idea of being able to leave a place at a moment's notice. But she'd never *really* traveled alone. She'd always ended up calling up an old friend or boyfriend in another city, sleeping on someone's sofa until she finally had to go back home. Still, traveling seemed to promise, no matter how falsely, disguise. When she visited New York she pretended to live there, let her imagination and clothes become her costume. She thought of the way she and her sister, as little girls in that first apartment, had pretended to be the Trung sisters, so-called brave, building a fort in the living room that served as the cave where they would plan a mission to overthrow someone else's rule. Van too had a terrible secret. She knew what it was to be concealed. And that was how Linny decided where to go. She didn't even call first, just took the roads she knew to get to Ann Arbor.

# 13

# Van

Over the past two months Van had spent her weekend mornings lying in bed for as long as possible until hunger or the need to use the bathroom forced her to get up. The weekdays she could fill with work, seeing Gertz & Zarou through the transition from INS to DHS. Her other hours needed escapism. She felt like her father when she searched for action movies in the video store, but they were a reason to avoid the present-day of her house. The world of a movie, the world of her clients: Van would rather live there.

But this Sunday Van remembered: Linny was in her house. The knowledge gave Van a feeling of safety, broadening as the daylight seeped through the wooden shutters in the bedroom. The previous night when Linny had shown up unannounced Van had surprised herself by not being bothered. She didn't mind the company, and was glad to find that Linny's motivations for being there didn't seem to come out of some misguided sense of pity. "I just wanted to get away," was all Linny said. "Can I stay the weekend here?" None of this could have happened a year ago, or even a few months ago, not with Miles in the house.

Van put on her old fleece robe, the one Miles disliked, especially when she wore it past noon, and went downstairs to the kitchen. Guessing that Linny was still asleep, Van did a quick tour around the first floor, glancing out windows in each direction, trying to see the place from her sister's point of view. She noticed the brown, brittle houseplants in the corners of the front hall, touched the fine layer of dust that had settled on the living room table. The house cleaner hadn't been there in a long time, not since Miles left, and Van finally realized that he must have canceled the service. She thought about calling them, but something inside her said, why bother?

In the TV room Van picked up the notepad she had written in after her one stilted phone conversation with Na Dau. He had been difficult to reach, and Van had left several voice mails, uncertain if she even had the right number, before he called back. He had laughed at her when she said that she'd rather talk in English. There wasn't enough left in the reserve of her knowledge of Vietnamese.

"You the fancy lawyer lady," Na had declared, his words thick enough for Van to wonder if he was drunk. "Now you help keep me out of jail."

Van had gathered enough information to conclude that Na's situation, a first-time OWI, would probably result in no more than a $500 fine and probation.

"It's very unlikely that you'd go to jail," she assured him.

"So my green card is good."

"Yes. Just don't get into any more trouble. Don't drink and drive. Don't do anything wrong. It could affect your status or your future application for citizenship."

"What you mean, 'status'?"

Van tried to explain that his status as permanent resident could be in jeopardy if he got picked up for further offenses. "Your OWI is just a first-time misdemeanor, so you're going to be fine. But you do have to be careful."

"I'm not worry. I can't get deport. I heard the government can't deport to Vietnam, so it's all good."

Van envisioned Na drinking and driving again, ignoring her, believing he was untouchable. Just like her father, in his way. So many of these Vietnamese men she knew in her father's generation seemed purposely reckless, as if daring some other upheaval to happen to them. She could guess why Na drank so much: it was a way to forget himself, the daily struggles in a bewildering, English-demanding nation.

She tried to explain to him that even though Vietnam still refused to accept deportees from the U.S., such immigrants could be held in detention centers.

"What, you mean like jail?" His voice still sounded lazy, laughing. "Then you bail me out."

"Nobody could bail you out if you're detained. Do you know what I mean?"

"What you think, I'm stupid?"

Van sighed. What had happened to the earnest Na Dau from her father's citizenship ceremony? "I just want to make sure you know the difference. Detainment isn't subject to the same laws as your basic jail time. You don't necessarily get a lawyer. For instance, there's this detention facility that was opened in Guantánamo Bay, in Cuba." At work, Van had started reading online legal forums, where a number of immigration lawyers had been talking about habeas corpus and the status of detainees being held at Guantánamo. It was going to be a huge issue, people were saying. Van had been saving this information into a growing pile, along with the news items she collected about Asian workers getting smuggled into the country and families who perished trying to cross from Mexico.

Van told Na that most immigrants from countries that didn't accept deportations were simply released, which was called a "cancellation of removal." But those who had committed serious crimes could be held almost indefinitely.

Na's voice sounded angry when he asked, "Why no one told me this before?"

"Don't worry," Van tried to tell him. "You'll be fine. All you have to do is be careful."

Hanging up the phone a few minutes later, Van wasn't certain that Na had fully understood everything she'd said. Still, she figured it was better for him to be worried than not. Maybe he would be more cautious now, tame his reputation.

Van was thinking about Na, how his two fists rose into the air at her father's announcement at the party, when the front door opened, setting off a loud series of beeps from the security alarm. Van jumped up, already panicking, when she heard Linny's voice saying, "Hey, how do you stop this thing?"

How had Van forgotten to check the lock on the front door? She hurried over to punch her wedding date numbers into the security pad while Linny carried two bags from Whole Foods to the kitchen.

"I thought you were asleep," Van said.

"I've been up for a while. Did you know your eggs were from over a month ago, and you're out of coffee?"

"I don't drink coffee." A little stir of agitation: Why didn't Linny ever remember this? "Did you really go out and leave the door unlocked?"

"I was only gone a little while. This is probably one of the safest neighborhoods around."

"No neighborhood is."

In the kitchen Linny unloaded groceries and set up a chopping board, knives, and little bowls on the counter near the gas range. No concealing, now, the bare refrigerator, the freezer containing little more than stacks of frozen pizza. Van waited for Linny to drop a remark about them.

"This is a nice kitchen," was all she said. She'd said the same thing the other two times she'd been in the house. "You don't use it much, huh?"

"I just do basic stuff. Miles did most of the real cooking." Van hoped Linny hadn't noticed her accidental use of past tense. She didn't know how to speak about Miles, where to fit him in the grammatical time line.

"Yeah, I know he liked to think of himself as a really good cook." Linny started throwing round slices of pancetta into a pan, mixing egg and cream for an omelet.

"He's got some specialties."

Linny rapidly chopped up a spray of green onions. "I bet he likes to take some time to cook up a nice risotto or osso bucco, right? Man, I can't tell you how many guys I've met who're all into their osso bucco. It's a real guy thing, this quest for specialized, so-called authentic cooking, with all the right equipment and ingredients and putting everything together just so. They think it's about the food but you know it's just the same old ego."

Van couldn't deny that there was something to that description of Miles. She never could quite keep up with his expanding knowledge of which restaurants to go to in which cities. He knew how to select ripe mangoes at the store and make his own ice cream. How did he manage it?

Van perched on one of the leather counter stools and set her notepad aside. She watched as her sister grated a block of cheese and, without hesitation, flipped an omelet over. It arrived on a plate thin and glamorous-looking, if an omelet could be called that, unburned and untorn, a yellow hemisphere. Van remembered reading somewhere that a simple, perfect omelet was a test of a chef and it gave her a new sense of respect for what lay before her.

"I got some orange juice too," Linny said. She dropped butter into the pan to make another omelet.

"How'd you get this to turn out so nice?"

"I'm using your crepe pan."

"I have a crepe pan?"

"It was in your cupboard. Hold on a sec, I forgot the toast." She popped two slices of bread in the toaster, but Van started eating the omelet anyway. She ate fast, pushing the bites into her mouth. She finished before the bread was toasted.

"That was fast," Linny said.

"I keep forgetting to eat," Van explained, though it was more than that. She hadn't consumed much beyond pizza, burgers, and soup in the past couple of months, and at the party in Wrightville she hardly ate at all because everyone asking about Miles made her nervous. Linny's being here marked the first time eating seemed something more than necessity, filling the stomach that must be quelled.

Linny slid the second omelet onto a plate. With her hair pulled back she looked as neat and efficient as a talk show hostess and suddenly Van could picture her sister in a white chef's outfit, cooking up roasts and vegetables every day in an echoing restaurant kitchen. She hadn't thought much of Linny's job, had never asked many questions about it. But it occurred to her, now, how pleasant it would be to have a pile of ready-to-cook meals sitting in her freezer. Linny would be rolling up her sleeves, filling all the pans with ingredients. She gleamed forth energy, ability. When had her slacking-off, college dropout sister transformed into this?

Linny brought out more food from the grocery bags. Cheese and olives, some sort of fig spread, a bag of cinnamon pita chips, a mini-cheesecake, a melon that she swiftly sliced into cubes. Van started eating it all, reaching forward to pop open the bag of chips. She crammed her mouth full, let crumbs spray onto the counter.

Linny's cell phone trilled inside her handbag. She grabbed at it to check who was calling, but let it go to voice mail.

Something about that gesture made Van slow down her eating. She wondered why exactly Linny had come to Ann Arbor, bringing all this food. "What are you doing today?" she asked, half-expecting her sister to say she was going to visit an old boyfriend in town.

Linny shrugged. "Hang out."

"I have to do some work."

"Sure."

Linny spent the afternoon watching TV and murmuring on her cell phone while Van sat with her laptop in the kitchen, reading immigration articles on LexisNexis. There were months, years of new reports and memos she could catch up on. Gangsters running indentured servitude rings. Special visas for migrant workers. Refugees coming in from Sudan and Somalia. Trucks and boats stuffed with "illegals" from China, many of them suffocating before reaching New York. And the expanding fallout from the new war in Iraq. Now the status of every brown-skinned immigrant was called into question.

Every article made Van feel anxious, part of that same indignation that had propelled her in law school. Who was on the immigrants' side, the refugees' side? How did anybody manage to get by in this vast country, the most foreign one of all? The immigrant words swam in front of her eyes, asking for elucidation. *Undocumented. Aliens. Lawful Permanent Resident.* Somewhere in all of this, Van opened her e-mail and searched for Jen Ye's address in her files. Jen was still working at the DA's office in Detroit, and in her last correspondence, somewhere around New Year's, she had again brought up getting together for lunch. Van wrote her a quick note, suggesting dinner after her father's TV show tryout. She considered e-mailing a colleague from the International Center too, because she had been thinking more about what it really meant for INS to get absorbed into the Department of Homeland Security, and how the war in Iraq and post-9/11 policies would affect immigrants and would-be immigrants in the area. What stopped her was the memory of Vijay Sastri, whom Na Dau had unintentionally invoked, and the shamed, hurried days in which Van had run away from the Center.

Linny was watching *The Thin Man* when Van wandered into

the TV room. *I'm hungry*, she wanted to announce, but it made her feel like her father. The way he'd suddenly appear in the kitchen, demanding, *Where's all the food?*

"How's Na Dau?" Linny asked.

"He should be fine."

"Lucky him. He's got rich relatives and free legal service, too."

"I'm not being suckered into it. I'd do the same for a friend or a relative."

"It makes me wonder what the hell is going on with Dad and the Baos. Maybe Dad feels guilty."

Van reached for the throw blanket but didn't sit down. "I'm still not buying this thing with him and Nancy. I highly doubt Rich would have stayed his friend."

"Maybe he didn't know. Or maybe enough time has gone under the bridge. Or water, or whatever that saying is. It's been, what, twelve, thirteen years?"

Van kept glancing at the television, distracted by Nick and Nora's banter. Myrna Loy was so gorgeous, and even in black and white film her satin gown glowed vibrantly. Linny's phone made a little gurgling noise and Van asked, "Who do you keep talking to? You're like a college kid."

Linny seemed a bit embarrassed. "Just Tom," she said, not answering her phone. Then she got up, started to collect the remains of crackers and cheese from the coffee table. "Maybe we should go out. Mom used to say that if we watched TV all day then we had to go out and make up for it."

"I don't remember her saying that."

"Well, she did. And anyway, I have an idea."

The edge of excitement in her sister's voice made Van wary. "Don't you have to get back to Chicago soon?"

"We should follow him."

She meant Miles, of course, and Van wondered if Linny had guessed how much that very idea had been in her own mind, ever since her initial failed attempt. As afraid as she was of getting caught, she was even more afraid of seeing where he would go.

"Don't you want to know?" Linny asked. "I would."

"It's Sunday."

"We'll do it tomorrow."

Van couldn't help her twinge of suspicion. "Don't you have to work?"

"I can take another day. It doesn't matter."

Van was a breath away from saying, *What, did you get fired? Why did you really drive all the way here?*

"Listen," Linny said. "I'll make dinner tonight and we can watch something super trashy, like that Will Smith movie about aliens attacking the world which I know you probably like because Dad loves it. And then, tomorrow, we'll go to Miles's work and follow him."

Linny, in her way, made it sound so easy—sensible, even. Her smile was the very one that made people like Tom Hanh pursue her all the way out of town. Perhaps Linny was the one, Van thought, who should have been the lawyer. It was that face again, the winning smile, the repeated persuasiveness of beauty. But the implicit point was undeniable too: like it or not, Linny had become a part of Van's secret.

And so the next evening Van found herself sitting in Linny's car, waiting for Miles to step into the parking lot outside his law office. She had rolled the windows down to feel the cool May air and Linny thought the blossoming magnolias on the street provided a bit of cover from Miles's possibly glancing their way. Van had left work early for this wait, an hour and a half now. She and Linny had been alternating between Van's NPR and Linny's CDs, getting out every so often to feed the meter where they'd stationed themselves.

Van was shocked when Miles did appear, walking the brief distance from the building to his Land Cruiser. There he had been all along, going to work, within easy reach of Van. She almost felt offended by how out in the open he was, so recognizable, so completely Miles. Her chest literally hurt to see him. Surely, she thought, he could sense this. He would know how she had endured the weeks and months of waiting. But Miles didn't look her way at all. He simply got into his car and started driving. Van was, plainly enough to make her eyes burn, invisible to him.

"This is crazy," she said as Linny put the Corolla into gear.

"I'll tell you what's crazy. Not knowing where your husband's been for two months, and him not telling you where he is. *That's* crazy."

They followed him down Huron Street, toward the entrance ramp to I-94.

"I have no idea where we're going," Van volunteered. She was stating the obvious, but the sentence seemed immense to her. She had no idea where Miles was leading them. She stared out the window at the miles of concrete walls they passed, built to provide some sound barrier between the freeway and housing divisions. She thought of how Miles always commented on these structures, on how odd it was to develop such neighbor-hoods and homes—to buy them, live in them—right next to the Interstate. "Who would want to live like that?" he had asked. He had been glad, triumphant even, to sail past them. *He* wouldn't live there.

They drove for half an hour, deeper toward the western sub-urbs of Detroit, taking the same exit Miles took toward the town of Birmingham. Van was glad her sister didn't say what she was surely thinking: that he was going somewhere definite, somewhere with purpose.

In silence Linny headed toward the center of the town, then east on a divided highway. When Miles led them onto a street of pretty bungalows set back on a hill, there were no longer any other cars between them.

"Don't let him see us!" Van whispered in a half shout, squishing herself down in the seat.

Linny slowed down. Miles made a right and she took her time doing the same. When Van looked out she saw a neigh-borhood of homes from the thirties and forties. The kind that Miles had increasingly admired in the last couple of years, the kind that had "character."

Linny parked the car behind a green SUV with the vanity plate *FUN MOM*.

Ahead of them, Miles was getting out of his car in front of a taupe-colored Arts-and-Crafts-style house with a broad porch. At least, Van thought it was Arts and Crafts, if she remembered correctly from his architecture magazines.

When she saw him step onto the sidewalk, she ducked.

"He's not looking at us," Linny told her. "He's going to that house."

Van peeked at Miles walking up the stone steps to the porch, then lowered her head again. "Is he going inside? Is someone there?"

"He went in," Linny said. "It looks like he had a key." She settled back in her seat. "Wow."

Van, folded into an uncomfortable position nearly underneath the dashboard, said nothing. She wanted to cry, but didn't want to appear to be even more of a mess than she was. It seemed unbearable to be caught in the truth of stalking her own husband. What she felt was the severest, strangest loneliness she had ever known, and Linny's presence—her witnessing all of this—only compounded it.

Linny said, "Should we wait until dark and look in the windows?"

"This is insanity." Van's voice broke a little.

"Stop saying that. You had to find out where he is. Now you know."

The trouble, of course, was that Van still didn't know anything. Was that woman Linny had seen with him inside the house? What were they doing, planning, in there? What would happen if Van walked right up to the front door and rang the bell?

"Drive by it," Van said faintly. As she spoke, an idea formed. "We'll look at the address and do a reverse lookup."

"Oh, that's good." Linny started the car.

Van took out her BlackBerry—a Christmas gift from Miles—and waited for Linny to glide slowly past the taupe house. Van strained to capture the whole building in her mind. It was neat and precise, with a swept porch floor, flowers in the yard, and potted plants hanging from the eaves of the porch. Someone loved this house, Van thought. Someone took care of every part of it.

Van did the reverse lookup in a matter of minutes. The name was clear. Even the phone number marched across the screen. *Grace Chang*.

Forty minutes later they were still sitting in Linny's car, back in the space behind the *FUN MOM* minivan. Dusk had begun to tug itself over the sky and Van felt, curiously, perversely, sheltered by it. She was glad to be in the confines of a car, a movable getaway. She could sit here all night in its protection, but Linny wanted to get some dinner, buy binoculars, then peer into the windows. Van had a sudden wish for some specialized Luong Eye that could see right through the walls of a house, transforming Van's sitting position into something useful.

Before they could agree on what to do, Miles appeared, suddenly, as if called out by them, on the porch. The woman was with him and Linny confirmed, needlessly, that it was the same one she had seen with Miles in Chicago.

Van knew she shouldn't be surprised, but she was. The physical fact of this woman was undeniable now. She was as willowy as Jen Ye but with Linny's long hair and tailored clothes. Van watched them walk down the steps and get into Miles's car. They looked so obviously together, so much a couple that Van was riveted. She was fascinated by this distance, allowing herself to pretend that she was merely watching a scene out of someone else's life.

It was Linny who said, after Miles and Grace drove away, "Let's go peek around the house."

Van shook her head. "The neighbors might see us."

"We're all Asian—they'll just think we're relatives or something." Van rolled her eyes but Linny added, "If you want to see it, you know now's the time."

Van pushed herself out of the car. Linny took the lead, striding along the sidewalk, right up the steps to the house. The front door, painted red, had an old-fashioned brass knocker. On the porch a pair of rattan chairs with fluffy striped pillows kept company with a table that held votive candles in need of replacing. Linny looked in the windows while Van imagined Miles sitting here with a book, in twilight—the blue hour, *l'heure bleue,* she had learned in a college art history class, the solitary moments Van had always associated with her mother. In the other chair, another woman—Grace. Neither of them aware that Van was watching, watching the neighborhood fall quiet in the dark falling around them.

Had she and Miles ever dreamed of this kind of companionship? Had they spoken of the long years ahead? Van wished their house in Ann Arbor had been built with a porch. Why hadn't they thought of a porch?

"Come here," Linny said. "Look inside."

Van had to stand on her toes to see over the plantation shutters. A stone fireplace anchored the square living room, and beyond that a gleaming dining table held a glass vase filled with huge pale blooms. Everything was taupe and beige and cream, accented with dark jewel tones. When Van put her hand on the window to steady herself her jade bracelet clanged against the glass.

"It's totally Pottery Barn," Linny said. She noted the high ceilings, white crown molding, magazines spread just so on the coffee table. These rooms looked clean, sanctioned. Some people had the effortless ability to beautify everything around them, to make all design bend for them. Van had known even as a child that she was not one of those people. No one had ever called her chic or admired her placement of a pillow in the corner of a sofa.

Van supposed that this house was a clear portrait of what Miles had always desired. Van could only be a ghost here. She was a tiptoe visitor, the Peeping Tom, the freak with nowhere else to go. Perhaps in these two months without him she *had* become invisible. She had disappeared from his mind. He had already started a whole new life, and he would never come back to Van's. He would never even think to call.

Van was so lost in this idea that she almost thought she'd conjured a vision when she turned from the window and saw Miles standing on the sidewalk with Grace.

It seemed a long minute before he finally spoke. "Is this a breaking-and-entering thing, or a stalking thing?" His voice so thick with derision that the woman, Grace, actually murmured something to him. It appeared to be one word of restraint, one stretched-out syllable: *Miles*.

Van felt her face getting hot, actually felt the red rising like liquid filling a container. She glanced at Linny and for a wild moment she considered running. They could jump the porch railing and get out of there, the way they had a few times, growing up, playing ding-dong-doorbell. They'd never gotten caught. But Van found herself frozen to the porch as Miles started up the steps. She was both scared and fascinated by this man, her husband. He did not bear the stony, impassive look from his office, the last time she'd seen him. Now there was anger. It took Van's conscious will to meet it. In so many ways his gaze was the very same one that had captivated her in law school. She could remember that feeling all over again. Sitting on that bench near the library. Being chosen, the spotlight on his stage. For years looking him in the eye—allowing him to look her in the eye—felt like nothing less than raw exposure.

His face made Van hold her breath. She had no idea what he was going to do. But he dismissed her entirely. He walked around her, aiming for the front door. It was a gesture that showed his awareness of what would wound her most.

Perhaps Van would have let it all play out like that. She would have just stayed rooted there while Grace trailed Miles into the house, the two of them shutting her out, emphasizing her pointless stand. It was Linny who reached forward and grabbed the woman by the elbow, saying, "Why don't you look at my sister?"

Grace gasped. And in that second she did, as if by accident, look. Van had dreaded this face-to-face, expecting to feel miserable hatred and jealousy. The very thought of Grace—perfectly Asian American in a poised, smooth-skinned way that Van had never been—had filled her with a desperate rage. And she wasn't wrong. Grace was her very name and Van, standing near her, felt every ounce of her own smallness. She was a clunky utilitarian van. The only thing left for her was complete humiliation. Abjection. It took her a moment to place, to name, the feeling. It flattened her, rendered her speechless.

Then Grace slipped away into the house, and Miles said, "You need to leave."

Linny was quick to reply. "What are you going to do, call the police? That'll be a great show for all the neighbors."

Miles ignored her. "I guess I should have expected that you would start stalking me, Van, but this is pretty psycho, don't you think?"

"I wanted to see where you were." Somehow Van managed to say this without sounding shaky.

"It's not your business. *I'm* not your business anymore. I've tried to spare your feelings, Van, so don't play the victim here."

"We've never had one real conversation about any of this. We said we were going to talk."

Miles sighed. His voice softened as he said, "I just said that to get you out of my office. I'm sorry, but it's the truth. I appreciate your giving me some space and not harassing me and calling me. You've been great about that. But I can't believe you've been hanging on to any hope. You have to have known it's over."

Van was keenly aware that Linny stood nearby, observing and listening. Now nothing could be disguised. Linny must know everything.

"And that woman?"

"Van. Are you really going to focus on this? *You* followed me here. Don't forget that. You brought this on yourself." Van shook her head but Miles didn't stop. "You're only hurting yourself. You're always focusing on the wrong thing. Grace is not the issue and I'll say that over and over again. So please leave."

With Miles it had always been better to go along, get along. Avoid courting the future apology. But in that moment Van realized: What did she have left to lose? In that long week since the citizenship party, she had been convincing herself that Linny's claim of seeing Miles with another woman had been a mistake, a misunderstanding. She had dug deep for that denial but there was no keeping it now. "I want to know how long you've been with her."

"Don't be childish," Miles snapped. "Don't make this ugly, don't make this a goddamn soap opera. I don't want to have to close the door in your face. It's pathetic."

Van ran through all the things she could say, but nothing seemed right. All she could think of were lines from television shows, movies, and yes, soap operas. Those were her examples, the only models of relationship behavior she knew.

"Why don't you answer her?" Linny spoke up.

"Stay out of this," Miles ordered. He looked furious, and Van suddenly understood: Miles could say nothing to Linny that mattered. There was something almost wildly gleeful about the thought.

Miles opened the front door. Not even facing Van, he said, "You can show up here all you like but you can't force me to talk."

She wanted to leap out at him, physically prevent him from disappearing from her sight. The only thing stopping her was the awareness of Linny. So Van didn't move; Miles did. He went in the house.

Van forced her body to pull away, to hurry back down the porch steps so as not to see Miles slamming the door behind him. When she stopped on the sidewalk, Linny, close behind, ran into her.

The house looked calm again. No signs of argument within, no signs of drama. Van imagined Grace sitting on the edge of her bed, tense, waiting. She was running hot water into a bath. She was perched at the bedroom window, surveying, taking in the lay of the land that was Miles's past.

"Are you okay?" Linny asked.

Van nodded. She had never been in this neighborhood before, never stood on this leafy street, surrounded by all the houses of families she would never know. She thought how she could have gone her whole life happily never knowing this place existed.

For nothing, now, bound her to Miles. Not a child. Not even a contract, really. Nothing that couldn't be broken.

While Linny was in Ann Arbor, Gary called six times. She refused to answer when his number came up and erased his voice-mails as soon as she heard them. *I'm smoothing things over,* he insisted. *I'm talking Pren down. By the time I'm done she'll be calling your work to apologize.* Linny had hidden in Van's bathroom to listen to the messages, as if her sister would be able to discern the whole situation otherwise. Instead of calling Gary back, she called Tom.

Two days after Linny and Van followed Miles, Linny returned to the kitchen of You Did It Dinners. Barbara, looking up from supervising a gaggle of moms, had nodded her assent. Later on, neither of them brought up the subject of Gary and Pren. Instead, Barbara talked about the future, looking ahead to the targeted opening of her new branch in Lincoln Square. Linny unofficially agreed to stay in the Oak Park location, and Barbara unofficially agreed to allow her. So for now Linny returned to her search for new dinner ideas, calling up recipe sites and reading through back issues of food magazines. She spent most of her evenings like that, taking notes and e-mailing Tom.

*It's not thrilling work*, she admitted to him. They'd been exchanging more and more messages since her father's party, talking on the phone at night.

*What* would *be?*

She sent him links to sites she'd bookmarked more than a year ago. The Cordon Bleu Institute in Chicago. The French Culinary Institute. The Culinary Institute of America.

*The CIA*, Tom typed back. *Serious stuff. New York?*

But Linny wanted to stay in Chicago. All of her years in Michigan, the city had seemed a beacon, a promise that she still wanted to have fulfilled. Here, in the middle of the country, an unlikely avant-garde spirit had risen, taking shape in neighborhoods edged by skylines, flatness interrupted by heights, midwesternness mixed with modernity. Linny had almost begun to take it for granted. It had taken Wrightville and Ann Arbor, seeing her father and sister, to make Linny long to stop wasting so much time.

More than once, Linny had almost told Tom about Gary. She just didn't know how to explain it. Nor could she say why she had the compulsion to confess, except that it had something to do with sensing that the pattern of her days in Chicago was shifting. If she told Tom the truth, as she might have back when they were fifteen, what else might change for her?

Look at how Van had already changed. That evening of the confrontation with Miles and Grace, Linny had driven Van back to Ann Arbor in silence, thinking her sister was in full retreat mode. The quiet between them dominated as it always had, seemed to expand like a bubble until it became a fearsome thing to break. When they got back to the house Van started to march up to her bedroom but got no farther than the stairs, where she suddenly sank down. For a moment she drew her legs up to her chin.

She surprised Linny by saying, "I would absolutely destroy his things if it weren't such a fucking obvious thing to do."

Linny, relieved that Van hadn't burst into sobs and relieved to hear her cursing, said, "It doesn't mean you can't do it anyway."

"Yes, it does. Because then Miles would say that's such a fucking obvious thing to do. And then *I* would be the immature one."

"It's funny to hear you swear."

"Miles said swearing was crass and the sign of an uneducated mind."

"Then he must be a hypocrite." Linny took a seat on a lower step, leaning against the banister.

"I should never have learned about the Trung sisters."

At this unexpected mention, Linny recalled the way they used to run around the living room of that old apartment, mixing up the Trung sisters with Charlie's Angels. Neither the Trungs nor the Angels would have walked away in defeat from Miles. "Just remember that they threw themselves off a cliff and drowned in a river."

But perhaps Van was not fully ready to sustain the anger she should have had. She pulled herself up like an old lady from a park bench and said, "I'm going to go to bed. I guess you're heading back to Chicago?"

"I don't know." She meant, *Do you want me to?*

"You should go." Van sounded weary, threatening to recede into some cold depth and take the whole evening with her.

"I can leave early in the morning," Linny suggested, wanting to say something else to bring back that momentary glimmer of fierceness. Van nodded, then moved up the stairs. At the very top she turned back for a moment.

"Will you do something?"

"Sure."

"Go to Dad's TV show audition."

There was no way Linny could say anything but yes.

On the day before the audition, Linny demonstrated a new chicken, roasted vegetable, and couscous dinner while Barbara took notes. They used to talk over every aspect of building a new dish, brainstorming—one of Barbara's favorite words—to reach the compound of ingredients that she judged would most satisfy the demographic. Now Barbara typed on her laptop, made a few noncommittal noises meaning *nice* and *possibly*, and let Linny go home early.

Walking her neighborhood to clear her mind, Linny told herself to expect the chilliness from Barbara. All she had to do was push through it. She would shop for Tom's upcoming birthday instead, focus on how bright the days had gotten: a glorious spring had arrived at last, bringing pansies from window boxes, kids selling silk-screened T-shirts at every corner. Near the five-point intersection where the El stopped, a restaurant owner, dressed all in white, stepped onto Milwaukee just as Linny walked past. They nodded at each other, a simple exchange that made Linny feel the satisfaction of being acknowledged. She headed down Damen to the row of new clothing boutiques that had completed the street's gentrification.

Linny was browsing a shop filled with sale sweaters and the

gleam of fresh summer dresses when the entrance of a woman with honey-red hair generated a call of hello from the hipster girl refolding clothes at the center table. Before she even looked, Linny knew it was Pren.

She had been expecting to see Gary in the neighborhood. Sometimes at night when the door buzzer sounded in the apartment next to hers she started, certain of Gary. In his most recent voice mail, left earlier that day, he had said, *How much longer do you think I'm going to wait for you to call me back?*

The scene with Miles and Van, all of it too close to Gary and Pren, had more than unnerved Linny. She couldn't talk about it to anyone but Sasha, who could only say, "Oh, lord, that poor girl. Poor sweet sad used-up girl." Well, there wasn't much else to say, was there? There was no resolution. Linny had never seen Van look so timid, so *small*. A violent feeling had surged up in Linny on that porch. If she'd been in Van's place she would have lashed out. Forget the semblance of control. She would have made Miles fear *her*.

But as soon as Linny imagined this she was chastened by her own role: as Grace. No getting away from that comparison. If Gary and Pren showed up outside her apartment, both of them screaming, their tall figures blocking out the store awnings across the street, what would Linny do? Gary would be Miles, trying to keep everyone quiet. Linny could no longer hold onto her excuses. *I wasn't looking for someone else's man*, she had defended herself to Sasha. *He approached* me. *What do I owe Pren?* And so what did Grace owe her sister? The question made Linny uncomfortable, spurred her to duck away, as much as she could, from Pren, who stood in the same shop, reaching forward to touch a chiffon dress.

Linny slid behind a mannequin dressed in a trapeze shift. Hiding was one of the few advantages to being small. But she couldn't avoid Pren's eye for long.

In the past, whenever Linny had run into her while dropping off a supply of dinners, Pren had been adept at making small talk. She never failed to compliment Linny's clothes or ask where she'd gotten her necklace. They had talked about Bucktown and Wicker Park too, how Pren adored the neighborhoods' shops and restaurants.

Now Pren's face drew down into a hard stare. She moved closer, fairly towering, smelling of honeysuckle perfume. This wasn't a woman who ran away. Pren said, "I'm sure the owner of that company told you we won't be needing those dinners anymore."

"I heard." Linny glanced past Pren, at the girl in tight jeans trying not to eavesdrop too obviously.

"I hope you don't think you're special. In fact, I'm glad I ran into you, because you should know that you're just another notch on his fetish belt. He's got a thing for you ethnic girls. Thai massage. All that stuff. Didn't you know?"

Linny felt her face getting hot. She thought about saying, *I'm sorry*, but the words seemed pointless.

"Thought you'd want to know." Pren turned away, but Linny stopped her.

"Wait," she said.

Pren glared. "Do you have something to say to me?"

"To him," Linny said. "Tell him not to contact me again."

Pren's lips seemed to furrow together, but she said nothing more. She pivoted, her expensive handbag flaring out. Her heels thumped on the distressed hardwood floor of the shop.

The girl folding clothes watched Pren go, heading north on Damen, and Linny knew she could never step in that store again. When she left she went directly back to the small space of her apartment where, at least, everything could be claimed as her own.

It took four and a half hours to drive from Chicago to the center of Detroit, and on the Saturday morning of the reality show tryout Linny spent most of that time thinking about Gary and Pren. *Another notch on his fetish belt*, she had said. The words, the idea, made Linny feel sick, as Pren had surely known they would. While Linny assumed that most white guys who hit on her were possible fetishists, she had never sensed that in Gary. He didn't fit the giveaway signs—didn't use the word *exotic* as a compliment or say stupid things like Vietnamese girls were the prettiest, or generally give off that subtle but clear vibe of guys who collected Asian porn videos. Was Pren lying, knowing just how to deliver a punch? Or was Gary really the kind of guy who boasted about dating various Latina, Asian, and black girls?

Linny knew she had almost reached the convention center when she caught a glimpse of the distant Ambassador Bridge that connected Detroit to Windsor, Canada. In the foreground the Renaissance Center, the skyscraper that used to have a revolving restaurant at the top, mirrored back the spring sky. It had once seemed romantic to Linny, before she knew what it was really like. Senior year in high school, she and her friends would drive all the way to Windsor because the drinking age there was eighteen. Some people preferred to take the eerie orange-lit tunnel but Linny liked the long wiry bridge and the way she could clearly see herself crossing from one country to another. Once in Windsor, they would head straight to the casinos, smoking and playing the ten-cent slots, pretending to be in Las Vegas. It had all seemed so innocent, full of play. The same as when Linny's guitarist boyfriend called her "Yoko Ono." She had laughed too, and it had taken years of dating enough guys to understand what the subtext meant. Linny wondered if Van had ever encountered fetishists— maybe the nerdy, engineering ones. As far as Linny knew, her sister had only dated one or two other guys before settling with Miles.

They had agreed to meet in the lobby of the convention center but the place was massive, a wide expanse of navy carpeting. Several conferences were going on, with signs pointing to hair care and chiropractic exhibits. Van had called Linny earlier in the week to report that their father's audition would probably fall around the midafternoon; somehow he had procured a number guaranteeing a tryout. He'd checked in with Linny, too, to make sure she would be there.

Linny was about to dial Van's cell phone when she saw her standing by a far pillar, under an electronic billboard that blinked *16th Annual DHA Members, Welcome!!!!* Linny walked toward her just as Van started moving in the opposite direction. Linny sped up, wanting to call out, *Wait for me.* It was like being ten years old at SeaWorld, where their mother had taken them one time, and not knowing how to find the actual sea lion shows. Back then Linny decided all she had to do was let her sister, who never seemed to get lost, guide the way. Sure enough, they found the sea lions. Van could read maps; she stayed on course.

Linny followed her into the ladies' bathroom. She reapplied her lip gloss and smoothed down her hair, motions that had become second nature to her. In one of the stalls a toilet flushed, sounding like a bowling ball hitting a strike, and Van emerged.

"Oh!" she said, startled, fixing the hem of her shirt over her pants. "I didn't know you were here."

"Just now. Have you seen Dad yet? I was shocked that he didn't call me while I was driving."

Van washed her hands and Linny was struck by how briefly she glanced in the mirror. Didn't pull any products from her bag, didn't even seem to care that the side part in her hair lay crooked. "They're already upstairs in the waiting area. You and I have to register first."

"What do you mean, 'they'?" Linny immediately thought of Nancy Bao but Van rolled her eyes.

"Your new boy toy Tom drove Dad here."

"Really?" Linny swiveled toward the mirror again, checking her face one more time before Van led the way back to the lobby.

"Are you two together or something?" Van spoke the words with a tone of something like distaste.

"I only saw him at that party," she answered. "We're e-mailing. Why? You act like there's something wrong with him."

She shrugged. "I thought you didn't date Asian guys."

"That's not true," Linny argued, though she had to admit Tom was the first Vietnamese guy she'd ever really been interested in. She could imagine, suddenly, how her mother would have smiled at Tom, a little dimple showing in her right cheek that conveyed her approval. She would have fawned a little, talked too loudly so other people would know about his dental practice. And here he was, wasn't he, a good Asian son, shuttling her own father to and from Wrightville.

It took them five more minutes of walking to locate the lone registration booth for *Tomorrow's Great Inventor*. It looked like one of those kiosks where people hawked credit cards on college campuses. The plastic sign drooped in the middle.

"This is it?" Linny had expected it to be something akin to *American Idol*, with teams of producers wearing headsets and lines of geeky guys holding on tight to their secret inventions. Her father among them would stand proud, attaining at last his long-held goal nurtured from years of infomercials.

The girl at the registration table had Linny and Van write down their information on clipboarded sheets. They signed a confidentiality agreement and video release form, then received adhesive tags printed with the show's logo.

"You're all set," the girl told them. She couldn't have been older than twenty. "You can go on to the Oakland Room upstairs."

"Do you know when the show will air on TV?" Linny asked.

The girl shrugged. "I'm not sure it's been sold anywhere. My aunt's a coproducer and I'm just helping out for the day."

Linny mulled this over as she and Van took an escalator to the second floor. She doubted her father knew about the status of the show. She began to worry about how he might react if he got rejected, if some young judge dismissed his lifetime of products for short people. Mr. Luong had never yet appeared to waver in his confidence about his inventions, yet this moment, this hour at the convention center, seemed all too typical: the big break he had aimed for could turn out to be another false hope, another rotted shoe pulled up on the fishing line.

As they headed down a carpeted hallway, Van suddenly spoke up. "Miles called me."

"What'd he say? What'd *you* say?" Linny talked too fast, glad that Van had brought up the subject.

They reached the doors of the Oakland Room. "Well, I took half the money out of our bank accounts."

"Good," Linny said. But then they were inside the waiting room and there was Mr. Luong, in the same navy sport coat from the citizenship ceremony, sitting next to Tom Hanh, who jumped up and waved. He looked like a bodyguard the way he hovered near Mr. Luong, and Linny realized he kind of was—he'd brought her father here, ushering him safely across the state. They stood out in the room of mostly white contestants, family members, and friends. Of course, the would-be inventors were easy to spot—gawky and fidgety, mostly a pale lot. Engineers past, present, and failed, Linny guessed. The last of the Science Olympiad hangers-on. Guys with video cameras were rolling tape but not much seemed to be happening. Linny felt a little let down, wishing for something grander for her father.

Tom crossed the room to greet them. "Hi, Van," he said. "Hi, Linny."

"You've known about this all along?" Linny asked.

"I helped him with the application a few months back," he admitted.

"How?"

"Nancy Bao. She came to get her teeth cleaned and asked for my help. I guess your dad doesn't use the Internet and Nancy barely understands e-mail, but she saw an ad for the tryout in a magazine. I was going to tell you at the party, but then I thought I would surprise you."

Linny was actually filled with relief that he was here. "Thanks for doing all of this."

Van, clearly losing patience, moved ahead of them to sit down with Mr. Luong.

"Hey, Dad," Linny said as she and Tom reached their row of saved seats. "Good luck today." She had never known how to greet him. Her voice came out stilted, careful-sounding.

"You girls been taking your time," he said with a scowl. He studied a crinkled page of notes, the cuffs of his pale yellow oxford shirt peeking out from the sleeves of his jacket. He had the Luong Arm and the Luong Eye near him, tucked in a box, plus a suitcase, and a ladder that stood behind the chairs.

"What's with the ladder?" Linny asked.

"Shh. It's for the show," her father said.

"I'm sure you'll do well," Van told him, like a schoolteacher. She knotted the straps of her purse in her lap.

"Did you see the cameras?" He nodded his head toward the video guys across the room. "Be careful what you say. They catch everything. They've got to make the best TV."

"Did someone already interview you?" Linny asked.

She was glad when he answered, "Not yet. I see some other guys talking to them but I'm going to wait. It's almost my turn." He pointed toward a set of double doors. At that moment they opened and a man in plaid pants emerged, unsmiling, carrying a contraption that appeared to be made up of small wheels. "Guess he got the reject too. So far that's everyone except two people." He looked back at the papers in his hand. Linny could see English and Vietnamese words mixed together, with underlines and exclamation points.

"We've been here about three hours," Tom said.

Mr. Luong had always claimed independence, saying no one could boss him or tell him what to do, but in truth, people were always helping him. Even when he and Mrs. Luong fought she still left meals for him and kept the rice cooker on warm. She made sure the basement bathroom was stocked with enough toilet paper and sometimes she left the newspaper leaning against the door for him. And how many times had she, Linny, and Van gone to the stairwell to listen for music? If the telltale Vietnamese folk and opera songs were playing, they knew Mr. Luong would be at work in his studio, which meant he couldn't be disturbed. They had flowed around him, treated him like a stubborn rock in a river. When late at night Mrs. Luong would sometimes awaken, frightened by the sound of explosions and fistfights playing out on the basement TV, she rarely told her husband to turn the volume down. Epic action movies were what he liked, disaster films, the more outlandish the better, and Linny and Van had watched them too. Even now Van was still sending him checks, and they both still traveled back home to clean up the house and look in on him. For all of his independence, Mr. Luong needed many people in his life.

Van, looking restless, checked her watch and excused herself. "I'll be back," she said to Mr. Luong before he could object.

Tom caught up Linny on how many people had gone to and from the audition area. Mr. Luong fidgeted, shifting his legs and reaching into his coat pocket as if he'd forgotten something important there. It took a while for Linny to understand: this was as important to him as citizenship, the first time he had truly struck free of his own basement. It was a moment of exposure, and Linny hadn't even considered that until now.

"So what do you get if you win?" she asked, wanting to encourage him in some way.

"Being famous and having a hundred thousand dollars," he answered. "That's a lot of commitment."

Someone flung open the double doors and yelled, "Number three-oh-six!"

A man with a layer of sweat on his bald head leaped to his feet. He had a giant metal case that looked like it held a trombone.

"He looks sick," Mr. Luong said. Then, "I wish we didn't wait so long."

"It's going to be fine," Linny said, though she didn't manage to make the words sound convincing. Was that all she could come up with? "I think your inventions are great. I use the Luong Arm all the time."

Her father's face swung toward her. "You do?"

"Yeah," Linny said, though it wasn't true. "And there are tons of short people out there."

"Of course. But don't say anything too loud. I don't want anyone to steal the idea. Where your sister go?"

A few minutes later the sweaty bald guy burst into the room and shouted, "I'm going to Las Vegas!" His family started shrieking and the camera guys moved in. Even Mr. Luong looked excited.

"*Now* it's finally like TV," he said with satisfaction. "Where's Van? Linh, go get her."

"I'm sure she'll be back."

"Go get her."

So Linny did as she was told and wandered out into the hallway, where Van, apparently, had been all along. She was leaning against the low windowsill, her arms crossed, backed by a view of long stretches of parking garage.

"You're missing all the excitement. Some guy just got the green light for the next round. He's all in a lather."

Van didn't crack a smile. "Did Dad tell you to go fetch me?"

"Of course he did. What the hell is wrong with you?"

"What do you mean, what's wrong with me?"

Linny had momentarily forgotten. "Sorry," she said. While Van stared into space, Linny went on, "I thought you were doing a good thing. Taking out your half of the money?"

"It's an aggressive action."

"You should have taken *all* of it."

"He might file now, after this."

"File for divorce? Why don't you do it first?" Linny couldn't believe that her sister, in spite of everything that had happened, still seemed not to grasp the state of her marriage. It gave Linny a strange sense of having changed places, of having become the older sister.

"You don't understand the way Miles works." Van opened her purse and let the magnetic closure snap it shut again. She did this two, three times.

"You know what I think of him. He's a phony. One of those I'm-so-self-aware Asian American guys."

"Actually, he's an optimist, even if that seems phony to you."

"I can't believe you're defending him."

"It was a mistake to follow him."

"Where is this coming from?" Linny leaned against the windowsill too, lowering her voice as two men rode up the escalator and headed toward the Oakland Room. They didn't look like inventors—more like Gary types, the kind who did vague finance work. One of them turned to stare at Linny and Van and when Linny looked back he gave a little smile.

"Jesus Christ," Van said, not missing a thing. "You're like Blanche Devereaux on *The Golden Girls*."

Linny laughed. "I love that show."

"I *know*. We used to watch it when we were kids."

"He was looking at both of us, by the way. If you pay attention, it's not hard to see what guys are thinking. Most of the time they're pretty transparent." Van emitted a little scoffing noise, the kind their mother used to make. "It's true," Linny insisted, though she didn't have the exact words to explain it to her sister. Maybe it took years of practice, years of gauging the expressions of interest that flickered over a guy's face. "Haven't you ever played the Asian card, just for fun?"

Van looked disgusted.

"You know how there are these white guys with Asian fetishes." Linny blushed, thinking of Pren and Gary. She knew she should shut up but she kept going. "You can manipulate them. For fun. Use that fetishizing against them."

"This is just—" Van uncrossed her arms, letting her hands fly out. "Absurd."

"You have to know how to keep the power."

"It's always a little game for you," Van burst out. "If it's not Tom, it's someone else. If it's not someone else, it's yet another someone else. It's not like that for everyone."

And that was when Linny finally began to understand: her sister thought she was losing a life, not just a husband. Linny had been so fixed on her own dislike of Miles that she hadn't truly considered that maybe the continuity of Van's days had depended on having him there, directing the next turn, the next event.

Linny's mind floated back to Tom in the waiting room, and what would happen between them from here. Soon he would visit her in Chicago, hurry up the three flights of stairs to where Gary had stood not so long ago, surveying her unmade bed.

It wasn't Tom, she realized, whom she had to tell about Gary and Pren. It was Van.

So she said it. "I just broke things off with a married guy."

"Why are you telling me this?" Van exploded. She pushed herself away from the windowsill, from Linny's proximity. "Are you trying to be smug? Are you trying to rub it in?"

"No! I was trying to tell you something else. To reciprocate."

"You're messed up."

Linny had never heard such trembling anger, such hurt, in her sister's voice. She wanted to lie to her, cover up what she'd said, smooth things out. But she couldn't. The thin veil that had bound them closer together these past few weeks was dissolving.

"It's been over for a while," she explained hurriedly, feeling like a little girl again, no longer the older sister. "It's got nothing to do with you."

But Van just got madder. "I don't want to hear it. There you were, acting all self-righteous to Miles. How can you call *him* a hypocrite? How can you have all these accusations about Nancy Bao when you're worse than she is? I don't have to stay around for this."

She ran to the escalator. Linny, following, wanted to respond in full—*I'm not Grace, Grace is not me, I'm not Nancy Bao; the situations are different*—but her voice faltered. A South Indian couple passed them on the up escalator and she didn't want them to hear. The woman, wearing a brilliant turquoise outfit, nonetheless stared right into Linny's eyes as if discerning the entire story.

"You can't leave. Dad hasn't had his audition yet," Linny called after Van as the escalator began to flatten out to the first floor.

"I don't care."

"He won't understand."

"Why don't *you* take care of things for a change?"

Van didn't even glance over her shoulder as she spoke. She kept walking, not the slightest hesitation in her step as she reached the row of revolving doors.

Upstairs, Linny took a minute to calm herself before going back into the Oakland Room.

"Where've you been?" her father demanded, getting up from his chair so fast he dropped his notes. "Where's Van?"

"She had to go." Linny retrieved the notes for him, noticing that one page had the Randy Newman line written in large print and underlined. Was he going to incorporate that in his audition somehow?

"Go where? I got to go in that room."

Tom, worried, said, "Is everything okay?"

Linny nodded as the headset guy popped into the waiting area and shouted her father's number.

"I told you," he said to Linny. Grabbing hold of the box that held the Luong Arm and Eye, he made a move toward the door, then stopped. He looked so nervous that Linny felt afraid for him. "I need to get all this in there," he muttered.

"I've got the ladder," Tom said.

Linny gathered up his notes and the suitcase, which was much heavier than she'd expected. "What's in here?" she whispered to her father.

"Dictionary," he said. "For showing off the Luong Arm."

The guy with the headset pointed at them. "Time's a-wasting. Let's go."

Linny and Tom ended up going into the audition room with Mr. Luong. Three bored-faced judges, all men, sat behind a long table, surrounded by cameras. Mr. Luong put his inventions on the desk set in the middle of the room and arranged the suitcase and ladder nearby. In the background, a huge screen printed with the block-lettered logo for *Tomorrow's Great Inventor* loomed.

"Who's the one trying out here?" demanded one of the judges, a bearded man with wiry glasses who was clearly the leader. His blue shirt had four distracting flap pockets.

"Me," Mr. Luong said. His voice seemed to shrink as he uttered the one syllable, and in that moment Linny knew: she could not leave him there.

"We're the assistants," she said to the row of judges. "Can we stay?" Remembering that they were men, she smiled at them.

The lead judge waved Linny and Tom away to the corner, out of the view of the cameras. "Let's get to it," he said impatiently, looking back to Mr. Luong. "Show us what you got."

Mr. Luong stood behind the desk. He tried to strike a shoulders-back posture, keeping his hands folded in front of him, and to Linny he looked like a kid in the final anxious round of a spelling bee.

"My name," he started, squinting at the camera lights, "is Dinh Luong. I am inventing products in Michigan and the

United States and I am a U.S. citizen. I have three products to-day to show for short people in the United States and America. Some people say short people are no reason to live, but I say short people have many reasons for becoming happy."

"Show us what you're referring to," one of the other judges interjected. He was the shorter one, thin and intense-looking. The third judge, the only one wearing a suit, laughed.

Mr. Luong fumbled with the box to reveal the Luong Arm. "This is my Luong Arm," he said. "It's very useful. I can dem-onstrate on many things how useful it is. All my inventions are very useful. I have the Luong Arm which is right here. Here I also have the Luong Eye and then I have the Luong Wall. So I have a big three, which is important."

Linny cringed at his deteriorating English and thickening accent, the way he was even now falling into an embarrassing Mr. Miyagi–like cadence. His eyes darted from camera to cam-era. For once in his life, perhaps the only time in his life, he was attempting to make good on two decades of promises; he was trying to stand in front of that panel of judges and pitch his work, let it go forth to critics, the world, when Linny and Van had never truly thought he could. And he was going to blow it all with his unsteady English.

"Listen, man, I can hardly understand you," the short judge said. "Can either of you?"

The lead judge shook his head. "Sorry, I don't think this is going to happen."

Linny made herself walk to the center of the room, right in front of her father, under the hot lights of the cameras. She said, "Let me explain. May I? There are three great inventions here, all designed to help short people make their lives a little easier. One is a Luong Arm, that can get things that are out of reach; another is called the Luong Eye, to help people see in a crowd; and the third is called the Luong Wall, which is basically a set of shelves that rise and lower with a remote control. All of these make it easier for short people to get what they need, or to have whatever they need come to them." The descriptions flowed with surprising ease, and when she glanced at Tom he nodded.

"Not bad," the short judge said. "Are you the translator?"

Linny glanced at Tom again, who gave her an encouraging smile. She didn't dare check her father's reaction when she said, "Yes. I'll translate."

The next few minutes blurred together so that later Linny wouldn't be able to remember what she'd said about the inventions. She only knew that her father moved away from the desk a little, not even once jumping in to add to her speech. She took over the whole thing.

Linny rushed through the description of the Luong Wall. She was more nervous about the thought of her father standing where she couldn't see him, folding his arms, than she was about the presence of the cameras.

"Let me demonstrate the Luong Eye," Linny said, bringing it to the judges' table. "You look into the viewfinder here, but the image you get is from up there. The height is adjustable. I can't tell you how many times I've wished I could see over people's heads in a crowd. Plus, it can collapse to fit into a handbag. It's very convenient." She realized this was true, though she had hardly ever used the Eye.

"Like a periscope," the short one said, testing it out. "Not the most necessary thing in the world, and a little unwieldy, but it seems to work okay. A decent gadget."

When Linny pulled the Luong Arm out of its box she realized it was a different, newer version from the last one her father had given her. This one had rubber grips and was made of a lighter material. "The Luong Arm is my father's original invention. As any short person knows, it can be difficult to reach things sometimes. Actually, it can be difficult even if you aren't short. The Luong Arm solves those problems."

"What do you use that for besides pulling something off a shelf?" the head judge asked.

Linny's mind raced. "You could use it to clean the gutters, or hang a painting, or change a lightbulb. You could use it to grab a cat out of a tree."

The judges laughed. "Okay," the short guy said. "Show us what it can do."

When Linny turned back to the desk she saw that her father had moved the ladder forward and positioned a thick dictionary—Van's, from high school, its gold tabs worn down with use—upright on the very top. Linny had never used the Luong Arm to grab anything more substantial than a bag of potato chips, and she wondered how many times her father had rehearsed this demonstration. She could see him finding the dictionary in Van's room and placing it on the Wall as a challenge, then picking up the Luong Arm, willing it to take hold.

Linny slipped her hand through the brace and secured it with the Velcro strap. Aiming the wand of the Luong Arm toward the dictionary, she secured its jaws around the wide spine of the book. She couldn't help imagining the thin metal snapping under so much weight, sending the dictionary thudding to the floor. But as she drew the Arm back it felt like a taut wire, the dictionary's solid mass—all those bound pages, all those words her father would never learn—becoming almost featherlike as she set it onto the desk.

"That's the Luong Arm," she said to the judges, as pleased and surprised as she had been the first time her father had shown her the invention and Linny had been certain she had inspired it.

She couldn't help smiling at her father, but his mouth was set in such a way to indicate any number of emotions—anger, betrayal, satisfaction, relief? As Linny turned back to the judges, who said they were impressed by what they'd seen, the peripheral vision of her father made her wonder how he would ever view *her* again.

When the judges invited them, with Linny as the presenter, they emphasized, to the second round of the competition, next month in Las Vegas, her father stood so still that the short judge called out, "Don't get so excited there, buddy!" Linny made a show of thanking the judges, going up to shake their hands, while her father silently gathered the Arm and Eye back in their box, refusing even to look at Tom.

The three of them should have been among the few cheering as they left the audition room. Linny actually did feel like celebrating, and Tom seemed to share the feeling, but Mr. Luong stormed toward the exit.

The camera guys zeroed in on them.

"These stupid TV people," Dinh Luong finally spat out as he reached the hallway. "They're all about the TV. My friends warn me. They said it. Watch out for the TV people. Well, they can take their Las Vegas somewhere else."

"Dad, I'm sorry," Linny said. "But it did go well. You made it to the next round." He snorted at that and she didn't want to say more, to have it preserved on film.

Her father set the box with the Luong Arm on the floor near the escalators. He looked flustered and confused. A camera guy zoomed in on his face.

"Could you say what you said again?" he asked. "Tell us what you're feeling."

Mr. Luong glowered at him. "I'm going to the bathroom," he announced.

Immediately the camera pointed toward Linny and Tom.

"Is that your father, miss?" the guy prompted. "How do you feel right now? How do you think he's feeling right now? Just talk into the camera—say whatever you like."

"Yes," was all Linny said. "That's my father."


Mr. Luong was quiet all the way to the parking garage. After securing the ladder in the back of his truck, he got in and rolled down the windows; he preferred manual ones, in case, he said, there was an accident that landed him in water. "What we waiting for? Where's Van? I want to go home."

"We can't go home yet," Linny said.

"We're going. I go."

"We have to find Van. Van's lost."

"What?" Mr. Luong opened the door and started to get out of the truck as if he meant business. Then he gave a scornful wave and stayed where he was.

Linny handed her car keys to Tom. "I'm pretty sure she went back to Ann Arbor. Will you follow us? My car's on level E, orange. Look for an old teal-colored Toyota. If *you* get lost, call me."

Tom took the keys. "Listen," he said. "It was good you jumped in. He'll see that eventually."

"Thanks," Linny said. "You know how he is." And she was startled to think that it was true.

Linny opened the door on the driver's side of her father's truck. "Will you let me drive?"

"No way. You already do a lot today."

"I'm sorry, Dad, but with the way you're acting you're liable to run off the road."

Mr. Luong sputtered at this, but slid into the passenger seat.

Driving to Ann Arbor, she ventured to say, "In a way, it all worked out. The judges liked your inventions."

"They're *my* inventions."

"I know they are. And they're good. You got invited to Las Vegas! It's a chance at the hundred-thousand-dollar prize."

Her father stared out the window. They were speeding past the gigantic Uniroyal tire that had once been a Ferris-wheel exhibition, perched at the edge of the battered expressway. Linny guessed that he was thinking about how the judges had made a point of congratulating *her* on the presentation.

"I'm not going," was all he said.

As they drove by the Detroit Metro Airport, planes swooping in overhead, Linny tried again. "I was only trying to help."

"You go help yourself then!" her father burst out. "You do go do that! Why don't you go finish college!"

It was the retort both he and Van would never give up.

"I'll finish college if you go to Las Vegas," she said. "I don't know what you did with that new Luong Arm, but that dictionary didn't even feel heavy. It was pretty amazing."

"Of course it works good." His annoyance made Linny feel guilty all over again, reminding her that she hadn't, for most of her life, believed his inventions would have a life outside their house.

He took his cell phone out of his pocket and switched it on. When it rang a moment later Linny recognized the loud voice of Rich Bao. Her father started talking a swift stream of Vietnamese and Linny, comprehending none of it, settled back in her seat. She thought ahead to how angry Van would be when they got to her house. She thought about Tom, and how long she could keep him with her before he had to take her father back to Wrightville. In her rearview mirror she saw him driving her car, keeping up, staying in the same lane. She wished she were in the car with him. They would turn down the radio and talk the whole way; it would be just the beginning of the conversation. Linny would say *I have so much to tell you*.

# 15

# Van

On the way back to Ann Arbor, Van had to drive past the university hospital, built on one of the few hills in town. It was where she'd gone to get her D&C and where she'd assumed she would one day give birth, wheeled around to a room with a view of the Huron River. Before the D&C, Van had searched all kinds of word combinations on her Internet browser: *reasons for blighted ovum; having a baby after miscarriage; D&C complications.* The searches had led her to a universe of message boards, galaxies of faceless women chattering all day and night, sharing everything from their ultrasound pictures to the dates they had sex. At first, the way these women charted out their reproductive sagas—signs of probable ovulation, hormone level numbers—gave Van a feeling of private hope. So many of these determined women had planned and won. But the longer threads devoted to infertility and repeated miscarriages were another matter. Here women commiserated over drug treatments and talked about progesterone levels and in-vitro fertilization. Some called miscarriages "little angels" and even named them. After a few days of reading their stories Van closed out all of the windows, vowing not to look again. She cleared the history on her browser. Miles would have hated all that sentimentality, all that effort when, as he had said, maybe some things weren't fated to be.

It wasn't until Van drove by the hospital, crossing the river, that her anger toward Linny began to lessen into weariness. Linny with that blurted confession, as though she'd wanted to share something she had in common with Van. That was Linny through and through, wasn't it? Just when Van thought she could begin to rely on her, Linny would show her true hand.

Now Van would have to call her father to make up an excuse for leaving before the audition. She'd have to call Jen Ye too, because they had agreed to have dinner afterward. Jen had responded right away to Van's e-mail, and this time Van didn't let the correspondence drop, filling her in on Na Dau's situation and even asking if she knew how things were going at the International Center. *You should stop by sometime,* Jen had written back. *Are you still keeping up with languages? My Spanish has finally improved. Btw I dated Paul, your IC colleague, for a while. He says they still miss you over there. Frankly they probably need you too.* It was an opening.

When Van made the turn onto her street she saw Miles's car parked in the driveway. She recognized that she should be startled by the sight, but she wasn't, exactly. Pulling out half the money from their accounts had been a final effort, a sign. And he had called her right away, saying, *Are you sure you know what you're doing?*

*It's just protection,* she had said, at first thinking, *Why didn't I do this sooner?* She could have kept him on the phone, kept him talking about money, made him explain himself to her.

But he wasn't having it. *If this is what you want,* he said. *Now we'll move forward.*

Money was something they had never argued about, except for his occasional questioning of the checks she sent to her father. Miles had often nagged her to get control over her father's finances, see if he had any life insurance money left (no way, said Van). She knew this was a good general idea—had even brought it up a few times, tentatively, though her father always dismissed her. He wasn't going to give up his financial information so easily. Still, Miles's objections were faint, hardly enough to cause tension in their marriage. Too many other things, it seemed, had come first.

Their untouched accounts had been a kind of test, since either of them could have drained all the money away in a moment. Miles surely had been trying to show her that he was too much of a gentleman to do anything like that. Which wasn't untrue—Van knew he never would have left her without money. He never even asked her to think about bills. He knew all along the money would just sit there, their years amassed in digits. He knew she would wait for him to make a move.

Taking the money had been the only way she'd known how to react to seeing Miles with that woman, Grace. Van had wavered between subjugating the entire episode, telling herself the humiliation could be forgotten and overcome, and letting it bloom into fury. In Linny's presence it had been easier to lean toward rage, but after Linny went back to Chicago, Van couldn't sustain the feeling on her own, not when its flip side revealed desire and fear, the old longing to affix her and Miles permanently back to the life they had once had.

She wondered if he could see her, if he was looking out a window as Van left her car right next to his, instead of in the garage, and went up the front walk. She used the front door, slipping off her shoes at the entryway. For a minute she waited for him to appear. She readied herself. But nothing happened. So Van went toward the staircase, then climbed it.

In the bedroom Miles was retrieving the rest of his clothes and shoes from his closet and folding them into suitcases. The image seemed so iconic—something she'd seen in late-night movies on cable—that she had to stop herself from saying, *What are you doing?*

As far as she knew, he hadn't been in this house in three months. Van could almost, still, pretend to herself that he'd been away on a long trip, but the fantasy had worn too thin. The bed wasn't made. Her robe hung over a chair. Those crumbs she'd never gotten around to vacuuming were visible on the floor. The room had changed into hers.

Miles barely glanced at her. "I should have done this a long time ago."

Maybe because that was the first thing he said to her, or maybe because he said it without even looking up, Van found her uncertainty tipped into irritation. "If you're still upset about the money, just say so."

He finally glanced at her, then back down at the belts he was coiling. "Why should I be upset? Now I know where you stand."

"I stand right here."

"I see that." He lifted a stack of T-shirts from an open dresser drawer. "You can have the house."

"I don't want it." She said the words loudly, before realizing them, before understanding their truth: she *didn't* want the house. It had never truly been hers. "I don't want the furniture either. I don't even like most of it. It's all evidence of your trying to make up your mind."

For a moment he looked taken aback, making Van feel a brief surge of power. She knew this feeling from the few arguments they'd had during their years together, and she also knew the rarity of it. Arguing was like any sporting match, and a well-scored point always brought satisfaction.

Miles could play the game better, though, or perhaps it had been easier to let him. The jolt of seeing Miles rattled faded fast. He started to zip up one of the suitcases. In the movies she'd watched, it would be nearly the end of the scene.

"You can go ahead and give me the blame," he said. "One of us has to file for divorce."

Had it been only a few weeks earlier, the statement might have crushed her. It might still crush her—she knew that. But now it seemed imperative to keep standing, to not crumple again within his plain view. When she didn't answer him, or took too long, Miles returned to the closet. He disappeared, heading all the way into the back, getting every last thing.

When he emerged with an old North Face fleece he said, "You know, I'm sorry about what happened at Grace's house. I lost my temper and the whole thing was unfortunate." Slightly, just so slightly, he altered his position toward her. His voice, his manner, became more expansive. He was not a litigator but Van guessed this was how he would work, seamlessly switching gears, changing tactics to get ahead of the argument.

"The truth is, if I hadn't looked for you, you wouldn't have explained a thing. Just like all that stuff with Julie." Van was surprised at herself, at her ability to bring up subjects she never would have broached before. She was, once again, in the position of having little left to lose. So why not say it?

"How long have you been fretting about Julie? She got married before you and I did." Miles made it sound like an obvious fact she should have known.

"Why didn't you ever tell me that?"

"What does it matter? You never asked, anyway."

Van recalled Julie's handwriting on the heavy envelope, the letterpressed card. The missing note. "It matters because after all these years it turns out I was your safe, dependable rebound."

"Don't be so simplistic. You always knew Julie was the last relationship before you. I never hid that." Miles spoke smoothly, double-checking his dresser drawers, closing the last one with his hip. "But I was ready to be serious, and as a consequence we got married when we were too young. We were both straight out of law school. At the time, I thought we did the right thing."

"Unless you're teenage and pregnant, who gets married to do the so-called right thing?"

"We're not the first or last to marry too young," Miles said, with the looking-back air of someone about to consign whole years to the closed-off past.

But Van didn't let this go so easily. "I think you didn't know what else to do."

"That's ridiculous."

"You had no other plan. And I went along because it was easier for me, too."

Miles shook his head. Had it been three months ago, or even three weeks ago, or any of the time they'd been together, she would have interpreted that shaking of the head as disappointment. That she had let him down by not seeing the clarity of his point of view. This rebellion—her refusal to acquiesce to his line of thinking—was so small but it felt significant. She wouldn't capitulate to his version of the life they'd had together.

Miles set the big suitcase on the floor, saying, "Don't you even make the bed anymore?"

It was a last jab. No doubt his eyes had cast over the piled-up papers in the kitchen, the open boxes of crackers on the counters. She supposed that Grace Chang always kept a meticulous house.

"Are you at least going to tell me how long you've been with her?"

"Not that it matters, but I've known her through work for about six months. I don't want you to think she's the reason for all of this. That wouldn't be accurate. She happened to be there. I'm not going to lie about that. But she isn't the reason."

Van thought that she would never again underestimate the power of pronouns. Me, her, you. His directness, whether or not she believed what he was saying, seared her all over again. How long was this going to last, these flinches and wounds, this having to reel back, gather herself in?

"Anyway," Miles said, "I'm not even sure about this . . . lawyer life. You know?"

"You didn't even want to be in law school."

"It was never the be-all and end-all for me." He sounded defensive now. "I've always had a hundred different interests. You know that."

"Yes. Your photography." She didn't restrain the hint of sarcasm from seeping into her words. Still, the moment of vulnerability in his voice made Van soften a little. She wished he had admitted it to her before. She wished he had been able, in their nearly five years together, to *confide* in her.

"I've thought about going back to San Francisco," Miles said.

So many times Van had imagined moving there with him, cramming together for the California bar while his parents found them a lovely town house with a view. In truth, she knew little about the Bay Area, and the times she'd been there had been insulated by the Ohs. She never could picture herself truly living there. Van was a midwestern girl, always had been. She'd heard the statistic that Michigan, with its depressed economy, was the state that more people left than anywhere else. But Van knew she would stay.

"You *should* go back," she said. "You don't even like the Midwest. You don't even know what you're doing here."

Miles looked startled by the sudden forcefulness in her voice. "What makes you think I don't know what I'm doing?"

"What makes you think I *don't* know?"

"Wow," he said. "You're all over the place."

"I already told you I'm right here." Van did not look away from his half-confrontational, half-bemused gaze.

"Then I guess I'll go."

Miles picked up a bag to sling over his shoulder but Van

stopped him with one more question. She needed to know about that empty picture frame he'd had on his office desk.

"I don't know," he said. "I stored away any photos I had a while ago."

"Pictures of us?"

"Probably. Why?"

"You had one on your desk. It was a frame with nothing in it."

"I don't remember."

Van smiled faintly. "You do. I know you do."

"I don't know what you're talking about." He was going to stick with that line, Van saw, and maybe she would never understand why. The frame, its emptiness, its story—these might remain a mystery to Van, like the mystery of her marriage, of being with a man who needed to cloak and reveal himself at will.

He lifted two oversized suitcases, the kind they never used for long international trips, like the ones they didn't take to Vietnam and China, and walked out of their bedroom.

"Take care," Miles said.

Had it been two months ago, or even two weeks ago, she might have listened for him to leave. She might have peeked out the window to watch him drive off. She might have cried. She might have thought, too late, of all the things she could have said to him, all the accusations. *You always kept me guessing. You kept me worrying about what you would think of me.* All of these words that were and were not her own. They were scripts she had picked up, cues from actresses with sturdily waved hair. For how else was Van going to know how to behave? Why else had she watched television and read all those library books in the first place, those growing-up years? Didn't everyone watch and read, keep their eyes open, in order to know how to be?

Yet if there was one thing Miles had shown her over and over it was that definitions were malleable. Meaning Van alone could not determine the weight of a sentence. Whatever words she tossed into the air were words Miles could transform. He might say, *I'm not responsible for your insecurity. You need to be stronger in yourself.* Their relationship, after all, had begun from Miles, spun out of his invitation. Van had accepted. She hadn't questioned. Maybe it was fitting that now she would have to work her own transformation on words.

Of course, she knew she would have to see him again. Maybe he'd send a moving company to fetch his papers, his box of framed photographs, all that furniture, but they'd have to see each other to figure out the settlement, that word of finality some of Miles's and Van's colleagues worked toward. For a little while longer they would still be bound—and then what? Neither had any reason to keep anything of the other's, not even to acknowledge the years they had, seemingly, shared.

Perhaps she had relied too much, as her mother had once briefly teased her, on pride and competition. They had fueled her through school, for the alternatives meant failure and shame. Of all the things Van had never gotten the chance to talk about with her mother, she thought most about that. Had her mother felt shame the way she did? Had her father? She thought of him, abandoned at the convention center in Detroit. She could see him fitting the pieces of the Luong Arm together, dreaming of wealth, as if the metal pincers at the end of the Arm would clamp themselves onto stacks of money sitting on a tall shelf, just waiting to be reached. He was not going to be pleased that Van couldn't prevent Miles from slipping out of her grasp.

What Van and Miles had now was the story of their marriage. The story was evidence. It seemed to her that he had already decided on his narrative; he knew what he would tell, when he had to, bearing it for the rest of his life. Van would be known as his first wife. His ex. How many people, for years on, would hear his version of events, how he married her too young, how he had tried to build something sturdy and noble but hadn't known what he was doing? A simple explanation. Even now Van was giving him the end to the story he was going to tell about her.

And what would her story be? Van didn't know yet, except that it would be hers. Miles would never get a rebuttal, never get a say in what she might choose to reveal. If there was one thing that probably bothered him the most about the end of their marriage it had to be that. And the fact that a story must be told. Neither could wave away their past years. They were historical facts, a mark on both of their permanent records.

At seven in the evening, daylight still reigned in the sky when Van stepped onto her back patio. She couldn't remember the last time she'd been out there. The gas grill wore its nylon protector, the cedar and wrought-iron tables and chairs shrouded in the dark green covers that Miles had so carefully fastened and removed with the seasons. Neither of them had been into gardening, though each spring Miles had hatched new ideas for the lawn-and-garden guys who rolled up in a rattling truck once or twice a week.

Normally Van disliked being back here by herself. Though surrounded by other houses, nestled right in the middle of the neighborhood, she could never get over feeling like a target, out in the open. Miles had always teased her about that same strange paranoia when she insisted on double- and triple-checking the locks on the doors. *Where did it come from?* he had asked. She claimed she didn't know, but then she had never told him about waiting for the bus with her parents and sister. She had never talked about the view of the prison and how urgently her mother had wanted to move to a house of their own. Mrs. Luong, with her job at Roger's and her consultations with the Oortsemas, was the reason they had. Van had known that even then. Her father would have stayed in the same apartment forever, ready to hunker down in the space he'd been given. Maybe that was what escape had done for him. And maybe something about it had filtered down to Van in the form of fear, caution, burrowing worry.

Van sat outside long enough to hear her a few neighbors' voices, cars sliding into garages, doors closing. She was staring at the trim wooden fence at the very back of the yard when she heard her own name. A shout. *Van.* Her sister's voice. Before she could even stand up she saw Linny, walking around the side of the house with their father and Tom Hanh. Van had almost forgotten Detroit, the convention center.

"Van," her father said. "I been trying to call you about Na."

Na had been pulled over the night before, Van's father said, for turning the wrong way onto a one-way street, and his alcohol level was higher than it had been for the first OWI. Rich Bao bailed him out of jail that afternoon, then left ten messages on the voice mail that Dinh Luong almost never checked. He had turned off his cell phone, preparing for the TV show tryout, and had forgotten to turn it back on until Linny was driving them to Ann Arbor.

Mr. Luong explained how Na had become obsessed, since getting that first OWI, with asking around for immigration stories gone bad. Na had heard about a guy from Thailand who'd been deported even after living in Oregon for twenty years as a permanent resident. He talked about people being detained at camps, with no access to a lawyer, for years. Instead of taking these as cautionary tales, Na seemed to be goaded by them as if drawn to a self-fulfilling prophecy. He became increasingly heedless and enraged. The evening before he got arrested again, Na had started a fight with two different guys at a Vietnamese restaurant.

Rich had told Na to stay at his house for a while, to keep low and not go anywhere. But Na wouldn't listen. He was gone before anyone knew it; they were certain now that he had left town. Rich Bao suspected California. Nancy, hysterical, called all of her friends and relatives there.

Na was afraid of going to the immigration jail, Van's father said. Afraid of being *detained*. He spoke the word as if it were fragile.

The words floored Van. She pictured Na saying this, enunciating it; she imagined the word being passed from phone to phone, immigrant to immigrant. She wanted to drop her head in her hands, cry. "I need to call him," she insisted. "It can still be okay. We can still fix this, if he comes back to Michigan immediately."

"Van, you cannot. Rich thinks Na threw away his phone. No answer."

"It's my fault," Van said. "I told him about detention centers. I was trying to warn him but I ended up scaring him. Now if he's ever caught he really will be in trouble."

"You were trying to be the good lawyer."

"I don't understand why he didn't call me." She could have kept him in the state. She could have kept him safe. "It's not even a worst-case scenario." She knew that even if they did find him—and they would, probably, since he'd always relied on money from his family—she would not be able to help him now. She had lost his trust. Na Dau would become one of those shadowy underground figures slipping in and out of restaurants, his every day weighed against the worry of being caught, pointed at, named illegal.

"Maybe I can still do something," she said.

No one responded. The four of them—Van, her father, Linny, and Tom—stood nearly in a circle in Van's backyard.

Finally Mr. Luong said, "It's the way it is. A bad day."

Remembering the convention center, Van asked, "What happened with that show?"

The look on her father's face, his stooped posture, made her regret the question. Mr. Luong shook his head. "My English is not good enough. They don't care. All they think is I'm not the true American citizen. I guess—they're right."

He had never brought up his use of English before, and the resignation in his voice overcame her. The only other time she had seen him this way—seemingly defeated, and accepting it—had been when her mother died. He had cried briefly at the funeral, but it had been enough to make Van feel helpless. She had never been able to ask him what he had done with the white mourning sashes they'd worn, that Linny had sewn from a pillowcase. Had he burned them one night, solitary in the backyard? This imagined moment was one of many that turned into a reproof whenever Van felt irritation toward him for not listening to her, for never saying a word of appreciation for all those checks she'd sent. And the shame returned to her now: for leaving him at the convention center, for not being able to help him procure the patent for the Luong Arm. For so many years she'd tried to appease her father—with her lists of short people, her law degree, even her choice of a good Asian husband—as if making up for all that she had assumed he would not achieve.

"Dad, you *are* a true American citizen," she asserted. "You've got the paperwork to prove it."

"No," he said. "Just normalized. *You* girls are born all-natural. You always know that's not the same thing."

Van and Linny stayed on the backyard patio while their father and Tom went out to pick up dinner. Linny pulled chairs from their covers, brought glasses of wine for both of them.

"Just keep drinking," she advised. "Na was unstable. Everyone knows that."

"But still—it's my *job*." She didn't know how to explain that Na's fleeing felt like more than a blown case. It was another loss in a long line of them. Her mother. Vijay. The baby who never was. And Miles. One by one she had failed all of them.

Linny said, "You're not still mad, are you?"

Though their argument in the convention center now seemed ages ago, hearing those words renewed Van's repulsion. She hated to think of Linny as a version of Grace, so confident in their bodies. She hated the idea of Linny being on Grace's side.

The difference, of course, was that Linny was her sister. That was unchangeable and, in truth, Van had never wished otherwise. "Not exactly," she answered finally.

They sat for a while, a pink sunset beginning to spread out over the subdivision.

"Almost Mom's favorite time," Linny said. "She would have liked this place."

"I'm not keeping it."

"You don't want this house?"

"It's too big. Miles did all the specs. But he doesn't want it either." She didn't elaborate on how Miles had kept looking for ways to improve it, and how Van had never quite gotten over the feeling of being a guest in someone else's domain. The house was like nowhere she'd lived before, full of unused areas, audacious proportions. And it *was* too big; it had put too much space between them.

"It is kind of a family house."

"We tried," Van said, answering Linny's unasked question. "It didn't work out."

Linny set her wine glass on the slate tile and Van was grateful when she shifted the subject, saying, "You missed a crazy show today in Detroit." She gave a rundown of the tryout and how she'd had to step in. "I wish Dad weren't so determined not to go to Las Vegas. He's really improved the Luong Arm. You wouldn't believe how easily it carried that dictionary. I could actually see people finding it useful."

"I bet that show never even makes it to TV."

"So if you don't like this house," Linny asked suddenly, "where are you going to go?"

"I'm not sure yet." But as Van said this she realized it wasn't exactly true.

When their father and Tom came back with Thai food they all decided to eat on the patio. Van could feel the summer approaching with its deceptive peak of days, and she thought about how all that long light made people forget that the sun had started its slow recession.

As they passed around containers of green curry, shrimp, and noodles, Van decided to wait until morning to tell her father about Miles. She wondered if he would blame her, ask if she'd taken care to be a good wife. She pictured Linny stepping in, saying, *Jeez Dad, don't be so mean*, her voice commanding in a way that Van's, somehow, never could be with her father. Or maybe he would surprise her. After all, he had never nagged her about having a baby. And it would only be a matter of hours before he realized that her kitchen had not been customized for a shorter person. Her father could just as easily be on her side, Van reasoned. She knew if she asked Linny right now to predict his reaction that both of them would only have guesses. They might never know a thousand things about his life, like whether anything had happened between him and Nancy Bao, or if he would ever travel back to Vietnam, or if he would ever admit why he refused to go.

Linny had sounded serious when she'd insisted that their father's inventions worked well, that they weren't as laughable as they'd thought them to be. Van, thinking of the seldom-used Luong Arm in her kitchen, wanted to believe that. She wanted something to replace the prevailing images she had of her father:

lecturing to them at dinner; struggling to explain what he needed at a hardware store; cooped up in his darkened basement. He had made sure Van and Linny knew they would never be tall enough, that they would have to work to get things that seemed out of reach. In response, Van had braced herself. She knew short people were supposed to be able to laugh at themselves, take a joke, brush off the comments, the people who kiddingly used their heads as armrests. *We live in a tall American world,* her father had often said, forever minding the shadows. Perhaps feeling inadequate went with the territory—had become their territory—when her parents crossed from Vietnam to America.

After dinner everyone but Van retreated inside to the TV room. She decided to wait, as she hadn't done in years, for the blue hour that had been her mother's favorite, deepening as the earth moved toward the solstice. Mrs. Luong would bring a lawn chair to the middle of the yard or, later, perch on the teak bench she'd set under the maple tree, ready to stare at the sky. *Gloaming; l'heure bleue*—Van had taught her these words. Her mother had loved learning them, even when she forgot their correct usage. For her, the words had been proof of Van's excelling in the American school system. "Everything seems to slow down when we're gloaming," she said once, maybe two years before Van left for college. "Stay out here with me." She always wanted company when she sat outside but rarely got it. Mr. Luong would be out with friends or in his studio; Linny would be out or on the phone with her friends; Van would be studying while watching TV. All excuses, a life of them, until it was too late. Only a few times did Van agree to sit in the darkening air with her, listen to her wander the subjects of work at Roger's, gossip about her friends, and how she had known all of her neighbors in Saigon. Van had been too selfish to pay attention. She hadn't known she would have such a small amount of time. The evening hour seemed long. Yet it disappeared in a moment, didn't it? Outside on her own patio, Van shivered in the dark. Her jade bracelet was cold around her wrist. The stars were becoming discernible, patterning the sky. At such times, her mother's shadowy profile would linger only a moment longer before retreating back to the house. It wasn't night her mother craved; it was the slow countdown, the space of half-light no one could ever keep.

For the first time in longer than she could recall, Van had several guests sleeping in her house. She liked the extra weight anchoring the floors, the fullness in the rooms. Past midnight, she slipped downstairs to check on her father, who'd insisted on sleeping on the TV room sofa. The flicker of lights as she reached the bottom step told Van that he'd fallen asleep while watching *The Bourne Identity*. She turned the television off; her father didn't stir. Van peeked into the backyard, the side yard, the front.

She would not mourn leaving this house, which had tried to contain, and couldn't, the marriage she herself had hidden from understanding. The house was all past tense. A former Miles. Even the walls couldn't commit, sometimes seeming beige, or latte, at times a mythical taupe. *Evening Fawn*. As if something rare or rarefied. The magical holding-of-breath feeling Van got whenever she did see a fawn, its stillness and quick movements equally stunning. To think that a wall, its role as barrier or blockade, could make or deliver such a promise.

No, she would not be sorry to leave. She would press the numbers of the alarm system one last time, disabling it. She and Miles had danced only once on their wooden floors, on their first anniversary, sharing a bottle of champagne. Even then Van had had a faint sense of enacting what she knew was supposed to be marriage. She'd carried a secret feeling of having somehow tricked him into all of it.

Then a blur of months, years. At the front window Van remembered she'd done this very thing—checking the window locks, seeing if any cars murmured by—the night after she lost Vijay's deportation case, after the screaming fight she and Miles had had. Her colleagues had said no one would have won the case, not when it involved a conviction for illegal possession of a firearm. The judges who ruled those cases were notoriously tough, Van had pointed out to Miles. But in defending herself she had given him more reason to highlight her guilt. *Excuses*, he said. *They accomplish nothing.*

And now Na Dau. Would he, like Vijay, waver into her dreams? What if he appeared at this window, this night? Would she be able to save him from running?

At the thought of this, something rose in Van—the same feeling that came over her when she read articles about racial profiling, or an op-ed in the *Free Press* about illegal immigrants "infiltrating" the state, or a piece in *The New York Times* on Somalian refugee boys struggling to get by in small-town Georgia. She remembered how swiftly anti-Japanese sentiment had swept through Michigan in the 1980s; people said then that any Japanese car in Detroit risked getting vandalized. In college, the Vincent Chin case had steered her to law school, to immigration studies in the first place. And the same kind of xenophobia could all be happening again, she knew, with the focus shifted toward the Middle East and toward Mexico and Central America. She thought of all the laws, past and present, stacked against brown-skinned immigrants, meant to keep them, at the very least, out of bounds and out of view. Laws made to exclude, keep out, guarantee fear. It was only in 1967 that the Supreme Court, in the fittingly named *Loving v. Virginia* case, had at last overruled state antimiscegenation laws. Van had felt at home among the immigrants at the International Center, the newly arrived, the first and first-and-a-half generation looking for that compromise between understanding and assimilation. East Asian, Southeast Asian, South Indian, Latino, Middle Eastern; short, dark-haired people, perpetually foreign in a foreign world—they were all in these States together.

Van stood in her house with her sleeping family for as long as it took to try to memorize the moment. It was something she wanted to keep of this place when she left it, when the rooms were all cleared out and the only thing she had to do was get in her car—a different one, she decided; she would trade in that handed-down Infiniti as soon as she could—and drive on, eastward, toward the spired shadow of the Ambassador Bridge that linked one country to another.

# 16

# Linny

On the first Saturday in August Linny and Tom arrived in Ann Arbor with bags of groceries and champagne. Van's house was nearly empty, almost all of the furniture carted away to a storage unit that Miles had rented. "I told him to take everything," Van reported, "except the big TV and the big sofa that goes with it." Those were going to her new condo in Dearborn, and whatever Miles didn't want would be sold, donated, or hauled back to Wrightville, for Mr. Luong wouldn't stand for anything to be thrown out.

"The buyers asked me if they could start moving in this week," Van said, lingering at the kitchen counter while Linny and Tom put together a plate of cheeses and prosciutto. "My place is all set, so I guess I'm moving early."

"It's a good thing we're celebrating today, then," Linny said. "Happy birthday."

Tom added, "We brought you a strawberry cream cake. Linny said it's your favorite."

Van peered into the cardboard box, taking a swipe of frosting. "You're going to have to learn how to make this," she said to Linny.

"I'm definitely taking pastry courses."

It was strange to think that Van would be moving so soon and that Linny would be starting culinary school in the fall. She'd already warned Tom that even if she failed miserably at it there was no chance of her returning to live in Michigan.

"It's not like I'm stuck there forever," he had replied.

"You have a whole practice there. And your parents."

"I'll take care of them wherever I am. Why do you think so many Vietnamese become dentists? People need them everywhere. We're a people who choose mobile professions. We never know when we'll have to make a fast getaway."

For now they were going to keep it safe, arranging his visits to Chicago and the restaurants Linny wanted to try with him. From where Linny stood in Van's kitchen, the idea of the future seemed almost suspenseful. Even Barbara had said something like that when Linny had told her about going to culinary school. By then Barbara had nearly softened back to her old self and tried to convince Linny to take on the management, after all, of the original You Did It Dinners. When Linny insisted she couldn't, Barbara finally agreed that they could try keeping Linny on as a consultant, see if they could work around her class schedule. "You have to do what you do when you're young," Barbara sighed. "Someone like you is probably made to go out on her own and achieve all sorts of things."

While it made Linny laugh to think of being viewed as an achiever, she did take the words as encouragement. Cooking school was one of the few things that didn't make her feel like she was simply settling or avoiding.

Van had joined a new immigration law firm that had sup-

port from a foundation, allowing the lawyers to handle pro-
bono and test cases in addition to the worker visas and permanent
resident applications Van knew so well. Both her new office and
her condo were close enough to the International Center for Van
to restart her classes in Arabic and Spanish. Her friend Jen Ye
lived nearby and was going to help her move in.

The only problem was money. With the pay cut she'd be
taking and without Miles to provide most of the income, she
could no longer afford to send her father a check every month.
Linny could contribute nothing—though she would still be
making a salary at You Did It, she was taking out a major loan
to go to school.

"Dad is the only reason I'm asking for alimony," Van said.
"The house will be paid off in a few years, but he still needs to
live on something."

"You should ask for alimony no matter what," Linny insisted.

But the divorce was far from being settled, and in the mean-
time they both worried. What would their father do? The occasional tile and flooring work he did for friends—"freelance,"
he called it—would have to be increased, though they couldn't
imagine him doing that. Most likely he had, in spite of himself,
come to rely on those checks from Van.

That was why Van had gone back to Wrightville, a month
after the tryout for *Tomorrow's Great Inventor*, to find out once
and for all what his finances were. He had hedged, unwilling to
reveal any actual numbers. It was only when Van had told him
she couldn't send as much money anymore—he hadn't realized
that would be a consequence of the divorce—that he admitted
he needed it for his business.

"That's how he puts it, of course," Van had told Linny. "Money for his business. Not for him."

In his late fifties, with no signs of ill health, he should be working, Linny asserted.

Van pointed out that he probably believed he was. "He's got his own version of events, and the trick is to gain control of the narrative. It's what he's always done: use silence as a weapon of control. We can use it right back."

Which was just what Van had done, Linny realized, the day after the reality TV show audition, when she announced at breakfast that she was getting divorced. Their father had demanded to know when that had been decided. "I like Miles," he said. "He's a nice guy. What did you do?"

"Not helpful," Linny had interjected.

But Van seemed calm, much more than Linny would have imagined. "It's for the best, Dad. You're going to have to trust me on this one."

A troubled look spread over Mr. Luong's face and stayed there. He didn't offer anything more—not an *I'm sorry* or *what happened* or *what can I do*, the normal American things people were supposed to say.

"He'll probably just pretend I was never married at all," Van said to Linny later.

"Your dad and I have a plan," Tom had announced to Linny over the phone one day in June, not long after Van had come back from seeing Mr. Luong in Wrightville. "Why didn't we think of this before? LuongInventions.com."

Linny, sitting in a coffee shop while working on a few recipes for Barbara, had laughed. "Van and I *have* both thought of that before, but my dad doesn't know how to use the Internet. I tried to explain it to him once and he got confused and then mad and didn't want to hear about it again."

"I think he's open to it now. A lot of his friends are starting to e-mail each other and he's feeling left out. So I talked to him and he said yes. He could even sell his stuff on eBay or any number of sites. I had him come over to my building so I could show him how it works."

"Are you having meetings with my dad?" Her father, as far as she knew, had never even used a computer. Linny couldn't picture him suddenly running a Web business out of his basement.

"Apparently when Van was back in Wrightville she showed him how he can apply for a patent. Did you know the entire database is online, pictures and all? I think he's excited."

"Pretty soon we'll all be running his e-business." But it amazed Linny to consider that her father might, after all, be able to step out of the cast of too old, too first-generation immigrant.

"You and your sister might not have to look out for him as much as you think," Tom said.

There was something hope-giving about the idea of her father having his own website, a place where anyone in the world could see what he was working on. Even if it didn't yield any sales, it would open up his basement studio. Plus, her father still believed in the possibility of striking it rich and winning the lottery. And he had heard that the Google guys had made billions.

"You do realize you're becoming one of the many people who help my father and get nothing in return," Linny said. "Some people would call that enabling. That's what my mother always did."

"I like your dad," Tom replied simply. "Plus, his inventions make sense. Using the Luong Arm is like channeling Plastic Man."

Linny thought back to how Van, the day after the TV show audition, said she had to admit Tom was a decent guy.

To Tom Linny said, "All this and nice teeth too."

"See you soon?" He had driven to Chicago nearly every weekend since the TV show tryout.

"Oh, yes."

That week, waiting for Sasha outside Paolo Francesca, Linny spotted Gary and Pren crossing the street with their children, eating bags of Garrett's popcorn like any group of tourists. It was the first time Linny had ever seen them all together outside of their house, and she guessed they were even then heading back to its comfort and gloss, all that high-ceilinged space Linny had admired. She was strangely relieved to see them, to know that her brief appearance in Gary's life had not left a darker mark.

She turned, heading for the entrance to the salon, but before she could get away with it Pren spied her. She froze for just a second. Then she looked beyond Linny, pretending to focus on something else. She pulled a pair of sunglasses from her bag and put them on. And Gary—he actually stepped in front of the children and glared right at her. At least, she thought it was a glare. Did he think she was looking for him? Sasha emerged from the salon as the family walked beyond them, toward the brightness of Michigan Avenue, Pren and Gary keeping protective hands at the backs of their children.

After Linny's run-in with Pren she had deleted Gary's every

e-mail. She would never know for sure if Pren had thrown her a disturbing truth or a brilliant lie but she decided it wasn't worth the trouble of finding out. After a while, Gary's messages stopped. He didn't show up at her apartment again. He simply receded. In the end, Linny knew that when she thought of this time in her life she would think more about Pren than Gary. How many times had Pren endured this—how many more times would she?

*No easy resolutions*, Linny might have said to Van if she'd ever dared to bring up the subject again. They seemed to have tacitly agreed never to mention it and that was okay by Linny. They weren't about to start talking out everything.

At sunset they ate Van's birthday cake on the back patio, using the furniture that was being sold to a professor at the university. Then a cleaning service would come in to shine the floors downstairs and shampoo the carpets upstairs. "It'll be all new again," Van said with a hint of melancholy. Linny was impressed by what she could only call Van's fortitude. So far she'd never even seen her shed a tear for Miles, though Linny attributed that, more likely, to Van's inborn sense of privacy.

"I bought you some clothes for your birthday," Linny told her. "And you can't return them."

"I'm not talking about clothes again. Not if you want to hear about Dad and Nancy Bao."

Linny was surprised. "What about them?"

"I saw her when I went home to see Dad. She came over to the house, and she didn't know I was going to be there."

Linny exchanged a look with Tom. "I told you!" she exclaimed. "Why didn't you tell me this before? They really *are* still together."

"That's the thing I was trying to figure out, because I don't think they are. Nancy came over to take care of the *house*."

She explained how Nancy, surprised to see Van there, had told her that she sometimes stopped by to check on Mr. Luong, bringing him a few sweet bean pastries or a magazine he might like. She had been the one to tell him about the reality TV show audition, after reading about it in a newspaper. She had also been helping him tidy up the house a little, get things organized. She had kept the living room credenza dusted, the sticks of incense replenished.

When Van asked Nancy why she did all this, she simply said that people in the community cared about Dinh Luong.

"That's all I got out of her," Van finished. "She probably thinks we're bad daughters for not being there all the time to take care of Dad. And I think she must blame me for Na, which I guess is deserved."

"That wasn't your fault," Linny said quickly at the pained look crossing her sister's face.

"Anyway, this still doesn't answer the question about them. There may be nothing more than an old friendship. Maybe there *was* more once, but I don't think there is now. It just didn't seem like it."

"I did notice sometimes," Linny said, realizing it as she spoke, "that when I would visit Dad the house wouldn't be as dirty as I thought it would be. I thought it was you, or that he cleaned and shopped only when he remembered to or when he felt like it. But that doesn't mean there *isn't* something else going on with Nancy." She turned to Tom. "What do you think? You live in that town—you hear the gossip."

"I don't know any more than you do," he admitted. "I never saw your dad and Nancy in the car and I've never heard anyone gossip about them. Lots of people have said that Rich and Nancy hardly ever talk to each other but who knows what that means. Who does talk to Rich Bao?"

Linny couldn't help thinking the mystery extended beyond her father and Nancy, out to their friends, their community and generation, the stories they told and wove about Saigon. Maybe it was their own way of making sense of how they'd gotten from Vietnam to America. That whole generation had its own language, its own clinging to tradition. *What are your children going to understand?* Her mother had said, meaning they were going to be thoroughly American. The idea had scared her. It was one of the reasons she wanted Linny and Van to go to Vietnam with her.

Maybe Van was thinking about their mother too, because she said, "Look at the sky."

The stars had started to pop out even before the sun fully set. Linny wondered if her sister was trying to keep that last moment in Ann Arbor, trying to take it all in. "You know what? Mom will never know that all this stuff has happened. I feel like we should tell her that you're moving."

Sitting next to her, Tom took her hand.

"I used to think that all the time," Van said.

"Maybe that's why Dad stays where he is."

"Maybe."

But it seemed a revelation to Linny, a possible answer to his identity. All her life Linny had thought of him whenever she stood on her tiptoes, straining to reach a package of pasta or a box of tea on a high shelf. She thought of him when in a crowd, craning to look around people's heads, careful to keep track of elbows so as not to get slammed in the face. She thought of him too when entering a room with tiled floors. She had tried to see, or maybe couldn't help but see, the world from his point of view.

She remembered being a tiny girl, staring at people's legs while waiting for some parade—maybe a Fourth of July festival or the Tulip Time celebration in the lakeside town of Holland. All Linny recalled was seeing other people's thighs. Pant legs and skirts all around her, close enough for Linny to see the weave of cotton and the sparkle of poly. Her mother had kept her close, her father standing nearby with Van. On that one day they had seemed like sentries. And then Linny had grown up— though not as up as she had hoped and assumed. She remained, and Van too, the short girls their father had told them they would always be.

In the early shadows of dusk, Linny accepted this. Words hovered in front of her. *The Short Girl Café*. Bright reds and yellows. Oncidium orchids. And Linny, years from now, sitting down at a table with her father, her sister, Tom. And more. No menus, just rounds and rounds of plates brought out to them on the longest day of the year. Then they would go outside or up to a roof, just in time to get as much of the sky as they could bear. It's what Linny will have learned to wait for. All that blue. She will see it again and again, crossing the world to follow it home. Each time she will hold out her hand, wishing to save just a little of it, to try to catch the falling hour.

# acknowledgments

I would like to thank: Molly Stern, Nicole Aragi, Liz Van Hoose, Laura Tisdel, Juliet Annan, Barbara Campo, Dave Cole, Gabrielle Gantz, Jacqueline Fischetti, Caitlin Pratt, Alan Walker, Richard Kessler, Jim Hanks, Vicky Farah, Pavneet Singh, Theju Prasad, Incigul Sayman, Liz Han, Joseph Nguyen, Purdue University, all of my family, and especially, and always, Porter Shreve.

# MARINA LEWYCKA

**WE ARE ALL MADE OF GLUE**

Georgie Sinclair's life is coming unstuck. Her husband's left her. Her son's obsessed with the End of the World. And now her elderly neighbour Mrs Shapiro has decided they are related.

Or so the hospital informs her when Mrs Shapiro has an accident and names Georgie next of kin. This, however, is not a case of a quick ward visit: Mrs Shapiro has a large rickety house full of stinky cats that needs looking after that a pair of estate agents seem intent on swindling from her. Plus there are the 'Uselesses' trying to repair it (uselessly). Then there's the social worker who wants to put her in a nursing home. Not to mention some letters that point to a mysterious, painful past.

As Georgie tries her best to put Mrs Shapiro's life back together somehow she must stop her own from falling apart . . .

'Vibrant dialogue, a family in meltdown, a clash of cultures and wonderful cast of expertly observed characters. Pure laugh-out-loud social comedy' *Daily Mail*

'Hilarious. A big-hearted confection of the comic and the poignant' *Literary Review*

'A big, bustling novel, told with enthusiasm by a narrator who is warm, winningly disaster-prone and, crucially, believable' *Spectator*

# KATHRYN STOCKETT

**THE HELP**

Enter a vanished and unjust world: Jackson, Mississippi, 1962. Where black maids raise white children, but aren't trusted not to steal the silver...

There's Aibileen, raising her seventeenth white child and nursing the hurt caused by her own son's tragic death; Minny, whose cooking is nearly as sassy as her tongue; and white Miss Skeeter, home from College, who wants to know why her beloved maid has disappeared.

Skeeter, Aibileen and Minny. No one would believe they'd be friends; fewer still would tolerate it. But as each woman finds the courage to cross boundaries, they come to depend and rely upon one another. Each is in a search of a truth. And together they have an extraordinary story to tell...

'Outstanding, immensely funny, very compelling, brilliant' *Daily Telegraph*

'The other side of *Gone with the Wind* – and just as unputdownable' *Sunday Times*

'A laugh-out-loud, vociferously angry must-read' *Marie Claire*

# *He just wanted a decent book to read ...*

Not too much to ask, is it? It was in 1935 when Allen Lane, Managing Director of Bodley Head Publishers, stood on a platform at Exeter railway station looking for something good to read on his journey back to London. His choice was limited to popular magazines and poor-quality paperbacks – the same choice faced every day by the vast majority of readers, few of whom could afford hardbacks. Lane's disappointment and subsequent anger at the range of books generally available led him to found a company – and change the world.

*'We believed in the existence in this country of a vast reading public for intelligent books at a low price, and staked everything on it'*
**Sir Allen Lane, 1902–1970, founder of Penguin Books**

The quality paperback had arrived – and not just in bookshops. Lane was adamant that his Penguins should appear in chain stores and tobacconists, and should cost no more than a packet of cigarettes.

Reading habits (and cigarette prices) have changed since 1935, but Penguin still believes in publishing the best books for everybody to enjoy. We still believe that good design costs no more than bad design, and we still believe that quality books published passionately and responsibly make the world a better place.

So wherever you see the little bird – whether it's on a piece of prize-winning literary fiction or a celebrity autobiography, political tour de force or historical masterpiece, a serial-killer thriller, reference book, world classic or a piece of pure escapism – you can bet that it represents the very best that the genre has to offer.

**Whatever you like to read – trust Penguin.**

read more
www.penguin.co.uk